The Vanishing Point

The Vanishing Point

SUSAN BONNERS

Farrar Straus Giroux / New York

www.fsgkidsbooks.com

Library of Congress Cataloging-in-Publication Data
Bonners, Susan
    The vanishing point / Susan Bonners.
        p.   cm.
    Summary: While spending the summer in a New England coastal town
with another family, Kate sees the ocean for the first time, takes a
challenging drawing class, and buys a mysterious painting.
    ISBN-13: 978-0-374-38081-6
    ISBN-10: 0-374-38081-3
    1. Drawing—Technique—Fiction.   2. Artists—Fiction.   I. Title.

PZ7.B64253 Van 2005
[Fic]—dc22

                                                        2004056440

To the artist in us all

Contents

The Vanishing Point

✿ The Lark Ascending

KATE LOOKED UP just in time to see a June bug bounce off the porch screen into the darkness. She glanced at the clock, then forced her attention back to the open math book on the kitchen table. Her favorite radio program, *Evening Serenade with John Lowe*, would end in ten minutes. Kate hated doing homework once the music was over.

The playlist on *Evening Serenade* leaned toward well-known short classical works. At the commercial breaks, sponsors sold denture adhesive, hair coloring, pain remedies, and bran cereal. Kate figured that she was the only person under fifty who knew *Evening Serenade* existed.

The two and a half weeks left in the school term felt like a prison sentence. Why didn't everyone just admit that going to school after Memorial Day was a total waste?

The opening measures of *The Lark Ascending*, Kate's favorite piece, came over the radio. A solo violin was the voice of the lark, repeating its brief, wistful song over and over, higher each time as it circled into the sky.

The last note, pitched almost beyond hearing, was still hanging in the air when the phone rang in the living room. Kate heard her mother answer it.

"Anne, I was just about to call. How are you?" By now, Kate was used to the edge of concern in her mother's voice when she talked to Anne. Her oldest daughter's coming baby was the focus of her attention now. "What did Dr. Cunningham say about the vitamin B?"

Mr. Lowe's soothing voice came on, thanking the listeners, over his theme music, for tuning in. Kate wrote the last answer on her paper. She was closing the book when her mother walked in and sat down across from her at the kitchen table.

"Anne has finally set a date to start her maternity leave—August fifteenth. I hope she isn't cutting it too close. First babies are tricky to predict." Kate's mother fiddled with the saltshaker. "You know, Anne won't be able to meet us at the farm this summer. She's in a rush to finish the designs for two new clients before the baby comes."

Kate nodded. She'd already guessed as much. Not having Anne come for at least part of the annual six-week stay at their grandparents' farm was going to leave a huge hole.

"And I talked to Zorina this afternoon." Kate hadn't seen her second-oldest sister since spring break at Zee's college. "She's going to take the job at the riding school, but now they want her to teach for all three sessions. She starts the Tuesday after her graduation."

"Then she won't be coming either."

"No." Her mother put down the saltshaker. "Kate, I'm afraid that you may have to go to the farm by yourself this time. I'd come with you, but now it's definite that your father will be having the surgery on his back. Dr. Franey's office phoned this morning. Dad's scheduled for July seventh. He'll have to line up someone to teach his summer courses."

For months, the surgery had safely roamed in the indefinite future. Suddenly it had elbowed its way into the present.

"I feel terrible about this, Kate. You don't complain, but I know you've been unhappy lately. Can you tell me what's bothering you? Is it Dad's surgery? Or is there something more?"

Kate shrugged. She didn't know what was wrong.

"I know this sounds strange," her mother said, "since I've been so busy lately between my job and the computer course that we haven't really talked, but maybe you need some time alone to think things through. And it might be fun, visiting Grandma and Grandpa on your own."

Kate shook her head. "I'd rather be here if Dad's going to be in the hospital."

"I know you would, but he'll only be there for a few days." Her mother paused. "You know, the developer who bought the Buchanans' farm has made my folks an offer for the south pasture."

"They aren't going to sell it, are they?"

"I don't know. They're talking about cutting back on the planting."

"They talk about that every year."

"I'm just saying, maybe you shouldn't pass up this chance to go." Kate's mother stood up. "Well, think about it anyway."

That night, lying awake, Kate did a lot of thinking about it.

She'd never visited the farm by herself, spent whole days without the needs of others blundering into her private time with her grandparents, her voice lost in the noisy stream of conversation.

But what about the afternoons, when her grandparents needed to sleep, the long evenings after their early bedtime? Those hours had always been passed joking with her mother and sisters over silly games and impossibly difficult jigsaw puzzles, the need for quiet resulting in fits of suppressed laughter.

But that was all in the past. There wouldn't be another July afternoon when Kate would lug her suitcase up to the blue bedroom to find Anne's sun hat tossed on the bed. If Anne came at all, the room would be barricaded with baby furnishings. Kate would be relegated to the sofa on the screen porch.

And when conversation lagged in the August heat, and all the magazines had been read, Zee wouldn't be there to say, *Let's have a picnic by the river*, or *Let's see who can find the most four-leaf clovers*.

Once, her grandparents would have joined in. Now, they seemed happy to sit on the sidelines and watch their family having fun.

For so many years, time had seemed not to pass. But silently the hands of the clock had been moving all the while.

Light rain spattered the window of her father's study as Kate, curled up in the wing chair, finished chapter five of *Murder at the Davenport Museum*. With her mother attending her Saturday morning computer class, the house was quiet, ideal for focusing on the mystery she and her father were reading that week.

"Dad, I think I know who did it."

Her father shifted his position on the sofa and adjusted his back support pillow. "So soon?"

"Uh-huh. I noticed a clue that I'm sure gives it away."

Just then, Mrs. Getty's Airedale started barking wildly next door. Kate's father checked his watch. "Like clockwork. Kate, will you see if there's any mail for me?"

Kate put her book on the desk and ran down the stairs. Envelopes and magazines were pouring through the mail slot. As she began separating the envelopes into two stacks, she noticed "D. Lang" in a return address. Kate's mother exchanged letters with her friend Diane two or three times a year, even though they hadn't seen each other since the Langs had moved to another state when Diane's daughter, Alison, was in nursery school and Kate was starting kindergarten. Then, three years ago, the Langs had moved again, this time to a small town on the East Coast, and the letters had begun to include invitations for Kate to stay with them for the summer.

Mrs. Lang had extolled the sea air and the tidy beaches.

That sounded fine, but accepting the invitation meant forfeiting the visit to her grandparents' farm, or at least part of the visit, and so, each year, the invitation had received a polite refusal.

Kate put the letter on the kitchen table, along with her mother's other mail. Not everybody knew that her mother had taken over the yard work and minor household repairs, but companies that sold hardware, plumbing supplies, and gardening equipment had figured it out. Their catalogs were often addressed to her these days.

Kate carried her father's mail upstairs.

"By the way, Kate," he said, sorting through the envelopes, "the faculty meeting at Woodward ran late. I didn't have a chance to look at the drawing you brought home yesterday. Will you bring it to me?"

"Dad, is Woodward going to close?"

"I don't think so, but keeping a small college open is tough these days. We may have to cut some programs."

"Not American literature. Besides, you've been there longer than anybody else."

"Thirty-three years next September, but who's counting? Oh, I think I'm safe for the nonce."

"What's 'the nonce'?"

"N-o-n-c-e. The time being."

Kate went to her room and returned with the drawing

she had done in art class that week. Her father studied it for several minutes.

"This has some good things in it. Your weeping willow is really alive. The swan is a little flat by comparison. I don't sense it's there, the way I do with the willow. I'm not sure what you can do about that. Have you got a photo of a swan?"

Kate went to her room and returned with the picture she had been using, a watercolor reproduced in a perfume ad.

"I don't have a real photo."

"I see your problem. This is more of a design than a picture of an actual swan. Maybe you can find something in one of my nature magazines."

"I'll look." Kate tried to sound cheerful, especially now that her father was in pain all the time because of his back, but sometimes she felt a tide of weariness. As usual, her father had put his finger on the weak spot in the drawing, but no other student in her class could do as well. Anybody else's father would have put a drawing that good on the refrigerator door and proudly pointed it out to visitors. Kate's father had never put her artwork on the refrigerator door.

He had framed some of it though. About a dozen of his favorites were hung on the walls of his study.

Kate was in her room when her mother got home and came upstairs with the letter.

"I guess you saw the envelope from the Langs. They'd love for you to visit them. Listen to this—you and Alison could take lessons at the Art Association. This summer, they're offering a beginning class that meets once a week. Children and adults can sign up."

"Beginning class" did not sound appealing.

"It would be something different," her mother said, folding up the letter. "Besides, you've never seen the ocean before."

After that, Kate's mother didn't bring up the subject again, but as the school year ground to its close, the invitation was never off Kate's mind.

Alison was a year behind Kate in school. They probably didn't have a thing in common. What would they do all day when they weren't in drawing class? What if they didn't get along? They'd be stuck with each other for the summer.

Even so, the words "something different" kept coming back to her. Wasn't she better off choosing that instead of constantly hearing the echoes of good times that wouldn't come again? She decided to accept the Langs' invitation.

After she told her parents, things happened quickly. Plane reservations were booked, phone calls exchanged, lists made.

On the last day of June, Kate stood in the waiting area for Flight 571, clutching her new carry-on bag.

"You won't forget to send copies of your drawings," said her father. "Even the ones you don't like."

"I won't forget, Dad."

Her mother put her arm around Kate's shoulder. "We'll spend more time together when you get back. I promise."

A voice came on the microphone: "Passengers in rows ten and higher may board."

"That's me."

Kate's parents each hugged her as if she were going away for two years instead of two months.

She turned around and smiled just before she stepped into the jetway, so they'd know she was going to be fine. In the harsh light from the bank of windows, she suddenly saw how lined her father's face was, how hard he was gripping his cane. The next passenger was waiting for her to move forward. If she'd made the wrong decision, it was too late to go back on it now. Kate hurried down the carpeted tunnel.

When all of the passengers were boarded, no one else was sitting in her row. Kate was relieved. She didn't want to have to make conversation with a stranger.

The plane took off and climbed out of the overcast day into the blinding sunlight above the cloud layer. Kate flipped through the puzzle book her father had given her for the trip. Exactly one week from now, he would be wheeled into an operating room. He'd be joking with the nurses and the orderlies. Everything would be okay. Since her mother was head of the medical records department, she knew who the best doctors were. At the hospital, they did hundreds of these procedures a year.

Kate put the book in her lap and pulled the notes from Anne and Zee out of her backpack. Anne's was written in her graceful script on a card with Monet's *Water Lilies and Japanese Bridge* on the front.

Dear Kate,

Have a wonderful time this summer. Come back with stories to tell. When I see you next, you'll be an aunt. Can you believe it?

Love,

Anne

Zee's card featured a cartoon of a dinner roll on a deck chair. "Bun Voyage" it read on the inside. "Have the best summer ever!" was scrawled above the signature.

Kate put the notes away and tried working a few of the puzzles from the book, but she found she couldn't concentrate on them.

About twenty minutes before landing, the pilot came on the public address system and gave the weather at their destination. Heavy rain. Winds gusting to thirty miles an hour. Sixty-five degrees Fahrenheit. That seemed impossible, but when the plane descended below the cloud layer again, they were flying through a downpour.

They passed over the coastline, fingers of land that curled into the water amid a scattering of islands; then the plane doubled back in a giant circle, lower and lower. They were only a few breathtaking feet above the water when the runway suddenly appeared under them and Kate felt the bump of landing gear on pavement.

She spotted the Langs even before she was out of the jetway, a blond woman and a lanky, red-haired girl as tall as her mother, inches taller than Kate. They were holding a hand-lettered sign that said, "Welcome, Kate Harris." When Kate waved, they broke into smiles and waved back enthusiastically.

The girl stepped forward and took the carry-on bag out of Kate's hand. "Hi, I'm Alison. I bet you don't recognize me."

"Well, your mom sent a photo."

"Oh, yeah. My school picture. I'm rounding them all up so I can burn them."

Alison's mother introduced herself. Kate tried to keep up with a flurry of questions. How was the flight?—Fine. Did she have luggage to pick up?—No. Had they fed her on the plane?—Sort of. Did she need to use the ladies' room?—No. Mrs. Lang said something about their car having engine trouble, but Kate didn't really take it in.

With Alison in the lead, they followed the Ground Transportation signs to a bank of revolving doors and pushed their way out into a wall of noise—car horns, police whistles, bus motors—all magnified by a cement overhang that deepened the gloom.

"What luck!" said Alison. "There's the shuttle bus."

After the outer terminal, the bus seemed like a comfortable living room. Then they came to a stop.

"Tallyho!" Alison cried as she grabbed the bag and jumped off the bus.

Mrs. Lang disappeared into the crowd. Kate had to follow Alison like a day-old duckling waddling after its mother, down a flight of stairs to a train platform where they all met up again.

A short ride on a clattering train took them to still another train station.

"I promise this torture is almost over," said Mrs. Lang as they walked up to a ticket window. "If it hadn't been for the car conking out—"

"You might just catch the twelve-oh-five," said the man in the booth as he pushed her change under the glass. "Track Eight."

"We can make it!" Alison shouted. "Run!"

They ran all the way to the last track and down the platform, where a conductor waited, pointing to his watch.

"Thanks!" gasped Mrs. Lang as they stepped aboard.

The train pulled out as they collapsed into the facing seats at the end of the car. The conductor slid Kate's bag onto the overhead rack and took their tickets.

"I should call my mom at work," said Kate.

Mrs. Lang pulled a cell phone out of her purse and handed it to her.

After Kate had left a message on her mother's voice mail, Alison took the phone and punched in a number. "Hi, Dad. Mission accomplished. We're on our way . . . Oh, good. See you in about an hour." She flipped the phone shut and handed it back to her mother. "The car might be fixed by the time we get there."

With Alison and her mother facing her, Kate could see how much they resembled each other—the same light blue eyes, elfin faces, and fluffy hair. Mrs. Lang's youth and Alison's height made them seem more like sisters than mother and daughter.

Kate turned to the window. Rain snaked down the dirty

glass as they passed through a grim landscape of factories and warehouses.

Alison's mother caught her eye. "This isn't exactly the scenic route," she said. "It gets better."

They left the city behind. On either side of the tracks, mudflats stretched as far as Kate could see.

"The ocean's that way," said Alison, pointing. "We're at low tide now."

They went through a series of towns. Kate noticed a lot of empty storefronts at first, but the towns looked increasingly prosperous as they rolled on.

Kate saw no sign of the ocean. Here and there, on the inland side of the track, wooded hillsides had been carved out to accommodate large homes with wide verandas and walls of glass.

For a while, the landscape seemed more water than land as the train rumbled over inlets and ponds. Then the land took over again and they entered a small town. There were no glass-walled verandas here, just narrow streets with rows of small wooden houses.

"This is us," said Mrs. Lang as she began tugging Kate's bag off the overhead rack.

Alison pointed out the window. "Dad's here!"

The train glided past a dark-haired man in a faded blue shirt and jeans, leaning on a small red car. At first glance, he looked decidedly odd, with a huge nose and heavy eyeglass frames, his captain's cap at a jaunty angle. As they walked up to him a minute later, Kate realized that the nose was rubber and the frames were fake.

He tipped his cap. "Lang Seaside Tours. We'll show it to you if we can find it."

"Great getup, Dad. This is Kate. Kate, this is my dad."

He shook Kate's hand.

"Dad isn't always this silly."

"Yes, I am. I am very silly. Isn't that right, Diane?" He opened the car door for Alison's mother.

"Except when you're goofy," she said, sliding into the passenger seat.

Alison opened the back door behind her mother. "Sit here, Kate. You'll get the best view of the water that way. Dad, take Shore Road to Perry Street, and then go past the Art Association."

"Aye, aye, Captain." Her father saluted and put the cap on her, pulling it forward so that it almost covered her eyes.

Alison left it there and climbed into the backseat behind him.

Her father pulled off the fake nose and glasses to look over his shoulder as he shifted into reverse. Without the mask, he looked too young to be the father of someone almost as old as Kate. But then, the fathers of most of Kate's friends looked young to her.

When they reached the harbor, only a light drizzle was falling, but waves thundered against the cement seawall.

Alison's father swerved into a parking space. "Let's get out for a minute."

"I'll stay in the car," said Alison's mother. "I've seen the view."

Alison skipped ahead of her father and Kate across a stretch of grass to a paved walkway. As Kate pushed against the wind to the guardrail, she tried to relate the smell of the ocean to anything she had known before—crushed leaves or wet soil. It was like nothing else.

"Hold on to the rail," Mr. Lang said, raising his voice above the roar of the water. "We don't want to lose our guest. Not on the first day anyway."

Kate wasn't sure if he was joking or if people had actually been swept off the walkway.

"We call those breakers," he said. "See how the waves are breaking up into foam? Once a wave hits the shallows near shore, its underside starts to drag on the sandy bottom. But the surface is still moving fast." He demonstrated by sliding the palm of one hand against the other. "So the wave starts to curl. Then it comes crashing down from its own weight."

Kate wasn't sure she understood the explanation, but she could see for herself the power of the water. A nearby dock was taking a terrible pounding.

"See those things floating in the water?" Alison's father continued. "Those are buoys. They mark the navigation lanes in and out of the harbor. Some of them have flashing lights as well as bells."

Kate saw them—bobbing specks in a world without color or form. The reflection of gray between sky and ocean left no clear separation between air and water. The boom and hiss as each breaker collapsed into its trough held to a steady pulse, drowning out other sound.

Water beaded on Kate's face. Her hair hung in wet ringlets that funneled water into her jacket. She couldn't tell if the water was rain or spray from the ocean.

Alison's voice seemed to come from a distance. "Kate? Ready to go?" As Kate followed Alison and her father back to the car, she realized that she tasted salt on her lips.

They drove on. Once they left the shore, the streets angled up sharply. Most of the town seemed to be clinging to the side of a steep hill. After the level grids of pavement that Kate was used to, the geography seemed crazy.

"There's the Art Association," said Alison. She reached past Kate to roll down the window. "Slow up, Dad."

He pulled over and stopped. Kate had to lean out of the car to see the whole building, set grandly on a raised lot.

"That's locally quarried granite you're looking at," Alison's father said, "including the columns at the front entrance."

Kate hadn't realized that the building would be so large or so formal.

"I just wanted you to see it," said Alison. "Let's get home. I'm starving."

Like almost all the other houses that Kate saw, the Langs' was wood frame with shutters, but theirs looked freshly painted. Instead of being dingy white, theirs was orchid with bright blue trim and dark green shutters. Flower boxes decorated all of the ground-floor windows, even the ones on the garage, which Kate knew had been made into a workshop for Mr. Lang's carpentry business. A large tree with shaggy gray bark dominated the postage-stamp front yard.

The place looked like a picture out of a magazine, and when Kate stepped into the enclosed back porch, she saw a pile of Renovator's Companion and Period Homes magazines in a basket on the floor.

In Kate's home, almost every piece of furniture was a giveaway or a thrift shop find, like her father's enormous desk, the conglomeration looking like a family reunion of eccentrics jostling around the high-ceilinged rooms.

By contrast, in the Langs' doll-sized house, things matched, like the bamboo-frame furniture on the enclosed front porch.

"Come on," said Alison. "I'll show you my room. We're going to share it." She picked up the carry-on bag, which her father had left in the kitchen, and led the way up the narrow staircase to the second floor.

"I decorated it myself," Alison said as they stepped into the tiny room. The walls were purple, making a remarkable contrast with the pale green woodwork. A bed on the right and a sofa on the left shared the nightstand in front of the single dormer window.

The tree in the front yard was so close that some of its upper branches brushed the windowpane.

"It's like being in a tree house, isn't it?" said Alison. "That's why I picked this room."

"What kind of tree is it?"

"A silver maple. Silver on account of the bark."

Kate pointed over the tree. "Is the ocean that way?"

Alison nodded.

A set of shelves had been built to fit the room.

"Dad made those," Alison said when she saw Kate looking at them. "He made that night table in front of the window and my desk and the dining table downstairs and the kitchen cabinets and the addition on our house where my mom's office is. Now he's building a sailboat. Your dad's a teacher, right?"

"Yes. And my mom's the head of the medical records department at a hospital. Your mother's an accountant, isn't she?"

Alison nodded. "She keeps the books for some of the businesses in town."

As Kate kept up the conversation, she was taking a mental inventory of Alison's things, each one an important clue to the person she would be spending almost all of her time with now. She noted the tennis racket, the Rollerblades, and the binoculars. One shelf was devoted to a collection of shells.

"I found all of those myself," said Alison, "except for the big conch shell. I got that from my grandmother."

"You found them at the beach?"

"Uh-huh. It took a long time to get that many. Hardly any shells make it to shore in one piece."

"Would you show me where to look? I'd like to find a few to send my family."

"Sure. Anytime."

Alison stretched out on the sofa. "This is where you're sleeping. It opens up into a bed. It's really comfy. I sleep on it sometimes, just for a change. It's going to be like having a sister with you here. You're lucky. You have sisters. Do you share a room?"

"They don't live at home anymore." Alison didn't understand. Her sisters had become young women, while Kate had still been playing with dolls.

Kate felt awkward standing there in her wet jacket. She pulled out the desk chair and perched on the edge of it.

Alison rolled off the sofa bed. "I'll show you where to put your stuff."

In the closet, the clothing was pushed tightly together, making room for Kate's things, and the small dresser was half empty.

"Come and get it!" called Alison's father.

"We can do this later," said Alison, bounding down the stairs.

Kate slipped off her jacket and hung it on the closet doorknob. When she got to the dining room table, Alison had pulled out a chair for her.

"From now on, this is your place," she said.

Lunch was macaroni salad—although Mrs. Lang called it "pasta salad"—various cold meats and cheeses, and a long loaf of bread.

"It's a *baguette*," said Alison in an exaggerated French accent. "Ever since La Lune opened up, we've been getting a lot of weird food."

"It's not weird, it's Continental," said her father. "I for one am very Continental." He ruffled up his hair and made a funny face.

"I didn't say I didn't like it," said Alison. "I said it was weird. I like weird food."

During lunch, Kate saw how much Alison and her father shared a sense of humor. When the three of them were together, Mrs. Lang didn't seem like Alison's sister. She seemed like the mother.

Kate and Alison spent the rest of the afternoon taking care of Alison's fish. The main aquarium had sprung a slow leak. Allison had to catch all the fish and transfer them to one of the other two aquariums until the new one arrived at the pet store.

Dinner, Kate learned, was always at five-thirty at the Langs'. That was another thing that was different from home, where meals tended not to be discussed until one of her parents looked at the clock and said, "Can you believe the time?"

By five, Alison's father had the coals glowing in the backyard grill. Alison began setting the table. Her mother mixed up dips and side dishes. Kate felt as if she were watching a dance whose steps had become second nature.

After dinner, they played dominoes on the front porch. At first, the excitement of the game kept Kate going, but by eight-thirty she was fighting off yawns.

"Alison," said Mrs. Lang, "why don't you two call it a day? I'll go upstairs with you and check on the linens."

Kate said good night to Mr. Lang, then waited on the doorstep to the living room for Alison, who had gotten into a game of tag with her father, using a sofa pillow.

"Night, Dad." She turned as if to go. "By the way, you're it!" She pivoted around, threw the pillow at him, careened past Kate into the living room, and made a dash for the stairs.

An expert throw sent the pillow arching over Kate's head. It hit Alison on the shoulder.

"Gotcha!"

Alison turned, made a wild toss, and ran up the stairs, out of breath from laughing. Kate followed her, uncomfortable to be in the middle of the high jinks without being part of them.

From a neatly packed closet, Mrs. Lang was assembling an armload of bedding and towels.

Alison slipped past them into the bathroom. "I'll be done in a sec. Then you can have the place to yourself."

Kate said good night to Mrs. Lang and waited in the bedroom, studying a navigation chart of the harbor on the wall above the sofa bed. Its contour lines disclosed a world of underwater hills and valleys.

Alison reappeared in a long pink shirt. "It's all yours."

When Kate crossed the hall and flicked on the light switch, she didn't quite recognize the face in the mirror. The salt spray from the ocean had stiffened the top layer of her hair, but she was too tired to wash it. She splashed water on her face, changed into her pajamas, and halfheartedly brushed her teeth, automatically putting her wet toothbrush back into its travel case.

She tiptoed into the bedroom.

"I'm awake," Alison said, although she sounded as if she had been asleep. "Can I turn this off?" She reached for the switch on the lamp between the beds.

"I'll get it."

With the light off, Kate could see through the screen on the window behind the night table. Directly under the window was the front porch roof. The roof and the maple tree blocked most of the view of the yard below.

"I forgot to show you where to put your toothbrush and stuff," said Alison.

"That's okay. You can do that tomorrow." Kate climbed into bed.

"Did you bring a bathing suit? I can lend you one if you didn't."

"I brought one." Kate pulled the covers up. "Alison, do you know the person who's going to teach the art class?"

Alison didn't reply. In the light from the nearly full moon, Kate could see that she had gone to sleep. Kate closed her eyes and tried to sleep, too, but the events of the day kept running through her head. Dominating all of them was her first sight of the breakers. Through the open window, she thought she could still hear them.

But what was that distant clanging? Maybe the gates were coming down at a railroad crossing. She waited to hear the train whistle.

At the farm, lying in bed, Kate would hear train whistles all night long. They always blew at the Sawyer Street crossing in Grafton, five miles away. Trains barreled through the night, carrying loads of cargo—and people, too. Her grandfather had told her about drifters, some of them only a few years older than Kate, foolhardy enough to jump on freight trains as they picked up speed leaving the yards.

Just as she was dozing off, Kate realized what the sound was—not a railroad crossing but a bell buoy, somewhere out there in the darkness, clanging mournfully on the rolling water.

At the Edge of the Sea

THE HIGH-PITCHED SCREAMS of a flock of gulls awakened Kate the next morning. She checked the clock. Quarter to six. Alison's bed was empty. Kate could hear water pouring in the shower, then a squeak as it was turned off.

Alison, wrapped in a towel, padded into the bedroom. "Good, you're up. I'm going to take you out for breakfast. My treat."

"I can pay for mine out of my allowance." Kate's allowance, raised to ten dollars a week for the trip, would be dispensed by Mrs. Lang every Saturday.

"Don't even think about it." Alison pulled a pair of jeans out of the dresser. "I've already cleared it with Mom."

Kate started to make her bed.

"Don't bother with that now. We can do it later," said Alison. "Let's get going. I'll be downstairs."

Kate found clothes and dumped them on the hamper in the bathroom. What was the rush? She wanted to wash the salt out of her hair, but with Alison waiting, two minutes' rinsing in a hot shower had to do. Kate pulled her matted, wet hair into three sections and made a quick braid, then tugged her clothes on over damp skin. She switched off the bathroom light as she went out the door, then turned back, shook her toothbrush out of its case, and brushed fiercely for a couple of seconds.

As Kate hurried down the stairs, Alison leaned into her parents' bedroom doorway. "Bye, Mom. We're off to the Wheelhouse."

Her mother murmured.

They went out to the workshop. Alison's father was looking over the plans for a set of cabinets. Kate had never seen plan drawings before. They were elegant and beautiful, pared down to essential lines, but every detail precisely rendered.

Alison took a sip of his coffee.

"Yuck. How can you drink this stuff?"

"It takes years of practice. Where are you off to so bright and early?"

"We're going to see the sights."

"Which ones would those be?"

"Down Winthrop, left on Butler to Perry, then right, across Shore Road to the beach. Then along the harbor to the marina."

"Okay. Just so I know."

They said goodbye and started toward the harbor. Kate noted the street name—Winthrop—in case she got lost.

A ten-minute walk took them to a beach they had

passed the day before. Kate forgot about her damp clothes and tangled hair. She wished they'd gotten there even earlier. In the delicate light, the sky and the ocean had emerged from the gray void of yesterday afternoon into radiant blues and blue-greens. Everything was revealed in its true colors, fresh and unspoiled. The world seemed newly made just for them, limitless and private at the same time.

Despite the clear sky and falling off of the wind, waves were surging onto the beach.

Out beyond the foam-capped breakers, the ocean was rising and falling in great, smooth rolls like molten glass.

Seagulls swooped overhead, screeching. Kate had never seen seagulls up close before. She'd always thought of them as cousins of terns. Now she saw that gulls were nothing like terns. They were many times bigger, with lethal-looking, downturned bills ending in points.

She and Alison began to search for shells, but that morning they couldn't find a single one that had made it to the beach intact.

They left the beach and walked through a waterfront park to the bronze statue of a fisherman. Outfitted in a slicker and sou'wester and grasping the wheel of a boat, the figure leaned stoically forward into an imaginary gale. Plaques set in a semicircle around the statue's pedestal were engraved with lists of names.

"Those are the fishermen who died at sea," said Alison. "We have a memorial service here every summer at the end of the waterfront festival."

"Even if nobody died that year?"

"Every year we've been here, somebody has."

"This year, too?"

Alison nodded. "Two people, about a month ago. Fishing's dangerous."

"So's farming," Kate said. "My grandparents know people who've had accidents with combines and hay balers and machines like that."

They continued on past icehouses, boat repair shops, marine suppliers, and docks where fishing boats were tied up. It was like traveling in a foreign country.

The Wheelhouse turned out to be a coffee shop on Shore Road. From the overheard conversations, Kate guessed that the customers were mostly fishermen. With their faded shirts and weather-beaten faces, they reminded her of the farmers she saw in Grafton every summer. They had a favorite coffee shop, too, where they gathered at dawn to talk about crop diseases and harvesting equipment and bank loans.

"What are your sisters' names?" Alison said, between bites of her cheese omelet.

"The older one's Anne."

"She's the one who's going to have a baby."

"Uh-huh."

"You're going to be an aunt. That's pretty amazing. I used to think you had to be a grownup to be an aunt. Who's your other sister?"

"Zorina. Everybody calls her Zee."

Alison laughed. "A to Z. I guess your parents thought they were only going to have two. You must have been a surprise."

Kate nodded. Not everybody noticed the significance of the names. She couldn't remember how old she'd been when she'd noticed it herself.

"Do you have any pets?" Alison said.

"No."

Kate briefly thought of the photo of Anne and Zee playing with four marmalade kittens, the litter of a stray cat that Zee had taken in when she was ten, just before Kate was born. Anne was already in her second year of high school by then, trying to look sophisticated for the camera. The kittens had long since been given away, and the mother cat, too.

"Want to see a haunted house?" asked Alison as they were leaving.

"Sure. Thanks for breakfast."

"It was fun. I've never bought breakfast for anyone before."

Alison led the way, up one narrow street and down the next. At the intersection of Chandler and Kirk, Kate turned around. Below them was the harbor. She was surprised how high they'd climbed. As they got away from the town center, the lots, hardly bigger than the houses that sat on them, gave way to slightly larger ones. Some had small gardens.

"Are there any brick houses around here?" asked Kate. Next to the solid masonry walls of her own neighborhood, wood seemed insubstantial.

"I think there's a couple on Elliot Street."

Alison stopped at a corner and looked diagonally across the intersection. "That's it."

The three-story house was taller than the others nearby. Its mansard roof created a hulking silhouette against the sky. The boarded-up windows looked like so many shut eyes.

The overgrown yard must have been somebody's well-tended garden once. Now the lawn had turned into a hay-field. Rosebushes had ensnared the trellis while ivy was sending runners up the walls. Wisteria had wrapped itself around the feet of the twin stone lions guarding the front steps.

"Whose house is it?" said Kate.

"It belonged to somebody named Martin Quinlan. He died a couple of years ago."

"Was he old?"

"I think he was about seventy."

"Why are the windows like that?"

"Some kids broke in and started a fire. The lady who lives across the street spotted it and called the fire department. They put it out right away, but a lot of stuff got wrecked from the smoke and the water."

"Who owns it now?"

"I'm not sure. Somebody told my mom that Martin Quinlan had two stepbrothers somewhere and that they're in a big fight about who gets the place. It isn't really haunted. I just think it looks creepy."

To Kate, it looked like a house of secrets, turned in on itself, surrounded by a magic garden. Next time, she'd have to bring her sketch pad.

———

At lunch, Alison questioned her mother about the Quinlan house.

"Funny you should ask. I just heard that one of the stepbrothers is here from out of state to clean out the house and put it on the market. The estate must have been settled."

"Didn't the man who died have any family here?" said Kate.

"I guess not," said Mrs. Lang.

"Wasn't there something wrong with him?" said Alison. "Mentally, I mean."

Mrs. Lang shook her head. "I imagine that you've heard some people talking. He was a little slow but a very good-hearted person. I did some volunteer work in the office at the Art Association when we first moved here. Martin did odd jobs for them, so I saw him once in a while. A lot of people really liked him. When he wasn't working, he spent most of his time at the Wheelhouse. All the regulars knew him."

Later that afternoon, Alison's father came home from a carpentry job with a flyer. An auction of furniture and household items from the Quinlan house was scheduled for just over a week away, on Saturday, July 9, in the Mary, Star of the Sea church hall.

After breakfast the next morning, they loaded the car with blankets, suntan lotion, and a cooler of lunch food and drove to Thayer's Cove Beach. The huge swells had given way to gentle rolls.

"Now, don't get lulled into a false sense of security," Alison's father said. "The undertow is always a danger. Stay well inside the rope barriers."

"I don't think Kate knows what undertow is," said Alison.

"Yes I do," Kate said. "It's a current under the surface that goes back out to sea. They explained it in my swimming class."

"Terrific!" said Alison's father. "Have you ever felt one?"

Kate shook her head. The largest body of water she'd ever been in was Grange Lake, near the farm. The best afternoons in the world had been spent stretched out in knee-deep water with the gentle waves lapping around her shoulders and minnows nibbling at her feet.

"Alison, you and Kate stick together," said her mother as she spread suntan lotion on Alison. "Kate, you need some of this, too, although you won't burn as fast."

"I'm the freckle queen," said Alison, pulling her hair back with a band.

When they were both thoroughly smeared with lotion, Alison took Kate's hand and ran toward the water.

Kate was too surprised to resist. "Is it going to be cold?"

Alison didn't answer. She dragged the two of them into the surf until they were hip deep. The water was like an ice bath. Kate gasped for breath as Alison ducked under the surface for an instant and bounced back up.

"You're better off getting it over with," she said. "Feel the undertow?"

Kate felt it as each wave receded, a pulling toward the ocean.

"And there's riptides, too, but we won't go out far enough to run into one."

"What's a riptide?" Kate could feel her teeth chattering as she spoke.

"That's a current that runs along the shore and out to sea. If you got caught in one, you might not be able to swim back."

Kate scooped up a handful of water and tasted it.

"See? It really is salty," said Alison. "I was surprised, too."

Kate discovered that the smoothly undulating waves had surprising force. Resisting their impact one after another was giddy fun. By comparison, Grange Lake was a bathtub of warm, placid water. When Alison's mother called them in to have lunch a short while later, dry land felt like another world.

Kate quickly learned that fun in Alison's family usually involved running, jumping, or chasing after small objects with a racket or with bare hands. Besides swimming, the weekend was spent playing softball, tennis, soccer, and croquet.

Kate was afraid she'd be the one to fumble the ball and get the rules mixed up, but as it turned out, Alison's father was the only one in the family who was good at physical games. Although he clowned around a lot, Kate could see that he was a natural athlete.

Kate's father had once been an athlete, too. He'd played for his college basketball team. In his study, there was a faded photograph of him in his uniform.

The weekend extended into Monday, the Fourth of July. The morning was spent in Alison's failed attempt to teach Kate how to Rollerblade. With pads strapped over every exposed joint, Kate tottered down the sidewalk clutching Alison's hand.

"Don't worry, I fall all the time," said Alison. Kate knew that was intended to be reassuring.

The afternoon was spent back at Thayer's Cove. That evening, the town's volunteer firemen set off fireworks over the water. Kate was happy for all the distraction. Now that she had seen the Art Association's imposing façade and the first class was hours away, she had started to wonder how much was expected of beginning students.

❀ Taking the World Apart

THE NEXT MORNING, Kate and Alison joined half a dozen people in the Art Association's lobby. At first, Kate thought they'd run into a tour for seniors. At least two of the people looked as old as her grandparents. Then she saw that all of them were outfitted with pads of paper.

A girl who looked about sixteen years old sat at the reception desk. A shock of her hair was dyed neon pink, which made an interesting contrast with her green feather earrings.

Kate was tempted to turn around and leave, explain later that the whole thing had been a mistake, and get a refund if she could. She didn't intend to spend the summer in a class with people who had nothing better to do with their time.

A young woman walked briskly into the lobby. Instantly, Kate thought of her sister. Like Zee, she was small and dark, and her movements had a crisp energy, like those of a dancer. "I'm sorry I'm late. Are you all here for Basic Drawing?"

An assenting murmur went around the group.

A woman raised her hand. "Miss Everett?"

"Please call me Laura."

"Laura, I'm not sure I belong here. I'm afraid I can't draw a straight line. Is there a class for completely untalented amateurs?"

A ripple of laughter went around the lobby. Several people nodded.

"First," said Laura, "nobody is too inexperienced to be in this class. Second, I may not be able to turn you into Michelangelo, but however you draw, I can teach you to draw better. And third, if you ever have to draw a really straight line, use a ruler."

More laughter followed Laura's last remark.

"Please come this way," she said, "to the library."

They followed her into a wood-paneled room. Kate took

in the marble portrait heads and oil paintings on display. Except for the metal folding chairs and a blackboard in the center of the room, it looked like a wealthy man's home. With her running shoes and backpack, Kate felt like a tourist in a church she didn't belong to.

"Please sit down. In case you missed my name just now, I'm Laura Everett.

"I wish our class met every day instead of once a week, but this course is an experiment by the Art Association. Even though our time is limited, I'll be able to introduce you to various approaches to drawing. My method is very traditional, which is the way I was trained. It's true that the origin of an artwork is in the creativity of the individual. You have a vision of something—a bowl of fruit or a landscape or your mother's face. That's excellent, you have imagination. But to show that vision to someone else, you need skill. You need tools in your kit."

Kate wasn't sure exactly what Laura meant by "vision." She hoped she could figure it out as the class went on.

"I'll begin each session with a talk, which I will try to make mercifully brief, then we'll go someplace and sketch. But if you really want to increase your drawing ability, don't limit your sketching to class time. Try to do at least a drawing a day. I'll be happy to give you my comments on any work you bring in.

"Before we begin, could you all just say your names for me, starting over there on the left? And maybe something about yourself?"

The person in that chair was the only man in the class.

He gave his name as Bob Banfield, a retired engineer. Next to him was Delia Longwood, a retired elementary school teacher, then Louise Farley, a retired organist and vocal coach, Jean Randall, the owner of a local bookstore, and Irene Dixon, the former postmaster in town.

Kate wasn't sure how to describe herself, so she just said, "I'm in school."

"Me, too," said Alison.

Sitting next to Alison was a woman who looked about the same age as Kate's mother—Barbara Shelley, a real estate agent.

Laura maneuvered the blackboard so that it faced the class.

"To a great extent, learning to draw is learning to see, and it's a gradual process." She picked up a piece of chalk.

"Every object, no matter how complicated it looks, can be broken down into one or more of the basic geometric forms: the cube, the cone, the cylinder, and the sphere." As she named each one, she drew it on the board. "I challenge anybody to think of an object that can't be analyzed in this way."

"An elephant," said Alison.

"Excellent subject," said Laura. "I'd start with a cube for the body. Might want to fatten him up by using part of a sphere—with cylinders for legs. The head is a bit tricky, but I'd say it fits nicely inside the base of a cone. The trunk, of course, is an elongated cone. And there's your elephant."

Alison wasn't discouraged. At her request, a rabbit, a truck, and a waterlily appeared on the board.

Kate was embarrassed at first, but Laura seemed to relish the opportunity to demonstrate her method.

"Okay," she said, brushing the chalk dust off her hands, "let's go out and draw. Today we're going to Cranford Neck."

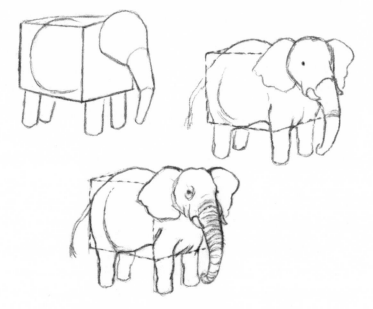

The class began gathering up their things, chatting enthusiastically, except for Kate. She continued to study the blackboard.

She had watched the demonstration carefully. She couldn't deny that Laura was skillful, her lines confident and strong. As she drew the basic forms, a person could feel them, solid and three-dimensional. The rabbit was as sturdy as the truck. But wasn't a rabbit a fragile thing—all nervously twitching nose and whiskers and soft ears? And yet Laura's rabbit was an excellent rabbit.

Kate picked up her drawing pad and joined Alison, who was waiting by the door.

Cranford Neck turned out to be a finger of land that extended into the water a few blocks away. Where a pier had been built over part of it, some of Laura's students set up folding camp chairs they had brought. Others found space on benches. They started drawing docks and shacks and dinghies. Alison set herself up in front of an overturned sailboat hull left on the rocky beach.

Kate wandered around. Picking the right subject for this first drawing was important. Despite her reaction to Laura's method, Kate wanted her new teacher to understand that she was a serious student. Twined around a post, she saw a vine of morning glories. She sat down on an old wooden box and began to work.

Kate lost awareness of the minutes passing as her pencil point followed the outline of the blossoms like a sightless person feeling an object to learn its shape.

"May I sit down?" Laura was standing behind her.

"Sure."

"Those are wonderful morning glories you've drawn. Very beautiful line."

"Thanks."

"I don't want to give you a hard sell here, but would you be willing to try something?"

"Sure." Kate didn't see what else she could say.

"Looking at the largest mass of the flower, which of the basic forms does it resemble?"

"I suppose it's a cone."

"Yes, definitely. It's a flared cone. Can you picture the cone at various angles?"

Kate shrugged.

Laura pulled out a spiral pad of her own and sketched a half dozen cones, each facing a different direction. "When I see a bunch of flowers, I often think they look like a group of people watching a parade. Each one is looking at something different. If you keep that in mind, your composition will have more variety."

Within the hard lines of the cones, she sketched curved lines to make the flaring trumpet shapes.

"By the way, the method I'm using is called 'crating.' In drawing a complex shape, it's often useful to picture the subject in a close-fitting container, like a crate. Draw the container, then draw the object inside it."

Laura stood up. "I've got to help the next person now. I'll try to get back to you." She tore off the drawing she had done on her pad and handed it to Kate.

Kate studied it. She had to admit Laura's drawing had a pleasing composition. The blossoms almost seemed to be in motion. But crating flowers? The idea was repellent.

Kate began a second drawing of the morning glories, building them inside the cone shape. They looked as if they were made out of steel. This method might work for Laura, but it wasn't going to work for Kate.

Maybe that meant Laura was the better artist. Maybe Kate's approach wasn't sensitive but merely sloppy. In her heart, she didn't believe that, but she felt that her own work had been diminished by comparison.

Laura walked to the center of the group. "This is the official end of today's class," she said, "but feel free to work as long as you like. I'll be here for another few minutes."

Kate didn't want to stay any longer. She was about to close her sketch pad when Alison came over. "I just did a lousy drawing of the hull. Laura said I'd picked about the toughest subject around here, but she was probably trying to make me feel better. How'd you make out?"

They compared drawings.

"Hey, you can really draw," said Alison, looking at the first page of morning glories.

"Well, I picked an easy subject," Kate said, feeling the discomfort she always did when singled out for praise.

Alison was right about the sailboat hull. Her drawing missed the graceful shape entirely. But the boulders that she had drawn in the background were lively and interesting. They seemed to be having a conversation among themselves.

"I like the way you've drawn the rocks."

"That's what Laura said. Maybe I should stick to simple stuff."

Before they went home, Alison took Kate to Kennon's Office Supply to make photocopies of her drawings. Next to the copier was a display of sketchbooks. Kate picked out a pocket-sized one and took it to the register.

When they got back to the Langs', their drawings were met with immediate enthusiasm by Alison's parents, which Alison seemed to take as a matter of course. Kate mumbled her thanks and escaped to the bedroom. Alison followed a minute later. She tore her drawing out of the pad and pinned it up on her bulletin board.

After lunch, Kate tried to draw one of Alison's angelfish.

"I wish it would hold still for a second. I'm not drawing it very well."

"The angelfish is probably a basic form Laura forgot to tell us about. You know, the cube, the cone, the cylinder, the sphere, and the angelfish." Alison pushed herself out of the recliner. "I just remembered. It's my turn to do the plants. I'll be right back." She went to the kitchen and returned with a small watering can.

Kate noted that the body of the can was a cylinder. The spout was an elongated cone. The handle was the circumference of a sphere. Well, maybe basic forms had a use—for simple, man-made objects.

Kate went back to the kitchen with Alison and began emptying the dish drainer. The colander was a half sphere. The cheese grater was an elongated cube.

"What are you looking at?" asked Alison as Kate studied the teapot from all angles. It was a sphere with a short, fat cone for a spout and a circular handle.

After Kate explained, they began taking turns to see who could come up with the most complicated object to analyze. Muffin tins, ladles, eggcups, can openers, and a waffle iron were hauled out of drawers and cabinets. As the game went on, they found it more and more difficult to find something challenging.

Finally Alison announced she'd had enough. "After this, I'm not sure I'll be able to look at anything and not see a basic form."

Kate knew that Alison was joking, but she wondered if there was any truth in the remark. Was that the life of the artist—forever taking the world apart and rebuilding it according to a scheme? Maybe she'd have to learn everything all over again. She reached into the soapy water and couldn't help noticing—the glass in her hand was a cylinder.

That night, Kate wrote her first letter home:

Tuesday, July 5

Dear Mom & Dad,

The trip on the plane was fine, except it was a little bumpy at the end because we were flying in a rainstorm. I'm sharing Alison's room. It's a very nice room—painted bright purple!

Alison has three aquariums with lots of fish. One of them was leaking, but her father brought home a new one. Setting it up and putting the fish back took a couple of hours.

I've been in the ocean. It was like jumping into an ice cube tray, although it's fun once you stop shaking. Guess what—it tastes salty!

Fourth of July was fun, too, with lots of fireworks.

The first art class was this morning. The teacher's name is Laura and she's very nice, but I don't think I'm going to do well in her class, since we don't draw the same way at all.

I'm sending copies of the drawings I did. I did the second one making the flowers out of cone shapes, the way she suggested. I think it looks awful, but you asked to see what I was doing in class and this is it.

Call me as soon as the operation is over.

Love,

Kate

A thunderclap awoke Kate the next morning. According to the marine forecast on the kitchen radio as she came downstairs, intermittent rain was going to fall during the day, with clearing by evening.

"Why don't you visit the Historical Society Museum?" Mrs. Lang asked as she set out the cereal bowls. "I think Kate would find it interesting. Then the two of you can go out to lunch on me."

Kate nodded, even though the museum sounded dull. At least it was someplace to go out of the rain.

After breakfast, she and Alison walked to the Historical Society sharing Mr. Lang's giant umbrella.

Just past the entrance, a woman in a flower print dress looked up from the reception desk. "Oh, hello, Alison."

"Hi, Mrs. Travers. This is Kate. She's staying with us for the summer."

"How nice." Mrs. Travers held up the book to show the cover. "Have either of you read any of these Inspector Trask mysteries? I'm just wondering if they're worth the time."

"I've read a couple of them," said Kate. "We—my dad and I—thought that the author kept too much information from the reader until the very end."

"Did you? Well, I guess I should give this one a chance as long as I've got it."

Kate opened her wallet and pulled out three dollars for admission.

"Oh, there's no charge," said Mrs. Travers with a smile. "I'll put your umbrella in the coatroom. Here's a map and a list of our special exhibits this month."

They thanked her and went through the turnstile. Kate was puzzled.

"My dad made some cases for their exhibits, so I get in free," Alison said quietly as they went into the first hall, devoted to ship models and navigation instruments. A diorama in the center of the room showed the harbor in 1800.

Kate had always loved scale models. She walked slowly around the diorama, studying every element—the men unloading fish from one boat, wooden chests from a second, women holding children by the hand, dogs trotting along unleashed, all of them fixed at a moment in time.

Kate circled the diorama again.

"I'm going into the next hall, just so you know where I am," said Alison.

Kate realized that she must have seemed like a sleepwalker. "Sorry, I'll be right there."

"That's okay. Don't hurry."

But the spell was broken. Kate followed Alison into the next hall.

Wooden figureheads were suspended from the ceiling. After the miniature harbor, the outsized carvings were a shock. Most of them were damaged in some way or badly weathered. Kate found their exaggerated features disturbing.

They went to the second floor. A sign was stenciled on the entrance to the gallery—"The Age of Sail."

"These are the cases my dad built," Alison said.

They contained hundreds of exquisite objects from the Far East arrayed on glass shelves: letter openers, earrings, bracelets, necklaces, pendants, combs to be worn in ladies' hair, belt buckles, perfume bottles, spice jars, baby spoons, ceramic bowls, teapots, teacups, boxes for snuff and boxes for letters, jars for sealing wax. Little white cards listed the materials: jade and moonstone and opal, porcelain, mahogany, and teak. Even Alison, who must have seen these things many times, seemed fascinated by them.

The objects had cards giving the sources: "Sarah Pickney," "The Estate of Eleanor Thayer," "The Estate of Margaret Hathaway," women who combed their hair and stirred their tea with treasures brought from half a world away. Kate had just started to read the informational sign when Alison came up behind her.

"It's twelve forty-five. I don't know about you, but I'm hungry."

"Is there someplace around here to eat?"

"Lots. The best one is up the street."

Mrs. Travers slipped a bookmark into her paperback when Kate and Alison got back to her desk. "That Inspector Trask is so clever," she said as she disappeared into the coatroom.

They thanked Mrs. Travers again and sloshed through the puddles to the Purple Cow.

When they walked in, Kate wondered why the place had been given the name. Everything she saw was glossy black and white—the old-fashioned tile floor, the glistening white walls, the black marble tabletops, the striped chairs. The Purple Cow's main attraction was ice cream, judging from the number of exotic flavors listed on the menu board.

"I guess we'd better get a sandwich first," said Alison. "Save room for dessert."

They decided to split the house special. "It's the best," said Alison. "I've tried them all."

Just then, the table by the window opened up. "Grab it," she said. Kate sat down in the nearest chair, feeling conspicuous to be occupying a table with no food in front of her.

"I almost forgot," Alison said, as she set the tray down a few minutes later, "tomorrow I've got an appointment in the city with my orthodontist. I'm hoping he'll say I don't need the retainer anymore. My mom and I have to leave after breakfast. We'll be back about three. You could come, but it's going to be boring. Mostly, we sit around the waiting room."

Kate thought of her father's operation. That was tomorrow, too. She needed to be by the telephone, someplace private.

"I'll stay here. I can read or maybe draw something."

"Okay. There's books in the living room. My dad will be in the shop working all day, so you won't be by yourself."

They split dessert as well, a hot fudge sundae since, as Alison pointed out, the weather was cold.

By the time they finished eating, the rain had stopped.

"Let's check out the water," said Alison. They headed toward Perry Street.

When they got to the beach, she shuffled through the sand to a spot just above the reach of the waves. "The tide's coming in."

"How can you tell?"

"Well, I can't really. I looked at the tide tables in the paper this morning. If we stood here for a few minutes though," Alison said, "you'd see it. Your shoes would get wet."

"It comes in that fast?"

Alison nodded. "Here it does. But my dad says that each place that has a tide is different. It matters how steep the ocean bottom is and lots of other things like that. Would you hold the umbrella for a sec?" As the water receded toward the shallows, she ran down the wet sand after it, then turned and ran back up the beach with the next wave racing after her.

"Try it," she said. "Leave the umbrella. It'll be okay."

Kate put it several feet into the dry sand area. They spent the next few minutes alternately pursuing and being chased by waves. It was a silly game, but soon they were both gasping for breath from laughing.

Alison shook her foot. "I just got water in my shoe."

"Me, too."

Suddenly Kate remembered. "Alison! Your dad's umbrella!"

About twenty feet up the beach, it tumbled lazily in the surf. They splashed their way to it through ankle-deep water, Alison in the lead. She grabbed the handle and righted the umbrella. Sandy water poured out.

"That was close," said Alison. "Thanks, Kate."

As they trudged up Winthrop Street a few minutes later, Kate could feel her wet socks rubbing tender spots on her feet.

"I think I'm getting blisters," she said.

"Me, too," said Alison.

When they got to the house, Alison turned on the garden hose and washed the umbrella and their shoes before setting everything on the back porch to dry.

Alison's mother called to them from her office as they came through the kitchen. "How was the museum?"

"Great!" Kate answered.

They managed to get upstairs without having to answer any more questions.

Before getting into bed that night, Kate saw the full moon near the horizon, huge and yellow. It was the moon and the sun, she knew, that caused the daily tides, exerting their gravitational pull through the incomprehensible distance of space. As the earth and the moon swung around the sun, billions of tons of seawater rose and fell, changing the shape of every coastline on earth, pushing salt water into the mouths of freshwater rivers, raising and lowering ships at anchor, and sweeping a forgotten umbrella off Perry Street beach.

✲ Sold

"REMEMBER," SAID MRS. LANG, as Kate checked the kitchen clock at breakfast the next morning, "you're in a different time zone here. It's earlier where your parents are."

Kate had forgotten about that.

Alison's father carried his plate to the sink. "If you want some company, I'm going to be gluing together a cabinet today, so it's safe for you to be in the shop, and you won't have to yell over power tools."

"Kate, leave the dishes," said Mrs. Lang. "Alison, we've got to step on it."

As they were going out the door, Alison turned around. "Don't worry, Kate. Your dad is going to be fine."

"Thanks."

After they left, the house was quiet, except for the bubbling of the aquarium filters. Kate washed the breakfast dishes anyway, partly for something to do.

She went upstairs to the bathroom and braided her hair, pulling out the hinged sides of the mirror to see herself from all angles. Her hair, neither blond like Anne's nor brunette like Zee's, was middle-of-the-road brown. People called the color of her eyes "hazel." What was hazel except a mishmash of colors?

She had one distinctive feature. Of the three daughters,

she was the only one to have inherited their father's cleft chin.

Kate went to the bedroom and checked the clock. Five after nine.

She went downstairs to the living room and began searching the bookshelves. The books had been arranged by subject—navigation, woodworking, accounting, and field guides.

Kate was about to go upstairs for her puzzle book when she found a history of the town and a book on the geology of the region. She took both and settled into the recliner.

She opened the first book and skipped to the second chapter. It told the story of sea trade in the 1840s and '50s. In the days when Panama was a jungle and not a canal, elegant sailing ships known as clippers raced around the tip of South America to San Francisco and on to Shanghai and Hong Kong, returning with exotic goods destined for the homes of the wealthy, as well as tea and spices for millions of kitchens. Paintings of the town's harbor done in those days showed a forest of masts as ships tied up at every available slip on the docks.

Before long, the clippers had to compete with steamboats, sturdy vessels that chugged steadily through the water in high winds or dead calms. When the Union Pacific and Central Pacific Railroads met in 1869, goods began to travel overland as well. The clipper ships all but vanished within a decade.

When the coming of rail turned the prosperity from sea trade into a thing of the past, the town still had its fishing industry. Then the fish, which had once seemed abundant beyond calculation, began to disappear.

Kate could see that, since the book was locally published, the author tried to put the best face on the situation, applauding the town's history as an art colony from its earliest days to the present, when the stock of cheap houses was luring young people into the area, people who wanted to renovate the aging cottages that had once belonged to fishermen. That explained something Kate had been wondering about—why many of the houses looked so neglected and other ones, right in the same block, had been fixed up, like the Langs'.

Kate checked the time. Ten twenty-five.

She turned to the book on local geology, which described the land as a veneer of sandy topsoil on bedrock, its coastline continuously remade by the surrounding ocean.

Kate put the books back on the shelf. The quiet had become oppressive. She went out to the shop to talk to Mr. Lang. She found him clamping two pieces of wood together.

"I was just about to see if you needed anything," he said. "Did you find something to read? I'm afraid most of our books wouldn't interest you."

"No, I found a good one with a chapter on the clipper ships. Alison told me that you're building a sailboat."

"Uh-huh. My own design. I should be able to get it certified next month and take all of you out on it."

"Where is it?"

"At a place I'm renting near the waterfront."

The telephone in the shop rang. Alison's father wiped

his hands and picked it up. "Tom Lang. Oh, hi." He glanced at Kate. "Uh-huh . . . uh-huh . . ."

Kate sat very still. She watched Mr. Lang's face closely.

"Well, that's terrific news. She's sitting right here. I'll put her on." He handed the phone to Kate.

"Dad?"

"Hi, Kate." Her mother's voice had the bright tone that Kate associated with the need to be upbeat. "Dad's a little groggy from the anesthesia, so I won't put him on, but he's fine. He's out of recovery. I'm calling from his room." Kate could hear women's voices and a hospital public address system paging a doctor. "The operation went very well according to Dr. Franey. I'll call again later, and you can talk to Dad then. How are you doing, Kate?"

"Great. Tell Dad I'm really happy he's okay." That sounded like a greeting card, but Kate knew he would understand how she felt.

"I'll tell him. I'll talk to you later, sweetheart."

"Talk to you." Kate handed the phone back to Mr. Lang. She wanted to jump up and down and yell, but she could only have done that if she were alone.

The mood at dinner that night was unusually cheerful. Everybody made jokes and laughed a lot. Alison announced she was going to make a bracelet out of her discarded retainer. Her father suggested they turn it into a hood ornament for the car—"to remind me where the money went." Kate realized that the Langs must have been worried, too, more than they let on.

The promised phone call from Kate's mother came just after eight-thirty. When Kate took the phone, she heard more of the hospital noises in the background.

"Kate, I'm going to pass you along to Dad for a quick hello."

"Hi, sprout." Her father's voice sounded like that of a very old man. "How are you doing?"

"Fine, Dad. Are you all right?"

"Well, the hospital food I had for supper didn't kill me, so I must be doing okay. I'm getting out on Monday if everything goes according to plan."

"Shouldn't you stay in longer, so they're sure you're okay?"

"Don't worry. We're only five minutes from the hospital if anything goes wrong." There was a pause. Kate could hear her father saying something to someone in the room. "They want to give me some more of their magic potions, so I'll have to say goodbye."

"Bye, Dad."

On Friday, Kate's mother called in the late afternoon to reassure her that her father's recovery was going along as planned, but he was sleeping, so Kate couldn't talk to him.

Saturday morning the topic of conversation at the Langs' breakfast table was the auction at the church hall starting in an hour. Mr. Lang explained that he sometimes bought tables and chairs as examples of good workmanship or simply because he liked them. Occasionally, he refinished a piece and sold it.

The rest of them decided to go for fun. Kate had never been to an auction.

"I've heard that a professional auctioneer has been hired for the occasion," said Alison's mother.

The church was close by, but they drove in case they needed to carry something back in the trunk. When they got there, the hall was already filled with people. Rows of folding chairs had been set up facing a lectern.

Besides the tables and chairs that Mr. Lang was interested in, the furniture included bureaus, bed frames, a wooden chest, several large mirrors, and a desk with lots of compartments. Rolled-up rugs and a number of picture frames had been stacked against one wall. What the frames contained was a mystery in some cases, thanks to a heavy coating of soot. Kate's first impression was that everything there was made of soot: pots, pans, dishes, silverware, lamps, furniture. For the most part, objects seemed to have been cleaned only enough to reveal what material they were made of. The whole place had the smell of smoke about it.

From the remarks Kate overheard, a lot of people weren't there to bid. They were just curious to see what had been in the Quinlan house.

"Most of this had to have come down in Martin's family," Alison's mother said. "I doubt he ever bought anything besides the food he needed and a pair of socks every now and again." She picked up a teapot. "This is probably sterling silver. From what I hear, Martin's mother always liked good things."

In Kate's opinion, the same could not be said for her taste in paintings. Of the ones that could be seen through the grime, several were sentimental depictions of children with inhumanly large eyes, red lips, and golden ringlets. Two paintings featured artificial-looking rainbows, and one landscape included trees on which every leaf had been painted separately, the way a little child would do it.

Alison thought they were dreadful. "I like the dirtiest ones best," she said. "You can't see a thing."

Kate and Alison found seats together in the fourth row. Alison's parents sat several rows behind them.

At the lectern, a man in a suit clapped for quiet. "Ladies and gentlemen, we're going to begin. Please be seated. There's no need to shout your bid. Just raise your hand when I call out a dollar figure. That will indicate your willingness to pay that amount for the item. But please, good people, make sure that that willingness is backed up with the ability to pay. I know many of the items look unprepossessing in their present state, but I am sure that most if not all of them will clean up quite nicely.

"Let's begin. I have here a claw-foot tea table with curved legs. The edge of the table is carved in the so-called piecrust fashion. The wood appears to be mahogany. I'm going to open the bidding at fifty dollars. Do I have a bid at fifty dollars?" He scanned the audience. "Yes, I have a bid from the gentleman to my right. Do I have sixty? Yes. The lady in the third row. Will anyone go seventy? Very good, sir. The gentleman to my left will go seventy . . ."

Kate had imagined that the auction was going to become boring, with the auctioneer's nasal voice reciting the same formula over and over. Instead, she found herself getting so caught up in the excitement, she could hardly keep up with the bids. The furniture was auctioned first. One item after another was brought to the side of the lectern, to be carted off by the new owner a minute or two later. Mr. Lang made the highest bid on a captain's chair.

When the last piece of furniture was gone, the auctioneer turned to the lamps and kitchenware.

Mrs. Lang appeared at the end of the row where Kate and Alison were sitting. "Your father and I are going," she said in a low voice, "but you and Kate can stay if you like."

Alison and Kate looked at each other. "Want to go?" said Alison.

"I'd like to watch a little longer."

"Me, too."

"See you at home," said Mrs. Lang. "Lunch at one o'clock." She left.

The tables began to be cleared of items at a rapid pace, with whole tea sets and dish sets sold as one. The paintings were next.

The first ones to be auctioned were the cleanest. They went for about forty dollars apiece. Kate figured that people were buying them for the frames, most of which looked well made.

Then the auctioneer began selling paintings partly obscured by smoke damage. Those went for less, about thirty or thirty-five dollars. Then a painting totally hidden under soot was held up.

"A work, presumed to be an oil painting, sixteen by twenty inches, in a simple wood frame. I'm opening the bidding at five dollars."

Kate heard a woman behind her whisper to someone, "That frame would be good for Mark's graduation picture."

This was probably the first and last time Kate would be at an auction. What was the harm? She raised her hand.

"I have five dollars, in the fourth row. Will someone make it ten?" The auctioneer pointed to the woman behind Kate. "I have ten with the lady in the blue dress. Do I have fifteen?"

The woman was sure to outbid her. Kate raised her hand.

"Fifteen with the young lady in the fourth row. Do I have twenty? Twenty? Anyone?" The auctioneer held his gavel poised. Kate felt her face get hot as her heart began pounding. "Sold!" He brought down the gavel with a crack. "For fifteen dollars to the young lady in the fourth row."

Kate couldn't believe it. In less than a minute, she'd given up all her allowance for this week and half of the next for a painting she couldn't see and probably would hate if she could.

"Have you got enough money?" whispered Alison.

Kate tried to think. She had just gotten a ten-dollar bill from Mrs. Lang that morning, and she had three singles left over from the previous week. "I think I'm two dollars short," she whispered back.

"I've got it," said Alison, pressing two crumpled bills into Kate's hand.

"Thanks."

Kate could still feel her pulse in her ears as she made her way out of her row to the table that had been set up for payments. She handed over the fifteen dollars. A young man who had been assisting with the furniture gave her the painting. Kate felt the powdery soot coming off on her hands. She tried to hold the frame away from her clothes.

"Here," said the woman who had taken the money, "I have a plastic bag that might fit." She slipped the bag around the painting, trying not to touch it herself. "Perfect."

"Thanks." When Kate turned around, Alison was standing by the door.

"You know," she said as they left, "my dad can clean that frame for you. It might be nice."

Kate appreciated Alison's efforts to make her feel better, but just then, she was overwhelmed with the feeling she had been foolish and irresponsible. True, the allowance was hers with no strings attached. That was the point. She was supposed to learn how to spend a fixed amount wisely. Well, she'd gotten a fifteen-dollar lesson this week.

"I can loan you something, so you'll have some money until next Saturday," said Alison.

Kate shook her head. "That's really nice of you, but I can't start borrowing money from you. It wouldn't be right."

"What's not right?"

Kate couldn't explain.

When they got home, they could hear Alison's parents

talking in the shop. Alison opened the back door quietly. They went upstairs and counted all the change in Kate's backpack, plus what she had in the pockets of her jacket and pants. It totaled sixty-eight cents.

"You can't even get a single-scoop cone with that," said Alison. "You'd better let me loan you some money."

Kate finally agreed to a four-dollar loan, to be paid back the following Saturday.

"I won't say anything about the painting if you don't want me to," said Alison. Kate thought about that. She wanted to dump the painting in the garbage when no one was looking, but she decided that she'd better tell Alison's parents what had happened.

Kate showed them the painting at lunch.

"We can salvage the frame for sure," said Mr. Lang. "I don't know anything about cleaning paintings."

"I wonder who would," said Mrs. Lang. "Tom, do we know anybody?"

"I don't think so. Try the phone book."

"I bet Laura would know," said Alison.

"Laura?" said Mrs. Lang.

"Our drawing teacher. We can ask her on Tuesday."

"That's a great idea," said Mr. Lang.

Kate nodded. It was a great idea. But no amount of cleaning could fix what was likely to be underneath the dirt.

The forecast for the rest of the weekend was rain, which had started falling during lunch. Mr. Lang decided to use the time for working on the boat. Mrs. Lang took Kate and Alison to a local historic house.

They spent Sunday poking into the shops downtown. At first, the sand dollars and glass fishnet floats and driftwood looked exotic, but after Kate saw the same things in two or three stores, they didn't seem quite so special.

Steering her umbrella around other pedestrians, Kate realized that this was the second week of July, and they hadn't had a single day of unbroken blue sky. On the brightest days, the sunlight was still punctuated by clouds. Even when rain wasn't falling, water hung invisibly in the air, curling the pages of books and magazines and rusting the heads of nails in the woodwork. The celestial almanac in the daily paper was all but useless, the night sky clouded over more often than not.

On Monday morning, the rain let up. While Alison's father went back to his cabinetry job, the "womenfolk," as he called them, drove to the quarry.

Long abandoned, what remained was a man-made amphitheater cut into the granite hillside. Shrubs dotted the walls. Their roots split the rock as effectively as wedges once had, however slowly, and softened its fracture lines.

Every whisper resonated. At intervals, drops of water rolled off leaves, making an irregular patter like the ticking of a clock whose spring was nearly unwound.

Kate wished her mother and father could be there. They would think it was wonderful. Maybe when her father was completely recovered, he'd be able to hike again, the way he had before, leading Kate and her mother through tangled vegetation and up steep inclines, suddenly stopping and holding up his hand for quiet because he'd heard a bird call or seen a movement in the brush.

When they got home, a letter had arrived for Kate.

Fri., July 8

Dear Kate,

You'll have to forgive any lack of clarity in this letter. I think I'm still coming out of the anesthesia.

I have your letter in front of me. I found your drawings quite interesting. It looks as if your teacher is using a more structural approach to drawing than you're used to. Don't be too quick to dismiss what she says.

I've never said this before, but I think that a sense of underlying structure is what's missing in your drawings. Also, you shy away from subjects that you're not good at drawing. You tend to stay with what you know.

If you had a surer sense of form, you would have the freedom to choose subjects that you might be afraid to tackle now.

By the way, the drawing that you've labeled 2 is better than you think. It may not have much surface prettiness, but it has dimension.

I hope you are having the time of your life.

Love,
Dad

Kate read the letter three times. Then she hauled her carry-on bag out of the closet and put the letter into the inside pouch. She had been hoping that her father would say something encouraging about the drawing done in her own style and that he would dismiss the other one as stiff and mechanical. She had imagined him telling her to stay with her own natural gift. Instead he was siding with Laura.

The comment about staying "with what you know" stung. That wasn't only about her artwork.

Kate's mother phoned after dinner. "We're home. I'm going to put Dad on, but don't talk too long."

"Hi, sweetheart. I felt like I was in for life, but they gave me time off for good behavior."

"I'm glad you're home. Dad, I saw the best place today. It's an old granite quarry. You'd love it."

"Sounds interesting. When is your next art lesson?"

"Tomorrow."

"Great. Your mother wants to say goodbye, so I'm signing off. Give my best to the Langs."

"I will. Bye, Dad."

If her father had been well, he'd have wanted to hear all about the quarry. He would have picked up immediately on what a special place it was. Despite her mother's brittle optimism, Kate knew that he had to be feeling very sick to have cut the call so short.

Kate's mother came back on the line. "How are things going?"

"Okay."

"You sound a little down in the dumps. Are you sure everything's okay?"

"I'm fine."

They talked a minute longer, then Kate's mother asked to talk to Mrs. Lang. Kate went out to the shop with Alison to watch Mr. Lang work on the captain's chair he'd bought. As the auctioneer had suggested, it was cleaning up quite nicely.

✿ Unexpected Entrances

THE ART LESSON the next morning began, like the first one, in the wood-paneled library. Laura sat on one of the metal folding chairs with a large drawing pad propped in front of her, and the class clustered behind her. About fifteen feet away, the young receptionist, the streak in her hair now a brilliant chartreuse, held an open umbrella as if she were standing in the rain.

"For this first one, Darlene," Laura said to her, "imagine that you're on the way to work and the bus is late."

Darlene grasped the umbrella handle with both hands and leaned to one side as if she were trying to see around a corner. Laura dashed out a few lines that caught the tilt of her body.

"Now imagine that you're waiting for the bus after you've shopped all morning and your feet are killing you."

Darlene's shoulders sagged. She let the umbrella rest against her neck.

"Perfect," said Laura.

A succession of drawings, each one hardly more than a scribble or a stick figure, appeared on the page as Darlene used the umbrella as a cane, twirled it on her shoulder like a parasol, and held it in an imaginary high wind.

"Gesture," said Laura, "that's what we're after this time, not form. Forget form—for today." She flipped the pad closed and reached for her bag. "Thanks, Darlene. You're a great model.

"Okay, everybody, we're off to the harbor. With any luck at all, there will be lots of people there. Of course, you can do a gesture drawing of a boat or any other object, but this technique is particularly good for getting the essence of a live model."

"Laura," said Miss Longwood, "what happens if the person we're trying to draw moves?"

"Ah," said Laura, "that's one of the benefits of this technique. It teaches you to capture a pose with your first few lines. You'll find you work with a lot more energy and concentration when you know the model may disappear at any time. If that happens, try to work from memory. But don't fuss over a failed drawing. Go on to another one."

"Scribbling sounds like my kind of thing," said Alison as they followed Laura out the door.

They reached the waterfront a few minutes later.

Kate and Alison found a bench to sit on facing the bronze statue of the fisherman. A steady stream of people came up to the monument, many of them pausing at least long enough to snap a photo.

At first, Kate's attempts to imitate what Laura had done failed completely. The paper was soon filled with meaningless tangles of lines. Alison seemed not to be having much success either.

"I think I need something simpler than a person to draw," said Alison. "Something that holds still." She went off in the direction of the piers.

In the two lessons so far, Kate didn't see that she'd had much chance to show what she could do. She felt as if she were taking a test and all the questions were exactly the things she hadn't studied.

She was about to try another location when her attention was caught by an elderly man walking up to the monument. His short-sleeved shirt revealed arms frail with age, but he held himself tall, his shoulders back. He stood for several moments, apparently reading names on one of the plaques. As he raised his hand to his face, Kate thought he was going to shade his eyes from the sun. Instead, he saluted. The movement was quick. Kate didn't think anyone else saw it. Then the man walked on.

Kate sat up, poised her pencil over the paper, and thought for a moment. She flicked out a few lines. They would have no significance to anybody else. But looking at her drawing, Kate saw the man saluting.

The next few drawings were disappointing. Kate figured that the good one had been an accident. Then a woman came by pushing a stroller. She knelt down to retie her toddler's shoe. With one line, Kate established the stroller handle. A simple curve was the woman's back, another outlined her head, two dashes were the child's waving arms. The woman stood up and moved away. Where had the child's legs been? Kate indicated them as best she could remember.

She turned to a terrier whose owner sat down to rest in the shade of a nearby tree. A triangle defined the sitting dog's body. A single short line showed the lift of his muzzle. Two quick dashes became the ears, cocked forward.

She looked at her three good drawings. A sort of magical transformation had taken place. A few scrawls had become a kind of code. Within a few minutes, she filled a second page. By that time, she was genuinely tired.

She went to find Alison and saw her sitting on a bench across the street from the Wheelhouse. Laura was looking over her shoulder.

"You've really got it," Laura was saying.

When Kate joined them, she saw that Alison's haphazard style had produced a drawing of the building that was messy and smudged. Lines careened around the page and sometimes off it. Kate couldn't find a single right angle. The walls slanted dangerously, the roof was out of kilter. It was a perfect portrait of the place.

"It's great," Kate said. "You should frame that one."

Alison was obviously pleased.

Laura turned to Kate. "I noticed you drawing up a storm over there. Could I see what you were working on?"

Kate hesitated. In the face of Alison's go-for-broke drawing, the exhilarating sense that she had discovered something had evaporated. The paper contained nothing but random marks—a lost language that even she couldn't translate.

But when Kate opened the pad, she found that the magical transformation was irreversible. The first thing she noticed were two tiny commas—they were the terrier's ears and always would be. The rounded W on its side was the woman's head and back. The man who had saluted stood as a proud capital T.

Laura examined the pages for a minute before she spoke.

"I'm so happy to see what you got out of the session today," she said at last. "I was afraid you were put off by last week's class."

Kate began explaining what the lines were.

Laura put up her hand. "The important thing isn't that I know what these lines represent, it's that you do. You're the one who needs to remember what you saw. It's so difficult to hold on to that first vision."

There was that word again. Did Laura mean only the scene, with all the elements in it? Somehow, Kate suspected the word meant more than that. She was framing a question when Laura said, "I see Miss Farley waving over there. I've got to go."

Then Kate remembered. "Miss Everett—Laura—could I ask you something?"

"Of course."

Kate briefly explained about the painting.

"As it happens," Laura said, "I do know someone who used to restore artwork professionally. He's retired now, but he might be willing to give you some advice." She tore a scrap of paper out of her pad. "This is his name," she said, scribbling it down and handing the paper to Kate. "I'm sure he's in the phone book. Let me know how you make out."

"I will. Thanks." Kate looked at the name, Churchill Avery.

Kate was reluctant to call somebody she didn't know, but Alison went for the phone book as soon as they walked in the Langs' back door.

"Found it!" Alison held her finger on the listing.

"Found what?" called her mother from her office.

Alison gave her the name.

"Oh, for advice on the painting. I should have thought of him myself. I saw him at the Art Association once or twice."

Alison held out the phone.

"I'll call after lunch," said Kate.

"Why not now?"

"Well, I need to think about this."

"What's to think about? Call."

Kate took the phone and dialed.

"Hello?" The voice was an older man's but energetic.

"Hello. I'd like to talk to Mr. Churchill Avery."

"Speaking."

Kate cleared her throat. "My name is Kate Harris. You don't know me, but I got your name from Laura Everett at the Art Association. She's my teacher."

"Laura, yes. What can I do for you?"

"Well, I have a painting. Actually I bought it at an auction. It's got a lot of soot on it because it was in a house where there was a fire."

"Would that be the Quinlan house?"

At first, Kate was surprised. Then she remembered that this was a small town. "Yes."

"And you'd like to know how to get the soot off."

"Yes. Laura said you were retired, so if you'd rather not—"

"I'd be happy to show you what to do. Of course, it's a very time-consuming process. Tell me, is this a large painting?"

"Um, I think the auctioneer said it was sixteen by twenty inches."

"Good. A nice, manageable size. You don't want to embark on cleaning any murals. Let's see . . . Why don't you stop by here with the painting this afternoon? Do you know where I live?"

Kate checked the listing. "Four twenty-five Chandler Street?"

"Precisely. That's the corner of Chandler and Elliot. It's a blue house with bay windows. Two o'clock?"

Kate turned to Alison's mother, who had come out of her office. "The corner of Chandler and Elliot Street this afternoon at two?"

"Fine. Take Alison with you."

Kate turned back to the phone. "We'll be there. Is it okay if I bring a friend?"

"Certainly. See you!" With a click, he was off the line.

Churchill Avery's house was definitely blue. As she and Alison walked up to it, Kate thought of it as electric blue.

The trim was deep violet. Here and there were accents of red. At first, she found it shocking, partly because the house was so big—and three stories tall. Then she decided she liked it. She wondered what the street would look like if every house was painted a different bright color.

They went up the front steps. Kate pressed the doorbell.

"Coming!" said a voice from inside. The door opened. "Right on time."

Mr. Avery was a slender white-haired man. His pants and shirt were spattered with red paint.

"I'm Churchill, and one of you is Kate."

"I am. This is Alison. Alison Lang."

"Lang . . . Do I know your mother, Alison?"

"She said she met you when she did some work for the Art Association a couple of years ago."

"Yes, of course. Lovely woman. I do remember. Well, go into the first room on the left and I'll be with you in a sec." He disappeared into a room on the right.

Kate and Alison looked at each other, then started down the hall. The Oriental carpet was so thick it was like walking barefoot on a blanket. Paintings covered the walls. A kerosene lamp made of cut glass stood on a small table.

The indicated room, through a double door, was carpeted like the hallway and furnished with the kinds of sofas and chairs Kate had seen in period rooms. Every available tabletop and shelf was covered—*stuffed* was the word that occurred to Kate—with small objects like the ones at the Historical Society. And yet everything seemed to be in the right place.

"Wow," said Alison quietly.

Mr. Avery came into the room. "Please, sit down." He gestured toward the sofa. "Excuse my work clothes. I'm doing a restoration of my own." He sat down on an ottoman. "Is that the patient?" He reached for the plastic bag Kate held out to him.

"It's really dirty," she said.

"It certainly is," he said, slipping it out of the bag, "but I've seen worse, believe it or not." He balanced the painting in front of his face like a tray and examined the surface, tapping it lightly with his fingertip here and there. "The soot is just a coating. I don't believe the paint underneath was subjected to heat or damaged in any way. This is quite salvageable. Of course, the question is, is it worth your time to salvage it?"

Alison spoke up. "We thought the other paintings were awful."

Kate still wasn't used to the way Alison impulsively spoke her mind, but Mr. Avery nodded.

"An astute judgment, I'm certain," he said. "I wasn't able to attend the auction, but I got a report from the director of the Art Association. However, let's be optimistic. Perhaps Eleanor Quinlan had a flash of good taste. Perhaps this is the result."

He put the painting back in the bag. "I want you to take a look at a small cleaning job I'm doing for a friend."

He led them through the kitchen into an alcove that looked like it might have been a pantry. A painting about half the size of Kate's was on the counter. Next to it was a shallow dish and a bag of cotton balls.

"The problem in this case is a coat of varnish that has darkened with age. I'm removing it, as you see."

The painting was a country scene with a lake and some grazing cows. Much of it was devoted to sky. While the subject was visible, the colors were all some version of brown, except in a small area about three inches square in the upper-left-hand corner, where the sky was blue.

"That cleaned area represents two hours' work," he said. "Now, I'm not saying that your job would go that slowly. Removing a powdery surface layer is a lot different from removing varnish."

Two hours. Kate could hardly believe it.

"Start by mixing up a small batch of warm water, about a cup, with a few drops of mild detergent. I'll write that down for you in a minute."

He pulled a cotton ball out of the bag. "Take one of these, dip it in the soap solution, and squeeze it until the cotton is just moist. You're not washing the floor here. Then gently rub an area of the painting about as big as your thumbprint with the cotton ball, following the brush-strokes as much as you can. Turn the ball and repeat, until the cotton doesn't have any clean sides left. Throw it away and start with another cotton ball. Keep doing that until no more dirt comes off. Then move to the next spot.

"You can do vertical rows. You can do horizontal rows.

You can start in the middle or at the edge. It doesn't matter. In ten minutes, you'll be bored out of your mind however you do it. But at all costs, resist the urge to mop the whole thing and be done with it. If water gets onto the canvas, you'll have a disaster on your hands."

The possibility of the painting getting cleaned was looking more remote by the minute. Nonetheless, when Mr. Avery wrote the instructions on an index card and gave it to Kate, she carefully put it in her pocket. If nothing else, the card would be a souvenir.

On the way out, Mr. Avery stopped at the doorway to a room where the sheet-draped furniture had been pushed to the center. It smelled of fresh paint. "I'm redecorating. It's a bold choice, but I like it. What do you think?" The walls were deep red.

Alison was fascinated. "I love it."

Mr. Avery retrieved the plastic bag and handed it to Kate. "Keep me posted. And say hello to Laura for me."

They thanked him and left.

"I wonder," said Alison as they walked back up Chandler Street, "if I could talk Mom and Dad into painting the living room red."

Somehow, Kate didn't think so.

After supper that evening, Kate and Alison demonstrated the drawing method they had been taught that morning, each of them holding a pose for several seconds while the other attempted to record a few significant lines.

Then Alison's parents took turns guessing what the

scribbles in their drawing pads represented. Kate was surprised when Mrs. Lang spotted the terrier in the triangular form with the commas for ears. Most of the other sketches were incomprehensible to anyone who hadn't seen the subjects, but both Alison's parents were as enthusiastic as they had been after the first class. Kate still wasn't sure exactly what they thought, not the way she always was with her father.

She carried her drawing pad back upstairs. When she came down again, she had her little sketchbook with her. When a baseball game came on TV, no one noticed that Kate was filling up page after page with gesture drawings of Alison sprawled on the floor; her father sitting forward on the sofa, intent on the next play; and her mother lounging crosswise in the recliner, engrossed in the magazine on her lap.

Before going to bed, Kate wrote her second letter home.

Tuesday, July 12

Dear Mom & Dad,

It's been a pretty interesting week. First, even though I didn't mention it on the phone, I'd better tell you that I bought something I didn't exactly intend to buy. It was at an auction. It's a painting. The other paintings were selling for lots more than I bid. I was sure that somebody was going to bid higher.

I can't tell you what it's a painting of because it was in a fire and it's all black with soot. But the art teacher, Laura, gave me and Alison the name of a man who knows how to restore artwork. We showed him the painting this afternoon and he explained how to clean it. The job would probably take the rest of the summer, so I don't think I'm going to start anytime soon.

By the way, it's probably a terrible painting. All the other ones were, from what I could see. The frame might be nice.

The photocopies didn't come out too well this time because my drawings were so light. Even if you can see the lines, I bet you still can't tell what the drawings are. They're supposed to be people and a dog in the park. I had to draw them fast because they were moving.

There's a terrific museum here with model ships and all kinds of things brought back from China and Japan on sailing ships.

I hope you are getting better really fast, Dad.

Love,

Kate

Kate was the first one in bed that night. Alison came over and switched off the light. "I can find my way around," she said as she went into the bathroom.

Kate noticed that the sky was clear. That bright spot had to be a planet, not a star. Her father had showed her how to tell the twinkling of stars from the steady light of planets.

As her eyes became adjusted to the dark, stars appeared, many more than she could see from her bedroom at home. But then, city lights destroyed the perfect darkness of the night sky, replacing it with a dull glow.

Kate heard Alison switch the bathroom light off, then her footsteps crossing the hall.

"Alison, can you find your binoculars without turning the light on?"

"Sure, they're right here on the shelf." Alison slipped

them out of their leather case. "What can you see in the dark?"

Kate slid out of bed. "Can we put the lamp on the floor for now?"

With the night table cleared, Kate could rest her elbows on it.

"I think it's Jupiter—that big bright thing. Here, take a look. First you have to find it without the binoculars. Then don't move your eyes, just raise the binoculars."

"I've got it. Wow."

"Can you see any moons?"

"It's got moons?"

"Lots. With binoculars, you might be able to see four of them."

"You mean those little specks? Those are moons?"

"Uh-huh."

"I've got—one, two, three . . . four. This is great, except I'm getting a crick in my neck." Alison handed the binoculars back to Kate. "Thanks. My cousin sent me these, but I haven't really used them." She got into bed.

Kate slipped the binoculars back into the case.

"It's strange," Alison said, after a minute. "To think that you're looking at another planet and it's out there right this minute the same way we are."

"I know."

Alison kicked the tucked-in sheet loose. "You've been here almost two weeks. Nobody's ever visited that long, except for my grandmother. You're practically a member of the family." And then she was asleep.

Kate got into bed and pulled up the covers. She wasn't sure she felt exactly like a member of the family, but she no longer felt like an anxious-to-please guest. Her clothes were tucked away. Her comb and toothbrush had fixed places. Her towels hung from their own racks.

She had worked out with Alison's mother a set of household jobs that were hers, including folding laundry and weeding the garden.

The vividness of the first days had slipped away. The bubbling of aquarium filters, the distant hiss of the breakers, even the raucous voices of the seagulls had all become background noise.

The remaining days that week fell into a pattern. Kate and Alison left the house just after dawn each morning to search Perry Street beach for shells and look at the water. Nobody swam there. It faced the ocean head-on, with no offshore arm of sand to absorb the shock of the waves. Signs informed the unwary about the strong currents and lack of lifeguards.

Beyond the low-tide line, an old wooden dock stood above the onslaught of seawater, its supporting legs bristling with little shells. Kate asked Alison about them.

"Oh. I guess you've never seen barnacles before."

That was true, but Kate had read about them. Twice daily, as high tide submerged it, each barnacle would open its armor to release feathery appendages. Hour after hour, the appendages combed plankton from the water and drew it to the mouth of the animal inside. Then the armor closed again, retaining a ration of seawater to sustain the barnacle through the hours of low tide.

Alison showed Kate the miniature worlds sheltering under rocks and beach junk. One morning, they found a tide pool where the retreating water had marooned a rock crab until the next high tide.

Shorebirds sprinted back and forth in the surf zone, poking the sand for tiny insects and crustaceans. At first, they all looked the same. Then, from one of the Langs' books, Kate learned that each species had a bill designed to pluck up the particular food that was wanted. After that, the godwits, sanderlings, plovers, and sandpipers looked more and more different.

By the time workers were streaming into the Wheelhouse for their take-out coffee and glazed donuts, Kate and Alison would be on their way home for breakfast.

As the days passed, Kate's borrowed money ran down to a few coins in the pocket of her jeans, earmarked for the daily ice cream cone at the Purple Cow, where they had decided to eat their way through each of the 44 Fabulous Flavors by the end of the summer. Alison readily offered more money, but Kate was determined to keep to the original loan, so they spent the afternoons walking through the winding streets until they seemed to have covered every one of them.

Kate was already familiar with the town's public face, its monuments, plaques, and markers that schooled travelers in the area's proud past. Street signs directed the out-of-towner to the Art Association and Historical Society and other buildings of interest. And tourists came. Cameras at the ready, pockets stuffed with maps from the visitors' center, they filled the lunch places and souvenir shops like a cheerful invading army in Bermuda shorts.

Now Kate saw more of the private town that existed side by side with the public one—no plaques and no tourists, only a harsh landscape of peeling paint and cracked pavement. Unexpected entrances sometimes led to hidden courtyards where window-box gardens struggled to survive.

A few times on their excursions, classmates of Alison's had said hello when they met by accident, but nobody said, Come with us. Alison didn't talk to friends on the phone or make plans to get together with anybody. Kate began to wonder about that, but she could never ask about it.

✹ A Miniature Window

LATE FRIDAY AFTERNOON, Alison suggested that they visit her father at his rented space near the harbor. Alison had never gone there by herself before. She thought that surprising him would be fun. The door was open when they got there.

"Hi, Dad!"

He looked up from the wood he was planing. "Alison, how did you and Kate get here?" He did seem surprised. He didn't seem pleased.

"We walked. We were at the Purple Cow, so we came down Shore Road. Then we took Granite Street to Butler."

Mr. Lang went back to his planing. Kate was used to Alison's father exchanging quips with his daughter, always happy to see her. She wondered if he was irritated at their interrupting him at his work. Alison seemed puzzled, too.

Her father set the plane down. "Alison, I don't want you and Kate walking on Butler Road, not this far down, anyway. I think there's drug dealing going on near the newsstand."

"We didn't walk on that side."

"I don't care. It's not a neighborhood for two young girls to be in."

Alison looked upset. Kate had the feeling that her father rarely criticized anything his daughter did. He picked up the plane again. For a minute or two, the only sound was the wood being shaved.

"Dad, if it isn't safe, maybe you shouldn't be here either."

"I'm here because the space is cheap. And I won't be here that much longer."

"Do you mean we're almost ready to launch?"

"We are. Climb up here into the stern." He pulled a step stool over to the hull. Alison eagerly got into the boat. "This is the view you'll get when you take the tiller," he said.

"You're going to teach me how to sail, right, Dad?"

"Sure am." He turned to Kate. "Have you ever been on a sailboat before?"

"No. My uncle has a motorboat he keeps at his lake cottage. I've been on that a few times."

"Kate," said Alison, sliding over to the other side of the tiller, "you've got to try sitting here."

"Sailing's a great experience," said Mr. Lang, helping Kate into the boat. "You'll love it. Racing along, no roaring engine, just the sound of canvas rippling."

Sailing certainly seemed wonderful. And the boat itself, set on wood frames that fit the hull and held it upright, was beautiful. One wall of the shop was lined with pegboard. Each mallet, hammer, screwdriver, wrench, and pair of pliers had its own hook on the board, identifiable by the outline of the tool drawn there. Kate liked the sense of order, as well as the tools themselves.

"Why don't you two stick around for a couple of minutes?" said Mr. Lang. "I was just about to wrap up here anyway. I'll give you a ride home."

"Can we stop at La Lune?" said Alison. "I want to buy some weird food for dinner."

On Saturday morning, Kate repaid the loan to Alison. She also won the Harris-Lang Croquet Tournament, as Alison's father had designated it. Kate was surprised to find that she was good at any sport, but then croquet was not a fast game. Taking time to plan a shot paid off. She also suspected that Mr. Lang was not trying to play his best, but winning was fun. The trophy was a coffee mug with some dandelions in it.

Sunday everybody voted to go to the beach. This time,

they drove to North Beach, a short distance from town. The small lot was full, so they parked up the road. When Mr. Lang opened the trunk, Alison took a bag of food and started toward the beach. Kate scooped up an armload of towels and followed her.

Ahead of them, a pile of boulders separated the pavement from the sand a few feet below. Kate hugged the towels to her chest so she could see where she was planting her feet as she followed Alison over the boulders.

"Kate," called Mrs. Lang. "Wait for us. There's an easier way."

"I'm fine," yelled Kate over her shoulder. At that moment, her foot slipped into a crevice. She pitched forward, then hit the boulder in front of her with the palms of both hands.

"Kate!" In seconds, Alison and her parents were by her side. As Kate recovered from the impact, she realized that the towels had padded her fall. But her ankle was beginning to throb.

"Are you okay? Were you hurt?" said Alison. "I'm sorry. I should have taken you the long way around."

"It's not your fault," said Kate. "I think I twisted my ankle."

Despite Kate's insistence that she could walk, Alison's father carried her to the car, which made her feel like a toddler. Mrs. Lang gave Alison ice from the cooler to hold on Kate's ankle on the way back to town. Kate was grateful for the concern, but she was embarrassed to have been so clumsy.

Except for a case of poison ivy, the emergency room at Branford Community Hospital was quiet when they got there. The young doctor on duty examined Kate's ankle carefully, ordered an X-ray, then pronounced the injury merely a sprain.

"You did the right thing by applying the ice," he said. "We tell people to remember the word rice. Rest, ice, compression, and elevation. We'll get that ankle wrapped in an Ace bandage, and I want you to keep the foot up for the remainder of the day. Ice packs for twenty minutes at a time periodically until bedtime, when you take the bandage off for the night. Ice again tomorrow if you can. Stay off the foot until Tuesday morning. After that, you can go back to light activity. Your ankle will tell you how much."

Few words had been exchanged during the trip to the hospital, but on the way home, the Langs kept up a steady stream of funny remarks. Kate did her best to join in, but she was still angry with herself for derailing their trip to the beach.

Alison's mother suggested that this was an opportunity to get more work done on the boat. After repeated assurances that the womenfolk could manage by themselves, Mr. Lang dropped them off and headed for the harbor. They went in the front door since it was only a single step up from the sidewalk.

"Sit here," said Alison, steering Kate into the recliner and pulling out the footrest. "I'll get a bag of ice."

"I'm going to call your folks, Kate," said Mrs. Lang. "Do you want to talk to them when I'm through?"

Kate nodded. Alison returned with the bag and the terry-cloth belt from her bathrobe. Kate thought that Alison would be annoyed to be stuck tending somebody so inept, but Alison seemed to enjoy taking care of her. She molded the bag to fit the injured ankle and secured it with the belt.

"There," she said, tying three knots, "that ought to hold."

"I feel awful about this," Kate heard Mrs. Lang saying from the kitchen. "I should have stopped both of them from climbing on the rocks in the first place."

Alison's mother brought the phone to Kate. "Your dad's on the line."

"Dad, how are you? Are you getting better?"

"I am, but it sounds like I might have to lend you my cane."

"I'm okay. It was my fault. I should have been more careful."

"Kate, sometimes things happen. They aren't anybody's fault. I'm glad it wasn't serious. Your mother and I miss you terribly, sprout. I sent you a letter yesterday morning. I won't run up the Langs' phone bill telling you everything that's in it."

After they said goodbye, Kate automatically started to get up to bring the phone back to the kitchen. Alison took it.

"You're resting today," she said.

Kate was still on the invalid list the next morning as far as Alison and her mother were concerned. They insisted that she do as little walking as possible and hurried to get anything she might need.

The day, which had started with light rain, stretched out in front of Kate. Then she thought of the painting. Cleaning it would be the ideal job for someone who was stuck sitting down all day.

Alison volunteered to make a trip to the drugstore for a bag of cotton balls. While she was gone, her mother set up a folding table on the back porch, along with a couple of chairs and a footstool. Then she went to get dressed for a business appointment. Kate was just easing herself into a chair when Alison came in the back door carrying a plastic shopping bag. She shook out her umbrella.

"Have you got everything you need?"

"I need a water bowl and the detergent," said Kate. "And the painting. It's in the closet."

Alison pounded up the stairs and back down again. She handed the painting in its plastic bag to Kate and went into the kitchen.

Alison's mother came out of the bedroom. "Dad will be out all day. I'll be home around four. There's lunch stuff in the fridge. Alison, you know where it is. See you!"

Kate waved goodbye. She slipped the painting out of the bag and looked at her hands.

"Alison," she called, "could you bring some paper towels with you?"

"You got 'em." Alison came out with the water, the detergent, and the towels. "Where are you going to start?"

"I thought in the upper corner here."

"How can you tell which end is up?"

"By the way the wire to hang it was attached on the back." Kate wiped the loose dirt off the frame and turned the painting over to show Alison.

"Start in the middle. That's where the interesting stuff in a picture is."

At first Kate was annoyed by Alison's usual take-charge approach. But when she thought about it, she decided maybe Alison was right. If the corner was sky, she could spend hours working and have nothing to show for it but a small square of blue.

Kate opened the detergent and squeezed a few drops into the water bowl. She swirled the mixture around. Alison tore open the bag of cotton balls and handed her one.

"Should we count how many you use—just to see?"

"Well, I think I'll use most of this bag. It says there are three hundred inside. It'll probably be easier to count the ones that are left when I'm finished."

Kate dunked the cotton in the water, squeezed it hard, and began rubbing the first patch. Almost immediately, she had to turn the ball to another side. In less than a minute, she had to discard it and take a new one. It occurred to her that they weren't going to be counting the leftovers, not from the first bag anyway.

"If you want to call somebody to go downtown with, go ahead," said Kate. "It's going to be kind of boring to watch me do this."

"I'm okay."

"If you change your mind, that's all right."

"Wait a minute," said Alison, "you should have an ice pack." She disappeared into the kitchen. Kate started to object, but when Alison returned with the bag and the terrycloth tie, she put her foot up on the stool.

Alison finished tying the ice pack and disappeared into the kitchen again. She returned with a brown paper bag and dumped the small pile of used cotton into it. After that, they didn't talk for a while. The steady rain drummed on the porch roof. Patches of color emerged from time to time in the area Kate was working on, only to be covered again by smears of black.

At first, Alison watched. Then she went to the window and looked out over the backyard.

"We used to live in an apartment building," she said. "We didn't have a yard."

"So this is better."

"I guess. We were on the fifth floor. You could see really far from our living room window."

"Did you have a balcony?"

"A little one. My parents never let me go out there alone. They were afraid I'd fall."

"Were there a lot of apartments in the building?"

"Uh-huh. And there was another building right across the street. There was always somebody to play with."

"I guess there isn't anybody right around here."

Alison shrugged. "There's a girl on the next block, but we're not really friends."

"Does she go to a different school?"

"No. She goes to Parker. I just don't hang out with her, that's all."

"When did she move in?"

"She didn't. She's always been here." Alison continued to look out the window for a few more minutes. "Oh," she said, turning around, "I've got to take your ice pack off."

Kate bent down to untie the belt.

"I'll get that," said Alison. She slipped off the ice pack. "It's funny, but the new kids always hang out only with other new kids."

Kate was about to ask who the new kids were. Then she realized they must be people like Alison, who hadn't lived here all their lives.

"Of course, I have friends to hang out with," said Alison, "Margie Thomas and Beth Irving, but they're both away at camp this summer."

"When will they be back?"

"Not until the end of August. The funny thing is, they don't get along real well. Of course, they'll probably be superchummy by the time they get back."

Kate wondered if she'd been commandeered as a playmate for Alison. She pushed the uncomfortable thought aside. Now that she was here, the Langs genuinely seemed to like her.

"Do you miss your old place?" said Kate.

"Sometimes. What about you? Did you ever live someplace else?"

Kate started to say *Yes, I lived on a farm.* But that wasn't true.

She had never lived there, only visited. "No," she said, throwing another cotton ball into the paper bag, "I never lived anyplace else."

The sound of the mailbox being opened and shut came from the living room. Alison went to the front door. She returned with a stack of mail.

"Here's one from your parents," she said.

Kate wiped her hands and opened the envelope. Folded into the one-page letter was a photograph of her mother and Anne, standing side by side.

Fri., July 15

Dear Kate,

I'm very happy you're taking these art lessons. Your sketches remind me of calligraphy. Since you may not have ready access to a dictionary, that's "beautiful handwriting."

About the auction, you don't say how much you spent. I hope it wasn't so much that you've put a dent in your summer plans. In any case, you can value the experience as one of life's lessons. At least the cost was only in dollars and cents.

Talking to a conservator (he may refer to himself by that term) was an excellent idea. Whatever you decide to do with the painting, at least you learned something new.

It has already been a week since the surgery. I can hardly believe it. I'm feeling better, although the recovery is going slower than I thought it would.

Love,

Dad

There was a note at the bottom scrawled in her mother's bold handwriting:

Dear Kate,

We miss you like crazy. I'll send you a decent letter as soon as time permits. Anne came over for dinner on Tuesday evening, and Dad took the enclosed snapshot. She sends regards. So does Zee. Love your drawings.

Mom

Kate reread the letter several times. She noticed that her father didn't offer to send any more money even though he didn't know if she'd spent her entire summer's allowance. But that wouldn't have been like him. She folded the letter and put it back in the envelope.

Alison felt Kate's ankle. "I think it's time for another ice pack."

Kate sighed and put her foot on the stool.

"What does your dad say about your drawings?" Alison asked as she began her elaborate tying system again. "I'll bet he thinks they're fantastic. I'll bet your mom does, too."

"Well, my mom always says something nice. But I never know what my dad's going to say. He's kind of picky."

"He is? My dad isn't. He always says my drawings are great. I don't think they are. Not really. He just thinks they are because I'm his daughter."

Since Alison had seemed to take her father's enthusiasm at face value, Kate was surprised to hear her say that. She wondered how she would feel if her father was like Alison's, if each thing she produced wasn't judged by the same unbending standard he would apply to a stranger. Telling the truth was important, but sometimes a free ride would be nice.

Kate sat back and looked at what she had accomplished. A patch about twice the size of her thumb was opening up like a miniature window. Brown was the dominant color.

"At least it's not blue sky," said Alison, looking over Kate's shoulder. "This is going pretty slow, isn't it?"

By the time Alison started fishing around in the refrigerator for food, Kate had cleaned a rough square about two inches on a side.

After lunch, while Alison tended her aquariums, Kate opened up the square to about three inches on a side, revealing a jumble of shapes, predominantly brown but grading in places into reddish brown and purple.

Alison leaned out from the kitchen doorway. "Do you want a snack?"

"Alison, does this look like a hand to you?"

"Hmm. I don't see it."

"A hand from the side, holding on to something? Isn't that a wrist?"

"Maybe." Alison brought out a plateful of cookies, then went back to her aquariums.

As the hand emerged from the soot, Kate saw that it was graceful and delicate but oddly colored, dark against a lighter background, the top edge outlined in bright red-orange.

Blackened cotton balls half filled the paper bag. Kate felt as if she had been cleaning the painting her whole life. She reached into the bottom of the plastic bag.

"Should I go to the drugstore and get you more of those?" asked Alison when she came out for a look.

"No. I'm going to quit in a few minutes."

"Want to try using a sponge and wiping the whole thing fast?"

Kate would have loved to do just that. But she thought about Mr. Avery's warning not to soak the canvas. "No. I'll work on it again tomorrow."

"That is a hand, isn't it?"

"It has to be. And this is part of a sleeve."

A little while later, Alison's mother came home. She looked at the painting, then into the bag of discarded cotton. "You are patient," she said.

By then, curiosity, not patience, was what kept Kate going.

The Underlying Order

THE NEXT MORNING Kate sat on the edge of her bed and tested her ankle gingerly.

"Alison, thanks for putting on all those ice packs. It's a lot better today."

"Terrific. Can you walk to art class?"

"I think so."

They left early so they could take their time. Alison insisted on carrying Kate's drawing pad.

At the Art Association they met Laura coming in the main entrance. As they walked to the library, Kate told her about their meeting with Churchill Avery and how she'd started cleaning the painting.

"Yes, Mr. Avery's one of our local characters. Actually he's one of the new people. He's only been here about fifteen years," Laura said with a smile. "You may have noticed that people are a bit funny about that."

"Are you one of the new people?" said Alison.

"No," said Laura. "I was born here, although I've been away at school most of the last four years."

"Art school?" said Kate.

"No, I went to a small college, but I majored in art."

"Are you going to teach art from now on?" said Alison.

"I may be able to teach an occasional class here at the Art Association. Unfortunately, I can't support myself by teaching unless I get a faculty post somewhere, and that's very unlikely. Actually, I'd like to take some time off and do nothing but paint, but that's only a dream."

"What are you going to do?" said Alison.

Laura seemed embarrassed. "Well, I've applied for a full-time position with Cape Savings and Loan."

"What about your painting?" said Kate.

Laura shrugged. "I'm going to try to keep it up on the weekends."

Kate was about to say something, but then she thought it wasn't any of her business.

"I'd love to see this painting you're cleaning sometime," said Laura.

"Sure."

Chairs had been filling up as they talked. Kate and Alison took their seats. Laura pulled a piece of paper out of her bag and tacked it to the top frame of the blackboard. It was a child's crayon drawing of a house.

"My niece's latest artistic effort," she said, turning to the class. "She's five."

Laura walked up to a painting on the left side of the room. The subject was a colonial kitchen, with a pump and a fireplace.

"Mrs. Shelley, when you look at this painting, don't you feel as if you've just walked into that kitchen?"

"I never thought about it, but—yes. Yes, I do."

"And where do you feel you are standing?"

Mrs. Shelley thought for a moment. "I feel as if I'm standing just to the left of the table, about eight or ten feet from the fireplace."

"Does that feeling change when you move to a different viewing location?"

Mrs. Shelley got up and walked over to the painting. She stood to the right of it. She moved to the left.

"No. I feel I'm in that spot no matter where I stand."

"Thank you," said Laura.

Mrs. Shelley sat down. Laura walked on to a painting of a street scene. "Mr. Banfield, where do you feel you are in this painting?"

"Hmm. I'd say I'm on the second floor, looking out of a window or maybe sitting on a fire escape."

"Why is that?"

"Well, I seem to be on a level with the second-floor windows across the street. And I can see the tops of people's heads on my side of the street."

"Yes," said Laura, "that's where you'd have to be to see this view."

As she circled the room, the class took turns describing where they felt themselves to be in the indicated pictures.

Laura returned to the front.

"The feeling that you are viewing a scene from a precise location doesn't happen by accident. It happens because that's where the artist put the viewer by his use of perspective. That's our subject for today—perspective.

"Perspective is the effect of your point of view on everything you see—its size, its shape, and its place in your field of vision. Even when you're standing still, each shift of your eyes changes your point of view.

"We all have some knowledge of perspective from our life experience. For instance, my niece has grasped a few things." Laura turned to the crayon drawing. "The house is seen from a single direction. It sits firmly on a ground line. The upper story of the house is between us and the cloud, so the roof cuts in front of the cloud.

"This is a charming piece. So why should we bother to learn any technical perspective? Because this drawing shows the skill appropriate to a five-year-old. A practicing artist needs more awareness and more control of the subject matter.

"For instance, what if you had the idea to do a drawing showing the house from your pet dachshund's point of view? Would you have to lie on your stomach to do the drawing? What if you wanted to show the house from the point of view of the bird flying by? Would you have to rent a scaffold?

"With technical knowledge, you can show the different points of view of a person or a dachshund or a bird, and the only tools you'll need are a pencil, a straightedge, and your brain.

"But the best part is, a knowledge of perspective will help you draw more accurately—because you will *see* more accurately."

Laura took the drawing down and picked up a stick of chalk.

"Say I want to draw a long, straight road as if I were standing in the middle of that road, looking to the far horizon. First, I'll give myself an imaginary piece of paper." Laura drew a rectangle on the blackboard. Then she added a straight line running from one side of the rectangle to the other. "This is my horizon line for this picture. It represents the limit of what I can see before the landscape drops out of sight because of the earth's curvature.

"We know from experience that everything appears smaller as it recedes from us. How small can a thing get? So small that it has no size at all. It recedes to a point. This is the vanishing point." On the horizontal line, Laura put a chalk point, labeling it "VP." "Notice where the vanishing point is. It is on the horizon, the line that represents the limit of what the viewer can see. And here's my road." She drew two lines that converged on the chalk point.

"If there were a fence along this road, or a bicycle path, or railroad tracks—anything parallel to the road—all those things would recede to the same vanishing point."

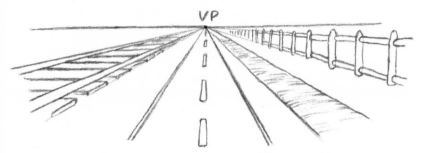

As Laura spoke, she drew them.

"This is called 'one-point perspective.' Have we lost anybody so far?"

The students looked around at one another. "I think we're still with you," said Miss Dixon.

"Good. So, if everybody knows all this stuff already, why can't everybody do correct perspective drawings? I think it's mostly because your brain keeps interfering. It keeps telling you, for instance, that the actual road is as wide at one end as it is at the other. It's remarkable how your *idea* of what's there can override your ability to *see* what's there.

"Keep in mind," said Laura, "that the system I've introduced today is only meant as a guide to help you see the underlying order of things. It doesn't show how the world actually looks, with its imperfections and messiness."

She reached for her bag. "I thought of an excellent place to go for sketching today, a place where a little knowledge of one-point perspective might come in handy."

The class trooped out the door behind her.

A five-minute walk took them to a street that dead-ended in a stone retaining wall about ten feet high. The wall was interrupted by a flight of stone steps, which Laura proceeded to climb.

When Kate followed her to the top, she found that they were in an old cemetery. Row upon row of headstones were set so close together that their edges almost touched. Probably the slate tablets had once stood in tidy formation. Now they resembled rows of broken teeth.

Most of them were from the 1700s and carved with variations on the same design: a skull surrounded by a few flourishes. "As you are now, so once was I" was a popular inscription. Only the ages at death fit no pattern. People lived to eighty-five or twenty-five or ten or died at birth or a month later.

When everyone had climbed the steps, Laura stationed herself edge-on to a row of headstones about midway into the cemetery.

"Will everyone come over here for a minute?" she said. "If you want to practice one-point perspective, face straight down any row the way we are doing now." She flipped her sketch pad open and began to draw as she spoke. "Remember, all lines that are parallel in nature converge to the same point in your drawing. The headstones have moved, but you can still imagine their top edges making parallel lines.

"You might try facing the broadsides of the headstones. To some extent, they are set in rows in that direction, too, but the pattern is harder to see."

"You cannot use one-point perspective if you face the headstones at an angle. I'll explain why in the next lesson.

"As you're drawing, think of the paper in front of you as three-dimensional space. Feel yourself drawing *into* it."

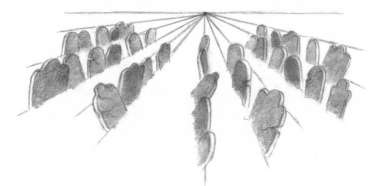

The students went to find good vantage points. Alison announced that she was going to sit in a patch of shade a short distance away. Kate didn't want to draw the headstones. She walked around looking for other parallels.

Alongside a tumbled-down fence, she found a bench and a line of stone planters. One end of the bench had been raised by the roots of an overhanging tree, and each planter tilted its own way, but Kate guessed that all these things had been set on the square in the beginning.

Drawing a whole scene, especially one with man-made objects in it, had always been difficult for Kate. Some objects might appear to float off the ground, while others sank beneath it.

Now she had a plan. Once she drew a horizon and decided on a vanishing point, she marked out space for the fence, the planters, the bench.

She began to imagine her drawing being animated, each object growing or shrinking as it advanced or receded between the converging lines, like a trolley car on cables.

After about twenty minutes, she set her drawing against the fence for a fresh look from a distance. She was immediately struck by its hard edges. It wasn't beautiful, except for the tree. That had come out well. But the rest was strange, even disturbing in its cold precision. Kate picked up the pad and started to rework the drawing, but she found that it resisted change. Once she knew where the converging lines were, she kept reverting back to them.

Alison came over from the other side of the cemetery and held out her pad for Kate to see. She had drawn the headstones from the broad side, their ranks extending back to the vanishing point, like an army on parade, many more headstones than actually were there. Comical ghosts peeked out from behind a number of them.

When Laura came over and saw Alison's drawing, she burst out laughing. "Very imaginative. I see you got the idea about one-point perspective."

Kate started to close up her pad. "Mine's not good at all. I don't like it."

"Before you throw in the towel, let me have a look," said Laura. She took the pad. "As a perspective study, this is fine. I think what's bothering you is the rigid quality. Ideally, you want to use the basic concepts of perspective without having them take over. That ability comes only with practice. Don't worry, you'll get the hang of it."

Kate nodded, but she didn't think she would. Her tentative way of drawing could so easily be overpowered.

Both the local and the national news that evening included reports of a tropical depression that was gaining strength as it moved out of the Caribbean.

Kate didn't pay much attention to forecasts. At home, her father rarely watched the weather report. He preferred to check the barometer in the front hall and watch the sky. At the farm, her grandfather paid more attention to what was coming from the north and the west.

That evening, Kate wrote her third letter home.

Tuesday, July 19

Dear Mom & Dad,

My ankle is much better. Except for a few twinges, I don't notice it at all.

Since I was not supposed to walk around yesterday, I started cleaning the painting. So far, I've uncovered a hand. The colors are mostly brownish. The restorer we talked to was cleaning a painting that was mostly brown because it was covered with old varnish. He said removing varnish is really hard. I hope my painting isn't like that. Cleaning off the soot is hard enough.

This week's class was on "one-point perspective." The drawing will show you what it is better than I can explain it.

We sketched in an old cemetery where the grave markers were set in parallel rows, since that's a good subject for using perspective. You can see that I drew a different view. At first I hated it because it looks more like a blueprint instead of a drawing, but I guess that's okay right now.

I hope you are getting lots better, Dad.

Love,

Kate

P.S. Have Grandpa and Grandma said any more about selling some of their land?

At breakfast on Wednesday, Mr. Lang asked Alison if she and Kate would paint the trellis he had put up earlier in the summer. It arched over the sidewalk leading to the front door, giving the house the look of a country cottage.

"I hear tell," he said, adopting a corn-fed rural accent, "that we've got a couple of them artist-types in the house. I'll bet they could do a bang-up job on the trellis."

"Sure," said Alison. "It's only a few feet of lattice stripping. How long can it take?"

That morning, they found out how long. Alison admitted she had failed to calculate that each piece of lattice stripping had two sides and two edges. After an hour of working in the sun, they had covered only about two-thirds of the outer face.

"Sorry I got us into this," said Alison. "I figured we'd be done in about half an hour. Maybe twenty minutes."

"That's okay," said Kate. She blotted her forehead with her sleeve. "It's a beautiful trellis."

"My dad made it."

"Did he design it, too?" The wood strips had been worked into intricate patterns that seemed, like the sailboat, not to fit in with his class clown personality.

"Yup. He worked it out on paper first."

They covered the last of the bare wood as Alison's father came home from a job site.

"Nice work," he said after a close inspection. "One more coat should do it."

"One more coat?" said Alison.

"Unless it's two. We'll see."

Alison groaned theatrically.

"The artist's life," he said. "Well, I've got things to do." He headed for the workshop.

"We owe ourselves double-scoop cones for this," said Alison, "with chocolate topping."

Banana Nut Crunch was that day's special at the Purple Cow. The shop had quickly become Kate's favorite place downtown. It was like a separate planet, with its own atmosphere and climate, pleasantly cool, in keeping with the needs of the planet's native inhabitants—the tubs of ice cream and sherbet. Despite the constant stream of babies and toddlers dribbling Dutch Chocolate and Raspberry Cream down their chins, the place always looked as if it had just been scrubbed.

Their favorite table by the window was taken that afternoon, so they ate their cones on the way to Perry Street beach. Kate found a spiral shell so tiny that it didn't seem to count, but it was the first whole one she'd found, so she kept it. Alison looked at the waves.

"The swells are kind of high today." She stooped down and picked up a half-buried shell. "Cracked. Too bad. When is your sister's baby going to be born?"

By now, Kate was used to Alison's sudden changes of subject.

"Around August twenty-fifth."

"Is everybody excited?"

"My mother and dad are. And my sister and her husband have been trying to have a baby, so they're really happy."

"Are you?"

Kate didn't answer right away. The conversations she and Alison had at the beach were special. With the surf blotting out all sound but their own voices and the cries of seagulls, they only talked about important things and always said what they were really thinking.

"I don't know. Sometimes I am because my sister wants a baby so much." Kate picked up another promising shell, but it was broken. "She looks a lot different. Her face, I mean. It's changed."

"Probably it will change back after she's had the baby."
"Maybe."

That evening, the news reported that the tropical depression had been upgraded to a storm. Coastal flooding had occurred in a few places as it moved north.

 Storm

THURSDAY MORNING, Alison and her mother decided to go shopping for some clothes Alison needed. Kate asked to stay home so she could continue cleaning the painting.

After Alison and her mother left, the sound of power tools occasionally came from the garage, but the house was quiet. Kate thought of turning on the radio. As soon as she finished the spot she was working on, she would get up. But that spot merged into the next and the next. The radio remained off.

A series of tiny circular shapes appeared. Kate realized that the sleeve she was uncovering was an old-fashioned one, with a row of buttons up the close-fitting forearm.

She abandoned the tidy vertical and horizontal rows she had been diligently expanding. She began to clean diagonally toward the area where she guessed the shoulder was.

Was the painting old? Or was it simply a painting of a woman in period clothing? How could anybody tell?

She had just reached a transition from the sleeve to what looked like a collar when Alison and her mother came home. Kate was both sorry and relieved to hear their footsteps. Her back ached. Her wrist was stiff. So was her injured ankle. She should have gotten up and walked around.

When Alison and her mother came to the table, their exclamations over her progress were surprisingly welcome.

"How do you stick with it? I'd have given up by now," said Alison. "It would be nice to see some colors some-place."

"I'll probably see something soon," said Kate.

She tried to get back to the job, but the excitement that had kept her going all morning was gone. She neatened up the table and quit for the day.

The afternoon was spent applying a second coat of paint to the trellis.

By evening news time, the storm was officially a hurri-cane, moving steadily up the coast. Every TV station had its raincoated correspondents yelling into microphones over the roar of the waves as raindrops spattered the camera lenses they faced. Behind them, seawater slammed against piers and jetties.

Kate began to follow the hurricane's progress as satellite maps and animations showed how a line of storms had de-veloped between masses of cold and warm air. As often happened, a spin had begun at a point in the line. Just a small accident at first, it was feeding on the air masses that surrounded it. And the bigger it got, the faster it spun, al-ways counterclockwise in the Northern Hemisphere.

Charted on the weather map, the hurricane seemed to dance on the water, gliding smoothly northward around its center of deceptive calm.

"Will the boat be all right, Dad?" Alison asked.

"All I can do is board up the windows and get the tools off the floor," her father said. "In fact, tomorrow I think I'll bring some of the power tools back here."

On Friday morning, first light was breaking when Kate opened her eyes. Usually she would have stayed in bed, drifting in and out of sleep until after sunup, but now she was wide awake. Alison was asleep, breathing deeply. Kate got out of bed, picked her clothes up off the chair, and went into the bathroom to dress. Then she tiptoed down to the back porch.

She studied the results of the previous day's work on the painting. She had definitely reached the collar now. From the position of the hand, the woman—Kate was by now convinced it was the portrait of a woman—appeared to be sideways to the viewer.

She reached into the plastic bag and pulled out all the remaining cotton. About thirty balls were left. Not as many as she'd hoped, but enough to make a start for the day.

She had been working about twenty minutes when a tiny area in the shape of a teardrop, lighter than the sur-rounding paint, began showing through the smears. She concentrated her efforts on the spot. It was an earring—a pearl earring, painted with such skill Kate could almost feel its satiny texture. She began to use the earring as a center point to work from.

She heard the cry of a seagull nearby, the first one that morning.

The woman's ear took another half hour to uncover. As Kate began moving into the area that had to be the side of the face, the first rays of sun hit the table. Her private world was about to disappear. She heard Alison padding into the bathroom upstairs, then water running. In the bedroom on the first floor, the alarm went off.

Kate was working on the cheek when Alison peered around the doorway.

"How long have you been up?" she said. "I thought I was the early bird around here." She came over for a look at the painting. "That's somebody's face, isn't it?"

"I think it's a woman wearing an earring."

"You're going to need more cotton balls. I can get them as soon as the drugstore opens."

Alison's mother, still in her bathrobe, joined them. "I can't believe you've gotten through the soot. I wonder what this is going to turn out to be."

"It's somebody's portrait, isn't it?" asked Alison's father, who had come out on the porch.

"The colors seem very dark," said her mother. "Unusual for a portrait."

Later that morning, while Kate continued working with a fresh supply of cotton balls—two bags this time—the Langs divided up errands. In anticipation of the storm, Alison's mother volunteered to walk to the grocery with the shopping cart while Alison and her father drove to the lumberyard for plywood to nail over the windows of the shop that housed the boat.

By then, Kate could make out most of the woman's face. The features were strong and definite. The woman's head was turned slightly toward the viewer, but the object of her attention was outside the picture, over the viewer's right shoulder. What did she see that caused her brow to furrow as it did?

Kate wanted to see the hair. She began working to the left, away from the face. Painted in brushstrokes that followed the flow of the strands, the hair was smooth and drawn back from the face, maybe in some sort of twist or braid.

Kate heard Mrs. Lang coming up the walk with the grocery cart.

"Good thing I went when I did," she said as she came in the door. "I got the last loaf of bread."

Kate went to the bottom of the steps and took a bag out of the cart.

"You must think we're in for the biggest storm ever," Mrs. Lang continued as she unpacked a bag containing batteries, bottled water, and utility candles. "Actually, we probably won't need any of this stuff. It's just in case."

She came out to see the painting. "Wow, you've really gone to town on this thing. I should have gotten more cotton balls."

"That's okay," said Kate.

Alison and her father were back before lunch. Alison was full of news about the preparations for the storm and how big the swells were.

"You have to come see them," she said to Kate. She turned to her mother. "Can we?"

"What do you think, Tom?" said Mrs. Lang.

"As long as you keep a safe distance," he said.

"We will. Oh, I almost forgot. I got three more bags of cotton balls." Alison dumped them on the table.

"Thanks." Kate wasn't sure if she was glad to see them or not.

After lunch, Kate and Alison walked to the beach. The sky, which had looked perfectly clear at dawn, was now veiled in clouds. The wind off the ocean was only a little stronger than usual, but it was constant.

When they got to Perry Street beach, Kate saw that they weren't the only ones who had come to see the swells. A number of people were gazing out at the incoming waves. Like the figures in the harbor diorama, they seemed suspended in time while the breakers thundered in. Even the seagulls were roosting. Out beyond the breakers, the swells that Alison had described rolled toward them, alternating with deep troughs.

Kate recognized many of the locations featured on the local news that night, as the owners of stores, boats, and waterfront houses rushed to barricade their property as best they could.

Saturday morning, thick clouds had settled in by breakfast time. Kate had just settled into her chair on the back porch when Alison jumped off the wicker sofa and disappeared into the house. She was back a minute later. "Mail call," she said, shuffling through the pile of envelopes.

"Alison," said her father, "we have to get a move on if we're going to get to Murphy's before it closes. I want to pick up a can of wood sealer in case they're closed on Monday."

"Okay." She dumped the mail on the sofa. "We're off. See you."

Her father was holding the door open for her. "Diane, don't expect us for lunch. Alison and I will probably get something downtown."

"All right, Tom."

After they left, Mrs. Lang sorted the mail. "Two things for you, Kate."

She held out the envelopes. Kate saw that her parents had each sent a letter. When she opened the one from her father, half a dozen photos slid out. They had been taken in the backyard in the shade of the elm tree. Four of them were of her mother and their neighbors, the Fitzgeralds, and a white-haired man who was probably a friend of the Fitzgeralds. She looked again. The white-haired man was her father.

It had to be just the light, or maybe the developing. That was it. When she examined the photo more closely, she could see that it was overexposed. The whole scene was washed out. The other two photos, close-ups of her father by himself, showed the true color of his hair, steely gray with silvery highlights.

They also showed how thin he was. Nobody had said anything about his losing weight. Was that because the doctor expected it and it was okay? Or because it wasn't?

Kate put the photos aside and turned to the letter.

Thurs., July 21

Dear Kate,

Your letter and drawing arrived this morning. The class on perspective sounds fascinating—the kind of thing that's right up my street. You'll have to explain the principles of it to me when you get back.

I continue to recover at a pace that makes the average inchworm look like a speed demon. As Dr. Franey cheerfully reminds me, getting over surgery takes longer when you're older, and I'm not a kid anymore.

I trust that you, by contrast, are tap-dancing by now.

On the other hand, I'm being so pampered, I'm almost ready to recommend surgery for the fun of it. Your mother has taken to cooking all my favorite dishes, including the dumplings and cream gravies that I thought were gone for good now that everyone has developed a phobia about dietary fat. I'm sure that somewhere Grandma Harris is nodding her head approvingly.

Cleaning the painting sounds like quite an undertaking. Don't worry about finishing the job there. You can always work on it when you get back.

The house is way too quiet without you. We miss you more than we thought possible.

Love,
Dad

Kate unfolded her mother's letter.

Dear Kate,

At long last—the promised letter.

The progress report on Dad is good. He's coming along steadily, if not quite as quickly as he'd like. So don't worry.

I want you to know, I look at your drawings, too. I don't have your father's keen eye for art, but I think they're very good, even allowing for the fact that you're my daughter.

But my opinion of your work, or your father's opinion, isn't the main thing. The main thing is that you enjoy what you're doing. I am concerned from time to time that you're so intent on doing a good job that you may be losing the enjoyment of drawing and painting.

I remember how much you loved crayons when you were little. I never saw such pure happiness on anybody's face as I did on yours when you were scribbling away with them. I do recall a couple of occasions when your enthusiasm extended to decorating the living room walls, but cleaning up after a budding artist was small price to pay for the privilege of living with one.

Anne is doing fine. She says she can hardly wait for the baby to be born. Zee is enjoying the job. They've already asked her to teach full-time in the fall. She's not sure about that. Both send their love.

Next weekend is my high school reunion. Don't ask me which one, I stopped counting after twenty-five. At any rate, we're going if Dad is up to it. We'll be back sometime on Sunday.

Kate, I feel I should prepare you—my folks are considering selling the south pasture. From a chance remark my dad made, I suspect part of the reason they're thinking of selling is to start a college fund for you.

I hope this won't put a damper on your summer, but you asked about it and I think I should tell you where things stand.

Say hello to the Langs for me.

Missing you more than ever,
Mom

"Bad news?" said Alison's mother.

Kate looked up. "No. Well, except that my grandparents might be selling part of their farm."

"Oh, I'm sorry to hear that. Are they going to retire?"

"I don't think so. I don't know."

"Are they still in good health?"

Kate nodded.

"That's good. How's your father?"

Kate hesitated, then handed the photos to Mrs. Lang.

She studied them for a minute. "Your father looks a little thin, doesn't he?"

Kate nodded again. She was glad Mrs. Lang hadn't said something about how terrific he looked, something just to make her feel better.

"That can happen after surgery, Kate. I know from my dad's experience after his heart operation. His recovery took most of a year."

"But he's okay now?"

"Oh, yes."

Then Kate remembered. "My mother says to say hello for her."

"How is she?"

"Fine. She's usually pretty busy with courses after work or on Saturdays."

"Yes, I know she's anxious to stay current. I'm sure that must be difficult for you, her being away so much."

Kate shrugged.

"I know she feels bad about that," said Mrs. Lang. "She wouldn't do it if she didn't think it was necessary, because . . . well, because she's put a lot into her job."

Kate knew what she had been about to say—because your father might lose his job at Woodward and she'd have to support the family.

"You know," Mrs. Lang continued, "that's how we met. I'd been hired to do accounting for the hospital. We met in the cafeteria one day. Your mother said she was looking for someone to tutor her in the latest computer operating systems. I was just out of school, so she hired me. I came to your house twice a week. You weren't even walking yet. That was quite a time—Alison in her infant carrier next to the computer and you crawling around on the floor."

"And Anne and Zee were there."

"Yes. Of course, they were teenagers. At least Anne was. They had their own lives. I didn't see much of them." She thought for a moment. "I suppose you didn't see much of them either. I guess it was more like being an only child, the way Alison is."

But it wasn't the way Alison was. Alison's birth was the beginning of the family. The walls of her home weren't covered with photos like scenes from a play that she'd arrived late for: Anne in a pinafore with a bucket of just-picked grapes, Zee taking their grandmother's Welsh pony, Butterscotch, over a jump. The grape arbor was gone now, and for as long as Kate could remember, the stalls in the barn had been empty.

"They didn't expect they were going to have me." Kate hadn't meant to say that, it just came out.

"You mean Anne and Zee?"

"My mother and father. I think I must have been a surprise."

Mrs. Lang paused. "Yes, I believe that your parents were surprised to learn another child was coming. In fact, your mother told me as much. But you have no idea how overjoyed they were when you arrived. They love you very much."

Kate knew that. But no matter how much people loved you, there were some things they couldn't give. They couldn't give you memories you didn't share.

Kate looked at the clock. Her mother would be at her computer class, but her father would be home. "Mrs. Lang, may I use the phone?"

"Of course."

Kate waited through three rings. Maybe she shouldn't have called. Maybe her father didn't have the phone right nearby.

"Hello."

"Hi, Dad. I—"

"You have reached the Harris residence. We can't take your call now . . ."

Kate scrambled to come up with a reassuring message. The tone came on.

"Hi," she said in her best everything's-fine voice. "Just wanted to see how you are. Call me when you can." She hung up feeling a sickening skid from false cheer to worried puzzlement. Her father was always home on Saturday mornings.

Kate went back to the kitchen, filled up the water bowl, and took it to the porch. The repetitive motions of cleaning the painting would help fend off the panicky feeling that had started when she saw the photographs. She mentally outlined a square and went back to cleaning in straight rows to reveal the area to the right of the woman's face.

She had been working for only a few minutes when a phrase from her mother's letter came back to her. The high school reunion "next weekend." That was this weekend. If they'd gone, that proved her father must be feeling better. If they'd gone.

In the meantime, she ought to do something, write a letter to her grandparents, explain that she didn't need a college fund. Her grades were always good. She'd get scholarships.

Kate sat back. The small circle she had just cleaned was distinctly blue.

"Ready for lunch?" Mrs. Lang called from the kitchen. She came out on the porch. "There's some color. Is that blue area sky?"

"I think so."

With only the two of them at the table, lunch was a

quiet meal. Kate liked that. The usual midday banter was fun, but Kate had found that it formed a barrier that was hard to break through.

While they finished a bowl of tuna salad, Mrs. Lang talked about her childhood moving from place to place, as her Army officer father was sent to different posts. "I guess that's why I fuss so much over this house," she said. "It's the first time I've lived anywhere I could really call home."

They talked about the differences between living in a small town and living in a big city.

"You know," Mrs. Lang said, "I sometimes wonder if we did the right thing by moving here. I love the house, and Tom is crazy about sailing, but I don't know that it's been the best thing for Alison. She's had a hard time making friends. People who were born here don't wear out the doorbells of newcomers."

Alison had said as much, but Kate didn't feel right repeating what she had said when they were by themselves.

"Maybe it will just take more time."

"Maybe. I went through so much of that myself, always being the new kid. I wish there were something I could do to help."

Kate didn't have any ideas on that.

After lunch, she went back to work, forcing her mind to stay on the surface in front of her. She was about three-quarters of the way down the square when she hit an irregular patch of brighter blue, then another. That was puzzling.

Next to the newly uncovered color, the area she had

been working on wasn't blue. It was nearer to gray. A few more minutes of cleaning solved the mystery. The blue-gray was cloud cover veiling the sky. Where the veil had shredded apart, the true color of the sky showed through— blue in the upper reaches, grading downward through hints of pale green and yellow, glowing red at the horizon, a red picked up by the undersides of low clouds that criss-crossed the sky. Was it sunrise or sunset? Kate couldn't tell, but finally she understood why the woman was painted in such muted colors. She was silhouetted against the sky, like the cluster of buildings in the distance.

Mrs. Lang was sitting on the porch with Kate when Alison and her father came home.

"Well," he said, "our hatches are battened."

Alison looked over Kate's shoulder. "You know what this looks like? The sun coming up over Rocky Point."

Her father came over. "It *is* Rocky Point. Look, there's the spire of St. Andrew's Church and the dome on the library."

"If we're looking east," said Alison's mother, "where's the clock tower?"

"It probably wasn't built then," said Alison's father. "This painting looks pretty old."

The rest of the afternoon, the Langs periodically checked to see what landmark Kate might have uncovered, but nothing as recognizable as the spire and the dome appeared, only more of the turbulent sky. By four o'clock, the cloud cover in the actual sky had thickened so much that the work became difficult. Kate quit for the day.

She thought of using the time before dinner to write to her grandparents, but when she sat down with paper and pencil, she found she couldn't focus her mind on a letter. She thought of phoning home again, even though she knew that that was pointless.

As the wind picked up, windows were closed. Mrs. Lang flicked on the dining room light while Kate was setting the table.

Kate's stomach was jittery, but she forced herself to eat. She didn't want to have to answer any questions about how she was feeling.

After dinner, Kate, Alison, and her father were playing cards on the front porch when a sudden gust of wind scattered the discards onto the floor.

"I thought that was shut," said Alison, pushing down a window that had been left open a crack. "We could move inside."

"Or," said Alison's father, "we could tell ghost stories."

"I've heard all of yours, Dad. You'll have to learn some new ones that I don't know."

Kate got on her hands and knees to fish cards from under the bamboo sofa. She hadn't really wanted to play in the first place.

"Are you feeling okay?" asked Mrs. Lang, when Kate told her she was going upstairs to get ready for bed.

"I'm fine. I'm just tired."

Kate was still lying awake when Alison got into bed half an hour later.

"I thought you'd be asleep," she said. "I won the last

two hands of rummy." She was silent for a minute. "I hope the boat will be okay. Dad's worked so hard on it."

"I'm sure it will be fine."

Neither of them spoke for a while. Then Kate said, "If the power goes out, will your fish be all right?"

She waited for a reply, then realized that Alison had gone to sleep. The window began chattering in its frame. Something metallic like a garbage can lid went clanking down the street. Shadows danced crazily on the walls and the ceiling as tree limbs were whipped back and forth.

The first drops of rain hit the window. In less than a minute, rain started to sheet down the glass until they could have been underwater.

Bursts of wind shook the house. All the windows had been shut, but somehow moving air was making the papers on Alison's bulletin board flutter.

Kate looked at Alison's drawing with its phalanx of gravestones marching steadily forward—or falling back. Which was it?

The vanishing point—everything receded to the vanishing point. Everything that got close to it would be pulled in. No, that was a black hole of space—an infinitely small point in the universe with a gravitational field so strong that anything coming near would inevitably be drawn in and disappear forever.

But the vanishing point was only an imaginary point. It didn't really exist. No matter how far back an object was projected, it could always be brought forward again. Nothing was lost.

A rending sound came from just outside the window, then a crash. Kate slid out of bed and looked into the yard. A huge limb had twisted off the silver maple. The trellis was ensnared in a tangle of branches.

That was what storms did—they destroyed things—trees and sailboats and pretty houses with trellises and window boxes.

Kate climbed back into bed and slid down the mattress until the covers were over her ears. She tried to sleep, but the image of the hurricane on the satellite map kept wheeling around in her mind. And at the center was the vanishing point, the tiny, voracious mouth into which everything was sucked—farms and morning glories and marmalade cats, plovers and seashells and little Welsh ponies—all whirling toward that point from which there was no escape.

✹ Picking Up

"KATE, ARE YOU AWAKE?"

Kate opened her eyes to find Alison silhouetted against the dawn light, looking out the window. "A big branch broke off the maple."

"I know. It happened last night after you went to sleep."

"I can't tell if it's wrecked the trellis or not." Alison pulled on her jeans. "I'm going out to see."

Just then, Alison's mother appeared in the doorway in

her bathrobe. "The rain has stopped, but the power's out," she said. "So don't open the refrigerator. I'll put food on the table for breakfast."

"Mom, did you see what happened to our maple?"

"Yes, I'm afraid we may lose it."

"It's just one branch, Mom. It'll be fine."

"Your dad's going to call a tree surgeon. We'll save it if we possibly can."

"Where is Dad?"

"He's gone down to the harbor to see if the boat's all right."

Alison pulled on her shirt and sandals. "I'm going out front."

"I'll be right there," said Kate, pushing off the covers.

By the time Kate got to the front yard, Alison had crawled under the canopy formed by the downed limb and was trying to free the trellis by snapping off small branches.

"It might be okay, I can't tell," she said. "I need a saw."

"Is there one in your dad's workshop?"

"Lots of them. I'll go and— Kate! There's a bunch of baby birds under here!"

"Where?"

"I almost stepped on them. We need a box—like a shoe box or something."

Kate ran to find Alison's mother. In a few minutes, a shoe box had been located and four trembling birds transferred into it one at a time from Alison's cupped hands.

"The parent birds might be nearby," said Kate. She'd read about the care of orphaned animals in a book in her father's study, probably a leftover from the days when Zee was bringing home strays. "If we put the babies someplace where the parents can see them, they'll feed them."

"Where could we put them? There are cats roaming."

Kate looked around. The front porch had a nearly flat roof. "How about up there?"

"It might work," said Alison. "We can reach it from my bedroom window."

They brought the box into the kitchen with the fledglings twittering anxiously inside.

"We could pad the box with tissues," Kate said. "And maybe we should feed them a little."

"Right," said Alison. "They're probably starving."

"What do we feed them?" said Mrs. Lang. "And how do we do it?"

All Kate could remember was a formula of egg yolks and milk, but she didn't know the proportions, only that it had to be thin enough to drop off the end of a matchstick, which was how the birds were fed. Mrs. Lang mixed up a batch, even though that required opening the refrigerator, warmed it a little, and gave Alison a matchstick.

Kate figured that the technique would never work. The birds had to be very frightened.

Alison maneuvered a drop of formula until it touched the beak of one of the birds. Instantly, it flowed off the matchstick. The bird swallowed. Alison fed a drop to the next bird and the next until each one had gotten a number of drops.

"Alison," said her mother, "you're a natural."

They put tissues in the box, and Alison carried it upstairs. After the box was set on the roof, Kate taped a piece of drawing paper across the window as a blind. Alison peered through a thin strip of uncovered glass. "How long should we wait for the parents?"

"I don't know. Hey, are your fish going to be okay with the filters off?"

"They'll be fine for a day or so. If the power's still off after that, I'll change some of the water. Kate, I'm going to stay up here. Why don't you eat breakfast?"

"I'll bring you something."

In the end, Alison's mother joined them, and they all ate breakfast—mostly fruit and bread—upstairs. No birds came.

The back door opened and closed. "Where is everybody?" Alison's father called.

"Up here, Tom," said Alison's mother in a stage whisper.

He trotted up the stairs and leaned in the doorway. "What's going on?"

"Shh, Dad, you'll frighten the birds away."

"What birds?"

Alison explained about the rescued fledglings.

"Why do I get the feeling this means more animals in the house? Hey, does anybody care how the boat is?"

"Sorry, Dad. It's okay, isn't it?"

"It's fine. The shop was ankle-deep in water, but the tide's going out now."

"How deep do you suppose it got, Tom?"

"The high-water mark looks about a foot above where it is now. The plywood on the windows held. We were lucky."

Alison stood up. "I'm going to feed the birds again."

"I'll put some of the formula in a pan of water to warm up," her mother said.

Alison brought the box back inside and carried it downstairs to the dining room table. The four babies were huddled together, peeping faintly. Kate didn't think they were likely to survive.

"We should put a lightbulb nearby to help keep them warm," she said.

Alison turned to her father. "We've got stuff like that, haven't we, Dad?"

"I have all kinds of lights I could rig up, but the power's off."

Alison's face fell. "I forgot about that."

"Wait, I have a big flashlight that might give off about as much heat as a small lightbulb. I'll put fresh batteries in it, but I don't know how long it will last."

Alison began feeding the birds. Despite their bedraggled appearance, they all opened their bills each time she brought the matchstick close to them.

"There's enough for everybody," she said. "No pushing and shoving, please."

After Alison had finished the round of feeding, she and her father figured out a place on the front porch where the flashlight could be clamped to a table lamp. Kate suggested placing the box so that only half of it was in the flashlight beam, allowing the birds to move away from it if they got too warm.

"Kate," said Alison, "how do you know all this stuff about taking care of birds?"

Kate explained about the book.

"I wonder if our library has any books like that," Alison said.

"Before it's feeding time at the zoo again," said Mr. Lang, "do you all want to walk downtown with me? The storm did some interesting things."

"Sure," said Alison.

"I'll see it later," said Mrs. Lang. "We have a dial tone. I've got some phone calls to make. I was supposed to have a meeting downtown tomorrow morning with a client, but I don't know what's happening now."

Kate thought of staying behind to call home. Maybe her parents hadn't gone to the reunion. She'd made such an effort to sound normal when she left the message on the answering machine, they would have no way of knowing how much she wanted to hear from them. She checked the clock and computed the time. If they were there, it was too early to call. At least a walk would pass the time.

"I'll come," she said.

Kate, Alison, and her father started down Winthrop toward the main street. All along the way, people were dragging garbage bags around their yards, tossing in broken flowerpots and sodden newspapers and other trash. The sound of power saws was almost constant, as decades-old trees were turned into woodpiles.

Downtown, people were sweeping mud out of storefronts, pulling nails out of plywood window covers, throwing ruined merchandise into heaps. Stretches of sidewalk had been wiped clean by the retreating water, while rivers of splintered wood and broken glass left other places impassable. A smashed lobster trap had made its way to the drugstore parking lot. Tangled mats of seaweed were everywhere, dotting the sidewalk, wrapped around lampposts.

When they got around the curve at the split-off to South Main, Kate saw that a large powerboat with an inboard motor was resting on its side in front of Murphy's Hardware. She recognized the store's owner standing in the doorway.

"Hey, Tom," he called, as they came closer, "like my new sidewalk display?"

"Another couple of feet and it would have been your window display."

"Right. How'd you make out?"

"Can't complain."

Then Kate saw that the boat hadn't made it to its resting place without mishap. It had split the beams holding up the overhanging roof of the Purple Cow, shearing off the entire front of the shop in the process. Their favorite table by the window had battered its way through the glass display case, while the striped chairs Kate had always loved were half buried in the mud that covered the floor.

The barbershop next door appeared untouched.

At South Main and Shore Road, two boulders that had been fixtures on Perry Street beach were sitting in the intersection, as if they had decided to take a stroll together through town. Alison's father led the way through the maze of debris, past the fisherman statue, to the docks. The bench where Kate and Alison had sat during the second art lesson was upended against a chain-link fence.

For all the preparations, in the end the stoutest barriers couldn't stop the surging water. What was spared and what was demolished made no sense that Kate could see. It was just luck.

"Dad!" Alison sounded alarmed. "Where's the Wheelhouse?" She pointed to a stretch of pavement.

"If I had to guess, I'd say about two hundred feet offshore."

A water-filled pit surrounded by foundation stones, along with a few pipes sticking up out of the pool, was the only evidence that the coffee shop had ever been there.

"That was one of my favorite places," said Alison. "Will they rebuild it?"

"I don't know," said her father.

They stood in silence for a few minutes. Finally Mr. Lang said, "I guess we should be getting back."

As they climbed the narrow streets again, Kate felt like a sleepwalker, unable to break through the membrane of her dream and return to the solid and familiar physical world.

When they got back, Mrs. Lang was out in the yard, pulling weeds as if it were an ordinary Sunday. "The ground isn't going to get any softer than this," she said. "Kate, your folks went to the reunion. Your mom called from their motel to see how we'd fared. She'll call again when they get home this evening."

"Did she say how my father is?"

"She said he was fine, although the trip wore him out a little."

Kate followed Alison in the front door. The fledglings began to peep when she looked in.

"They know me already," Alison said.

That seemed unlikely to Kate, but she didn't say anything.

Mrs. Lang set out peanut butter, bread, and fruit for lunch.

Alison was busy the rest of the afternoon, caring for the new arrivals and tending her fish. Her father started his own power saw and began cutting up the fallen branch.

Kate went back to the painting. She had been working for about half an hour when Mrs. Lang came over for a look.

"You must be going crazy by now, doing the same thing over and over."

"No, I don't mind." Just then, the canvas felt like a life raft. Kate had begun to find the work soothing.

The big area of sky in the upper-right-hand section undoubtedly did not contain any interesting figures or landmarks, but Kate didn't care. She moved slowly, cleaning upward, away from the horizon with its vivid colors, into the increasingly dark cloud cover over the woman's head.

She didn't take a break until after four. By then, Alison had managed several rounds of feeding. "They're looking better," she said after every one. Kate murmured a reply each time, but she avoided checking on the birds all afternoon, fearful of seeing them near death, despite Alison's positive reports.

"Come on," Alison said at last, stirring another batch of formula, "you've got to see them."

Kate followed her out to the front porch. As soon as Alison came near the box, wild cheeping began. Kate could hardly believe the change. The birds still looked bedraggled, but they were fluttering their wings vigorously, each one determined to be the sole recipient of the food. Completely calm and in control, Alison held back all but the intended target each time she carried a drop of formula into the box.

Mr. Lang came in an hour later and announced that the trellis frame was intact, although some of the decorative latticework would have to be redone. Like Alison, he seemed to have recovered his bearings. Now he was eager to clean up the wreckage and get back to work.

Dinner was leftover spaghetti noodles and tomato sauce, heated on a camp stove. They ate by candlelight.

"Why don't we do this every night?" said Mr. Lang. "I feel like we're in a romantic restaurant. Except for the Pinfeather Chorus over there. Are they going to do that all night?"

"Do birds usually cheep at night?" Alison shot back.

"Good point," he said.

"Kate, you're not eating," said Mrs. Lang. "Can I get you something else? If you'd rather have soup, we've got plenty."

"No, this is good," Kate said quickly, sitting up in her chair. "I like spaghetti."

"You look a little under the weather," said Mrs. Lang. "Do you feel all right?"

Kate felt all eyes on her. "I'm fine. Maybe I am sort of tired."

"You can make it an early night tonight."

"Except my mom's going to call."

"Oh, of course."

Just after eight that evening, the refrigerator and the aquarium filters started up. The streetlight on the corner flickered, then shone steadily.

"You know," said Alison's mother, "I was getting to like the power being off."

Kate had liked it, too. The steady glow from the candles had created a private space insulated from the disorder outside.

A few minutes later, the phone rang. Alison's mother picked it up.

"Hi. Yes, she's right here." She handed the phone to Kate. "Your mom."

"Hi."

"Hi, Kate. Is the power back on?"

"It came back a couple of minutes ago."

"That's good. We've been following the storm coverage on the news. Is there a lot of damage?"

"Downtown is kind of a mess." Kate knew she could never describe what she'd seen. "The maple tree in the front yard lost a big branch."

"Yes, Diane told me. We're just glad everybody's okay."

"How's Dad?"

"He's fine. Kate, Diane mentioned that Dad sent you the

photos from the Fitzgeralds' visit. Those were about the worst pictures of your father I ever saw. He's much better than he looks there. He's lost some weight, but the doctor isn't concerned, so I don't want you to be. All right?"

"All right. Can I talk to him?"

"He decided to lie down for a few minutes. Should I see if he's awake?"

"No, that's okay. Mom, please tell Grandma and Grandpa that I'll get scholarships to pay for college. They shouldn't try to pay for it."

"I'll tell them."

"Will you be talking to them soon?"

"Probably tomorrow evening."

"Don't forget."

"I won't."

Kate said goodbye and hung up. The call hadn't brought home much closer.

Before Kate and Alison went to bed, Mr. Lang replaced the flashlight over the shoe box with a small incandescent bulb on a cord, adjusting its position to regulate the heat.

"Mr. Tough Guy," said Alison's mother in an undertone to Kate.

When Kate woke up the next morning, Alison's bed was empty. She dressed and went to the front porch. Alison, still in her pajamas, was dispensing another meal.

"Now I know what they mean about the early bird," she said. "I got down here at five-thirty and they were cheeping their brains out."

"Want me to do some of the feeding?"

"No, you've got your own stuff to do. I can take care of this."

Kate went to the back porch and examined the painting. At the rate she was going, she figured the job would be done in three or four more days. Alison came to the porch doorway.

"What was the title of that book you read on orphaned animals?"

Kate found a pen and a scrap of paper. She wrote it down and gave it to Alison. "I think that's it."

The library didn't have the book as it turned out, but Alison came home later that morning with a stack of books on the same subject. Kate was surprised to see her poring over them.

Meanwhile, Kate's fingers performed the automatic motions of cleaning the painting while her mind floated free, almost unaware of what she was doing.

"Sorry I've been so busy with the animals," Alison said at lunch. "You must be bored stiff."

"No, it's okay. This way, I can get the job done."

While working on the figure late that afternoon, Kate discovered something new. The woman was wearing a cape, fastened around her neck by a brooch that was painted with the same care as the pearl earrings. The cape was brownish gray. Kate saw that she had been mistaken about the color of the blouse, thinking of it as brown. Next to the drab cape, the blouse was clearly a dusky rose.

Alison noticed it, too, when she came out to see Kate's

progress. "You got more dirt off the sleeve. It's changed color."

"No, I haven't touched it."

Kate found a discarded newspaper, tore off a piece, and made a small hole in the center. Then she laid the paper on the sleeve, hiding the cape. Surrounded by the paper, the sleeve was unquestionably brown. She took the paper away. The sleeve was definitely rose.

"It's sort of an optical illusion, isn't it?" said Alison.

Kate nodded. She realized that the same thing had happened when she'd discovered the patch of blue clouds, only to have them turn gray after she uncovered the brighter blue sky behind them. She'd have to show the paper experiment to her father when she got home.

By the end of the day, the fledglings were hopping around in the box, looking alert, and twittering in expectation of food whenever Alison was in sight. "They think I'm their mother," she said. By then, Kate had to agree. Nobody else elicited the same reaction from them.

For the first time in days, Kate got out her sketchbook and drew the fledglings, mouths gaping, wings fluttering. Look at me. Feed me.

That evening, Kate, Alison, and Mrs. Lang discussed what to do about the art lesson. Alison would have stayed home, but her mother said she'd take over the morning feedings.

"I've been learning from the master," she said.

✹ New Questions

THE NEXT MORNING, Alison wanted to give the birds one more feeding after breakfast, so they arrived at the Art Association later than usual. They were both out of breath as they slid into their seats.

"Hi," said Laura. "I was beginning to fear I might have lost you after last week's class. Technical perspective isn't everybody's cup of tea."

She picked up a piece of chalk. "The last lesson, we considered the view if you were standing in the middle of the road, looking straight ahead.

"What if you step off the road onto the left shoulder and look across the road at an angle? How do I draw my picture to show what you see now?"

There were no takers for that question.

"We have just entered the wonderful world of two-point perspective. That's what happens when the viewer is not looking at a subject straight on."

Laura drew a rectangle. This time, she extended the horizon line well beyond the left and right borders.

"The lines representing the road still converge at a point on the horizon, but now that point is *outside the picture* to the left." At the spot where the lines met on the horizon, she wrote "VP 1."

"What if another road crossed this one at a right angle? The lines representing that road would converge at a point on the horizon, too, *outside the picture* to the right." She labeled the point "VP 2."

"Now I'm going to put a building there. Remember— all lines that are parallel in the real world converge at the same vanishing point in your drawing."

By projecting lines from the two vanishing points, Laura constructed a cube.

"Voilà. Max's Corner Hamburger Stand, sitting squarely on its corner lot.

"Now," she said, "what happens when we bring the vanishing points closer to the borders of the picture?"

"I feel as if I'm a little closer to the hamburger stand," said Mr. Banfield.

"Yes, indeed," Laura said. "Now look what happens

when we shift the points in the other direction." She marked the dots so far out on the horizon she had to use a yardstick to project the lines straight.

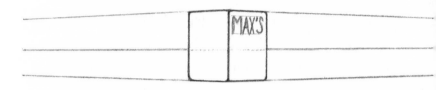

"Now," said Mrs. Shelley, "the hamburger stand looks farther away, even though it's about the same size."

"Aha," said Laura. "As you see, the distance that the viewer feels he is from the subject doesn't depend on how big the subject is. It depends on where the artist put the vanishing points."

Laura demonstrated the distorting effects of pulling the vanishing points very close to the center.

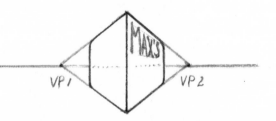

"Would an artist really consider all these possibilities before beginning a drawing?" asked Miss Longwood.

"No, not at all. An artist usually has a concept of the picture before setting pencil to paper. I wanted you to see the range of possibilities, as well as some of the weird results you can get if you push the method too far."

"Yes," said Mrs. Randall, "it seems to me that some of these versions were definitely more correct than others."

Sounds of agreement went around the group.

"Some versions are certainly more naturalistic," said Laura, putting down the chalk, "in the sense that they more closely approximate what we see, but none of them is the 'correct' one. The one you choose depends on the effect you want in that particular drawing."

"But," said Kate, "if you're trying to draw a scene exactly as it is, isn't there one way to do that that's better than all the others?"

"I'd say there's a range of possible ways to do that," said Laura. "Within that range, each way would look a little different, but they'd all look right."

"But only one would actually be right, wouldn't it?"

"No, there's no perfect way to duplicate in two dimensions a world that exists in three dimensions. The best you can do is create the illusion that you've done that."

"Are you saying," said Miss Dixon, "that a painting is an optical illusion?"

"Yes, if you're talking about painting that attempts to represent the world as we see it."

The statement seemed like a complete contradiction—painting that had the goal of showing reality was an illusion. The phrase "optical illusion" echoed for a moment. Kate struggled to organize her thoughts.

"But," she said, "a camera gives us a picture of exactly what we see, not an illusion." Laura couldn't evade the simple fact.

"A good photograph," she said, "comes about as close as possible to representing what we see. It helps that we're so accustomed to camera distortions that we no longer pay attention to them."

"Well, some kinds of special lenses distort things," said Kate. "You can usually spot those right away. Otherwise, a photograph shows what we saw." She was determined to set this piece in place.

Laura thought for a minute. "If I ask you to describe the carved wooden chair by the bookcase over there, would you continue to focus on me and try to see the chair out of the corner of your eye? Or would you turn your head to look at the chair?"

Kate tried to see where this question was leading. "I guess I'd turn my head."

"Yes. In real life, your eyes are in constant motion, and every movement is a shift in your point of view. When you take a photograph or do a drawing in perspective, you record the scene from only one fixed point of view."

"What has that got to do with distortion?" said Kate.

"A lot," said Laura. "You'll find that technical perspective has definite limitations. In terms of creating a natural-looking effect, the method works best in the center of the picture, where your main elements are. As you draw your way out to the edges of the picture, you'll find that objects start to look a little strange, as if they were being pulled out of shape. Photographs show this edge distortion, too."

"Is there anything you can do about that?" said Mrs. Shelley.

"There certainly is. You can do what artists have always done. You can cheat," said Laura.

Several people laughed. Kate was not among them. She was feeling more and more as if the rug was being pulled out from under her. No sooner had Laura given them a system that produced convincing results than she took it away again by saying it didn't really work all that well.

"For instance," Laura continued, "if you notice unnatural effects in your drawing, you can shift to different vanishing points for objects near the edge of the picture. In other words, you break the rules."

"Wouldn't that be obvious?" said Mrs. Shelley.

"Not if you do it right." Laura looked around the class. "From the puzzled expressions, I'd say I've spread enough confusion for one day. Suffice it to say, it takes a bag of tricks to make people think they see an exact replica of the three-dimensional world on the surface of a flat piece of paper or a canvas. We'll talk more about depth and different ways of showing it as we go on. Don't try to grasp it all right now."

But Kate did keep trying to grasp it. She was so perplexed, she couldn't even figure out what her questions were. She'd started that day's class feeling that at least she was going to learn more about recording things as they really were, and now Laura was saying that even a camera didn't do that.

"For sketching today," Laura said, "we're going to St. Andrew's Church."

As they walked the last two blocks, Kate thought the

neighborhood seemed familiar. "Isn't the haunted house around here?" she said to Alison. "I'd like to draw it. Want to come?"

"Sure."

Laura gathered the class together at one corner of the church property. "One more thing. Don't worry about actually putting in the vanishing points. Unless you make a very small drawing, they'd be off your paper anyway. I want you to do what's called 'freehand perspective.' Sketch the main outlines of the building as best you can from sight. Estimate where the vanishing points would be. Imagine your parallel lines fanning out from them."

"Laura," Kate said, after the rest of the class had walked away, "there's a house across the street that we'd like to draw, if that's okay."

"Sure, if it's right nearby. Just so I don't lose sight of you."

As she and Alison came up to the intersection, Kate saw that the magic garden was more lush than before. Vines were reaching for the FOR SALE sign that had been planted in the front yard.

A stone retaining wall diagonally across from the Quinlan house made a convenient place to sit. Alison began blocking in her first bold lines while Kate stared at her paper, trying to recapture her feelings when she'd first seen the house.

The light was entirely different. The cloud cover just then was casting a diffuse light over everything, wiping out its character. Even the stone lions had lost their menace.

By the time Laura walked over to them a half hour later, Alison had finished. Like her drawing of the Wheelhouse, the new piece showed a sagging and disheveled structure, perfectly rendered in her haphazard style.

"Great, Alison," said Laura, looking over her drawing. "I believe this is what the real estate section might refer to as a 'handyman's special.' " She turned to Kate.

"I haven't finished," said Kate. She noticed Alison glance at her watch. "But we've got to go."

"You could stop right where you are," said Laura. "Unfinished is always better than overworked. An unfinished piece gives the viewer's imagination something to fill in. It's beautiful as it is."

"I wanted it to look mysterious."

"I think it does," said Laura.

"Well, more mysterious then. And a little scary, too."

After Laura left them, Kate walked across the intersection and studied the house. From closer up, it loomed over the passerby. That was the view she should have drawn. The only reason they'd sketched from across the street was that the wall had been there to sit on.

Maybe she could come back another day.

"You know," said Alison on the way to Kennon's Office Supply a few minutes later, "I didn't think you could get more real than a photo. Did you understand what Laura was saying?"

Kate shook her head.

"And what about drawing and painting being an optical illusion?" said Alison.

At that moment, Kate realized why the phrase had rung a bell—Alison had used it to describe the way the colors appeared to shift in the painting Kate was cleaning. Was that an accident or something the artist had done deliberately? She'd have to ask Laura.

"I'm trying to figure it out myself," said Kate.

"If you do, let me know."

The downtown streets were lined with mountains of trash awaiting pickup. Damaged storefronts were once again protected by plywood. Kate was glad to leave it behind as they walked back home up Winthrop.

After lunch, Alison went with her father to help do the finishing work on the boat. Mrs. Lang had a new client, so she retreated to her office.

As Kate began cleaning the painting, her thoughts returned to that morning's class. Was she being blindly stubborn to reject what Laura was saying? After all, Laura had spent years studying these ideas, but Kate couldn't accept them until they made sense to her.

This was the first time she could remember being baffled by something explained by a teacher. She was used to doing well in class, being one of the star pupils. She had even helped some of her classmates who were having trouble in math. Now she understood how they felt. She turned her mind to the painting.

After a few minutes she began to see glimpses of bright red-orange just where the dark mass of the hair met the background. Then she realized, it was strands of hair catching the dawn light behind the woman's head.

She started following the thread of vivid color as it encircled the head. It skipped to the forehead and down the edge of the cheek, touching, here and there, the sleeves of the blouse and finally connecting to the highlights on the fingers. Now the strangely painted hand made sense. The dashes of red-orange looked natural on the backlit figure.

Kate had never seen a portrait like it. The woman peered out intently. Her hands gripped a black railing in front of her. On the eastern horizon, a red glow fired the undersides of a handful of clouds, while from the west a solid bank of cloud was sweeping in like a blue-gray cloak, extinguishing color. Who was the woman? Why did she seem so worried? Was she looking at something? Or looking for something?

As new questions pressed in, the confusion of the morning receded. After supper, Kate wrote her fourth letter home.

Tuesday, July 26

Dear Mom & Dad,

Downtown is still a mess from the storm, but not as bad as it was on Sunday. As soon as the garbage piles are picked up, it will look a lot better.

The class this week was on two-point perspective. I'll try to explain it if you want me to, but I don't think I really understand it, even though I thought I understood about the vanishing point after last week's class. We talked about photographs and whether or not they are true pictures of what's there, or if they distort things, especially at the edges of the picture. I don't mean photos taken with special lenses like your fish-eye lens or anything like that, just regular ones. What do you think?

The drawing shows the house where my painting came from. It didn't come out the way I wanted it to, but maybe I'll get a chance to do another one.

Love,
Kate

✿ Brushstrokes

ON WEDNESDAY MORNING, Alison went with her father to a marine supply store to buy some brass fittings for the boat.

Alison's mother came out to the back porch. "I'm expecting Mrs. Perry, the director of the Art Association, this morning," she said to Kate, "but we won't disturb you."

Kate had seen Mrs. Perry a couple of times, usually bustling in or out of her office, answering the phone with "Perry here." She was a tall woman, quite thin, always in a tailored suit, her perfectly combed hair a lustrous silver.

Mrs. Lang went back into her office. For the next hour, no phone calls came in. The doorbell didn't ring. Kate worked steadily.

When she had first exposed some of the cape, that part of the job had promised to be dull, adding nothing but an area of drab, neutral color. Now Kate began to see undulating shapes. A powerful wind was whipping the cape out like a pair of wings.

At eleven o'clock, the doorbell rang. Alison's mother hurried to answer it. Kate heard Mrs. Perry's voice. The first few words were indecipherable. Then she heard her say, "And she's been caring for them ever since? Isn't that amazing? Just look at the little things."

Kate heard footsteps in the living room.

"What a wonderful renovation you've done on this place, Mrs. Lang. Such a shame about the maple. Do you think it can be saved?"

"Well, a tree surgeon is coming out to look at it."

"Excellent idea. So many people wouldn't take the trouble to research the matter. The unnecessary removal of trees is a crime, don't you think?"

"Oh, absolutely."

Kate didn't want to be introduced, but the women were definitely coming her way.

"May I see the rest of the house? I saw it once, just out of curiosity, when it was on the market, shortly before you bought it. I must say, I never thought it would shape up so beautifully."

"I'm not sure Tom and I would have taken it on if we'd realized how much work it was going to be."

"But now you have a charming home. Is that another porch? I love porches myself. I practically grew up on our back porch." Mrs. Perry appeared in the doorway. "Oh, hello."

Kate pushed back her chair and stood up. "Hello."

Alison's mother slipped behind the woman onto the porch. "Mrs. Perry, this is Kate. She's the daughter of an old friend of mine. She's spending the summer with us. Kate and my daughter, Alison, are taking drawing lessons at the Art Association."

"Splendid! How are they going?"

"Oh, it's very interesting," Kate said, feeling that her reply was lame.

"Is that a class project you're working on?"

"No, just something for myself."

"Well, Mrs. Lang and I have some business to discuss, but I hope to see you at the Art Association."

They went into the office, closing the door behind them.

Kate returned to uncovering the cape. The artist's brush had moved quickly here, even an amateur could see the energy. The bold strokes of paint didn't merely define a piece of fabric. They were the force of the wind and the woman's inner turmoil. Following the paint tracks with the cotton, Kate imagined her own hand directing the brush.

The office door opened again.

"I'm so happy that you'll be doing this job for us," Mrs. Perry was saying. "I'm afraid the association has been terribly lax about record keeping."

Instead of going in the direction of the front door, the footsteps came to the back porch. Mrs. Perry reappeared in the doorway. "Mrs. Lang tells me that you're cleaning a painting from the Quinlan house. That's a very ambitious undertaking. I was at the auction, so I know the condition things were in. May I have a look at it?"

"Sure." Kate started to pick up the painting.

"No, don't bother. I'll come over there."

Mrs. Perry looked at the painting for what seemed like a long time. When she did speak, her voice had dropped several notes.

"I must say, I didn't think there was anything this good in the Quinlan house, not from what I could see of the other paintings at the auction."

"I've still got a lot of cleaning to do."

"There's certainly enough visible to see what a fine piece it is. If I had to guess, I'd say this was the work of Maude Randolph Whitney."

"I'm sorry," said Alison's mother, "I'm completely ignorant about painters. Is she well known?"

"Well, I wouldn't say she ever achieved a national reputation, but locally, she was quite well known. I believe she was even represented by a New York gallery for a period of time. And, of course, she was a member of the Art Association. She was born here. Her studio was a few miles north of town."

"She isn't living now?" said Kate.

"Oh, no. I believe she died sometime in the late fifties or early sixties, after a very long career. This looks like one of her early works. Assuming that it is a Whitney, of course."

"I suppose it would be signed?" said Alison's mother.

"Any Whitneys I've seen were. 'M. R. Whitney' was the form she used, always in the lower-right-hand corner." Mrs. Perry studied the painting a minute more. "I'll have to look this up in our file on Maude Whitney. She willed all her papers to the Art Association. If it's her work, there should be a record of it. And of the sale to the Quinlans, as well, naturally."

Mrs. Perry lingered a minute more over the painting. "Well, this has been a most interesting morning." The cheery tone had returned. "Thank you for showing me the painting. Do let me know if you find a signature. Meanwhile, I'll let you know if I find any information myself."

She turned to Alison's mother. "I'll go out the back door so I can admire your garden. Goodbye—Kate, is it?"

"Yes. Goodbye, Mrs. Perry."

Alison's mother walked Mrs. Perry around the yard, then came in by the back door again.

"Isn't this exciting, Kate? You might have a valuable painting."

Kate nodded, but she felt uneasy. Until now, the painting had been hers alone. She didn't like the idea of it turning into a public object.

Well, she had a lot of cleaning to do before she got to the lower-right-hand corner, and right now, she was in no hurry to do it.

Alison and her father were back before lunchtime. The household resumed its usual pace. The birds peeped for a feeding, power tools screeched in the workshop, Mrs. Lang made a few phone calls. Kate tried to regain the sense of solitude she'd had before Mrs. Perry's visit, but she found that was not possible.

On Thursday morning, Kate woke up with the idea of going to the library. She didn't want to wait for Mrs. Perry to send along information. She wanted to find out a few things for herself.

"Great," said Alison. "I'll come with you. I can drop off these books."

"You've finished them all?"

Alison nodded. "I want to see if I can find anything else."

When the library opened at ten, they were the first people there. After they explained what they were looking for, Mrs. Edgar, the librarian, set them up in separate rooms, Alison in the main reference room and Kate in Special Collections, where she had to sign a form stating that she understood the materials were not to leave the room.

"Here's our file on Maude Randolph Whitney," Mrs. Edgar said, putting a folder in front of Kate.

"Thank you, Mrs. Edgar."

"Please be careful with the material. Keep it in order. If you want to photocopy anything, bring it to me."

"I will."

Mrs. Edgar went back to her desk. Kate opened the folder; the contents were mostly photocopies of newspaper articles and clippings from magazines.

The stack had to be at least two inches thick. Kate hadn't realized there'd be so much information.

Glancing at a few sheets, she saw that the items were generally in chronological order, with the newest on top. She paged through them until she came to an obituary from the town's newspaper, dated October 28, 1961. She skimmed it for information.

Born in 1878 to a prominent local family. Studied painting with several noted artists of the period. Studied in France and Italy before returning to the United States shortly before World War I. Special subjects were the coastline and women in their homes. Her work was in a number of museums, as well as private collections. Mentored many young artists. Married Edward Ramsey, a heart surgeon, in 1918. Widowed in 1950. No children.

After reading the obituary, Kate opened the stack here and there, scanning headlines as she worked her way to the bottom, which had the effect of taking her backward in time.

September 17, 1960
Six Decades of Recording the Seafaring Life

February 4, 1943
Art Association Holds Auction for War Effort

August 23, 1935
Art Colony Thrives Despite Bleak Economic Forecast

July 12, 1920
Devastation in Europe Gives Birth to New Visions in Art

There it was again. Vision. Momentarily distracted, Kate flipped past the words "Red Sky" before she could mark the page. She started at the bottom of the stack, going more slowly this time. Under the headline "The Rocky Shore— Five Artists View Life on the Seacoast," she found what she was looking for. The article was dated September 9, 1913:

Maude Randolph Whitney continues to explore life in the maritime trades with insight and compassion. Her most recent work, "Red Sky at Morning," is a technically innovative portrait, being rendered almost as a silhouette. Just enough light illuminates the features of a woman, seen in three-quarter view, to show us a face etched by worry. Behind her, a disquieting, red-streaked dawn is breaking. Ominous clouds blanket the sky above, threatening to envelop the dawn light in their eastward movement.

The iron railing the woman grips is one surrounding a widow's walk, telling us that this is the wife of a seafaring man, likely a captain, judging by the quality of the woman's dress and jewelry.

The portrait's title undoubtedly refers to the old saying "Red sky at night, sailor's delight; red sky at morning, sailors take warning."

Breaking free from the naturalism of her former work, Whitney turns to a symbolic use of color. Blood reds and acid yellows that never appeared in a dawn sky here become powerful symbols of danger and distress.

In tandem with Miss Whitney's portraits of the wives of immigrant fishermen, this work brings us into the world of those whose lives are ever at the mercy of the sea.

Kate tidied the photocopies into two neat piles, divided at the 1913 article, picked up that sheet and the obituary, and went to find the librarian. She hoped Alison was ready to leave. She wanted to get home.

She found them both at the main desk.

"And then we had to build them a bigger cage," Mrs. Edgar was saying.

"Mrs. Edgar and her husband raised some orphaned baby raccoons," said Alison as Kate walked up to the desk. "Did you find anything?"

Kate nodded. While Mrs. Edgar went to make the photocopies, Alison held up a stack of pamphlets. "I've got all this new information."

On the way home from the library, Kate laughed at Alison's descriptions of Mrs. Edgar's life with the mischievous raccoons, but her mind was on the painting.

As soon as they walked in the door, Alison headed to the front porch to check on the fledglings. Kate set up on the back porch and began to clean the painting's lower-right-hand corner.

That part turned out to be a mosaic of light and dark green. If the woman was standing on a widow's walk on the roof of the house, the area could be the tops of trees around the house.

This had to be the painting described in the review. There couldn't be two so much alike. Unless this was a popular subject. Maybe lots of people tried it, like doing a still life with apples and a loaf of bread. Maybe—

Kate swiped over a brush mark in dark red. She took a new piece of cotton and concentrated on the spot. The mark became the upstroke on a y. She worked to the left, revealing a loop. That made ey. Every few swipes exposed a new letter, n-t-i-h, then the bold capital W, the R and the M. And there it was: M. R. Whitney.

"Kate," said Alison's mother, stopping by the doorway into the kitchen, "lunch in about a half hour."

Kate motioned her to come over to the table. She pointed to the lower-right-hand corner of the painting.

"Alison!" her mother called. "Come and see what Kate found."

"Is that the person you were looking up at the library?" asked Alison when she saw the signature.

Kate nodded. She pulled the photocopies out of her backpack and showed them to Alison and her mother.

Alison ran out to the workshop to tell her father. He came in with sawdust still on his shirt. "Looks like you got quite a bargain at the auction," he said.

At lunch, the Langs raised their juice glasses and toasted Kate's success.

"I'm so happy to see you rewarded for all the work you've done," said Mrs. Lang.

"Have you called your folks yet?" said Mr. Lang.

"Not yet. I thought I might surprise them with it when I got back."

"What are you going to do with it?" said Alison.

Kate hadn't thought about that. "I don't know. Just keep it safe, for now."

"You can keep it upstairs from now on," said Mr. Lang. "I'll put up a picture hanger next to the navigation chart. By the way, do you know the reason for that old saying about the red sky?"

Kate shook her head.

"The weather in this hemisphere generally travels from west to east. A rosy sunset means that you're seeing the western sky through dust. The dry weather has yet to reach you. But if the dawn sky is rosy because of dust, the dry weather has passed you and rain could be on the way."

The phone rang. Mrs. Lang picked it up in her office. "Kate," she called, "phone for you."

Kate hurried to the office. Had something happened to her father?

"Hello."

"Hello, Kate. This is Mrs. Perry at the Art Association. I was just wondering—now I see that you're doing an excellent job with the cleaning, really most impressive—but don't you think it might be a good idea to have a professional do the finishing touches? It so happens, I know just the person to call. I'm sure Mr. Avery—"

"I met him."

"Oh."

"He's the person who showed me how to clean the painting."

"Did he? So you see how knowledgeable he is then. If you'd like, I'll make the call and—"

"Thanks, Mrs. Perry, but I'll be finished in a couple of

days." Kate thought of telling her about uncovering the signature, then decided she wouldn't. She wasn't sure why.

"If you change your mind, do let me know and—"

"I will. Thanks again, Mrs. Perry."

After Kate hung up, she thought about the situation. She had intended to show Mr. Avery the cleaned painting from the beginning of the project. She still wanted him to see it, but she'd make the call herself.

On Friday morning, Mrs. Lang went to the Art Association to begin her new job. She returned just after noon, throwing her satchel on the porch sofa.

Kate looked up from her work. "Did Mrs. Perry say anything about the painting?"

"Not really. She said she won't have time to go through the artist's papers thoroughly until after the association's next show is hung."

"When is that?"

"The end of September, I think."

By the time Kate was finished that day, only a narrow border of black remained to be removed from the edges of the painting. One more day, she figured. Maybe two.

✵ A Work in Progress

SATURDAY MORNING'S MAIL included a letter from Kate's father.

Thurs., July 28

Dear Kate,

That sounds like a very interesting discussion you had in your last class. I'm sorry I wasn't there.

After I read your letter, I looked through some of our albums. I'm sending along three photos I found showing noticeable edge distortion.

I don't know if this comparison will help, but think of the flat maps of the world you've seen, the ones that are called Mercator projections. Since the landmasses are actually on a sphere—the earth—showing them as flat is a distortion, a distortion that gets worse as you go away from the equator to the edge of the map. On a Mercator projection, you've seen how Greenland, up near the top edge, appears to be bigger than Canada and the U.S. together. On a globe, you see that it is really about the size of Mexico.

Think of the world around you as if it were a painting on the inside of a sphere. Wouldn't flattening it out result in the same sort of distortion?

While you may not understand the entire theory behind technical perspective, you seem to be able to use it just fine in your drawing.

I am curious about this painting you are cleaning. Could you send us a photo of it? It wouldn't have to be completely clean.

This week, I was able to walk without the cane for short distances. Your mother is threatening to enroll me in a tai chi class. By the time you get back, I should be springing around like a superhero.

Love,

Dad

Kate spread the photos out on the table: a holiday party at their house, her father at his desk, and her mother with Anne when she was a toddler. Now that Kate was looking for it, distortion was plain to see at the edges of the photos. She had to admit—a camera didn't show what a person saw. She supposed that, as an artist, she should feel better about this. Instead, it brought back the sliding sensation of the rug being pulled from under her feet.

Alison snapped a few photos of Kate holding the painting, finishing the roll of film in the camera. "Dad and I are going to work on the boat. We'll drop off the film at the drugstore on the way. Want to come? You don't have to do any sanding or anything."

"Thanks, but I'll stay here."

About a half hour after they left, the front doorbell rang. From the back porch, Kate heard the voice of an older woman and thought at first that Mrs. Perry had come back. Then she realized that it was not Mrs. Perry's voice.

"Kate," called Alison's mother from the living room, "can you come in here for a minute?"

As Kate made her way through the house, she saw a woman who appeared to be in her seventies standing just inside the front door. Like Mrs. Perry's, her hair was white, but it was unruly. She wore an old-fashioned black straw hat and a worn blue sweater. Alison's mother turned to Kate with a confused expression on her face, then turned back to the woman.

"Uh, please come in, Mrs. Bennett. This is Kate. Kate, Mrs. Bennett is a cousin of Martin Quinlan's."

"Second cousin."

"A second cousin of Martin Quinlan's, you know, the man who owned the—"

"I remember," said Kate. Whatever this person wanted, Kate felt it couldn't be good. The woman didn't look happy.

"I'll get right to the point," said Mrs. Bennett. "I've heard a rumor that Martin stole a valuable painting."

Kate felt a thump in the pit of her stomach.

"Kate," said Mrs. Bennett, turning to her, "I believe that you're in possession of a painting by Maude Randolph Whitney called *Red Sky at Morning*. Mrs. Perry told Alice Franklin, the Art Association secretary, about it. Alice told Helen Travers at the Historical Society, and Helen told me and goodness knows how many other people. Helen's a talker."

"I was at the Art Association yesterday morning," said Alison's mother. "Mrs. Perry didn't say anything about the painting being stolen."

"Well, Alice told Helen that as soon as Mrs. Perry returned to the office after seeing the painting, she searched the files. She found the catalog for a show at the association in the summer of 1961."

Kate thought that her searching the files called into question exactly how busy Mrs. Perry was until the end of September.

Mrs. Bennett paused to catch her breath. "The show was a retrospective of the work of several association members, including Maude Whitney. A painting called *Red Sky at Morning* was in that show. It's described in the catalog."

"Was there a picture of it?" asked Kate.

"I don't believe so. At any rate, when the show was taken down in the fall, the paintings were delivered back to the artists. There are signed receipts from all of them, acknowledging the return of their artworks.

"Martin's signature appears on the receipts as the person who made the deliveries."

"But," said Alison's mother, "all the artists acknowledged the return of their paintings. Isn't that what you said?"

"Some of them inventoried the crates and listed each painting individually, and some of them merely signed for the lot without bothering to check that every painting was returned. Maude died only a month or two after that show was taken down. It's possible she never checked the contents of the crates."

"How were the crates found?" said Alison's mother. "After her death, I mean. Had they been opened?"

"Well, I don't think anybody knows. It was a long time ago, and Maude didn't have any descendants. I believe she named Phillip Lloyd as the executor of her will. He was head of the Art Association at that time. He passed away a number of years ago."

"So the possibility exists that Martin didn't return all the paintings to Miss Whitney and—"

"She never knew it. That's the rumor. Except it's absolute hogwash. I grew up with Martin. It's true he was a little slower than other children, but he was the kindest, gentlest person—and totally honest. He would never have stolen a matchstick, let alone a painting."

Kate saw that Mrs. Bennett was becoming more and more distressed as she spoke.

"People always thought Martin was a simpleton. Now they're going to think he was a thief as well, and it just makes my blood boil."

This last remark seemed so out of place with the woman's proper demeanor that Kate had to stifle a smile. Then she saw that Mrs. Bennett had tears in her eyes.

"I apologize for getting emotional," the older woman said, dabbing at her eyes with a handkerchief she pulled out of her sweater pocket. "But I was so very fond of Martin."

Kate hadn't especially liked Mrs. Bennett at first, but now she found herself wanting to help her. She tried to think of what she could do.

"Couldn't your cousin have bought the painting?" she said.

"I believe he did, but no one else will. Martin never bought things like that. Every stick of furniture in that house and every piece of artwork came down in the family or was purchased by Martin's mother. And I presume you saw her taste in art.

"Then there's the question of money. By the time Martin inherited from his mother, the estate consisted of the house and little else. He had only limited resources at his disposal."

"In that case," said Alison's mother, "and I don't mean to be rude—could he have afforded the painting?"

"He did do odd jobs, you know," Mrs. Bennett replied. Nobody said anything for a minute. "I admit it's puzzling." She shook her head. "I'm sorry, I didn't think anything through before I came here. I was just so upset."

"Mrs. Bennett," said Alison's mother, "I knew Martin slightly from doing volunteer work at the association, and I'm sure you're right about him, but I don't know what we can do about the rumors."

"Well, I suppose there's nothing anyone can do about people talking." She put her handkerchief back in her pocket.

Alison's mother looked at Kate. "If we think of any way to help you, Mrs. Bennett, we certainly will."

"I'll call my father," said Kate. "He'll have an idea. He always has good ideas."

"Thank you both. I appreciate your concern."

"Can I make you a cup of tea?" said Alison's mother.

"Oh, no, dear. That's quite all right."

"Would you like to see the painting?" said Kate.

"Why, yes, yes I would."

Kate led the way to the back porch.

Mrs. Bennett was silent for a minute. "What an unusual portrait. Very moving. I was in Martin's house on three or four occasions over the years after his mother died. I have to admit, I never saw this there. Of course, I was never on the second floor, where the bedrooms were.

"You know, the woman in this picture reminds me of Martin's mother, Eleanor. It isn't her, but the face is similar in certain respects, and so is the hair. Interesting." Mrs. Bennett seemed to be lost in memory for a moment. Then she came back to the present. "Thank you very much for showing this to me. I'll be on my way."

Before Mrs. Bennett left, she wrote down her phone number and gave it to Alison's mother. "Oh, I almost forgot," she said, pausing at the front door. "Alice Franklin told Helen that the first thing Mrs. Perry did after she found the catalog last Wednesday was to call Arthur Burke."

"Arthur Burke?" said Alison's mother.

"He does legal work for the association. That seems peculiar, doesn't it?"

Kate didn't like the sound of that at all.

"Mrs. Lang," she said, as soon as Mrs. Bennett had left, "can I call my dad?"

"Sure. You can use the phone in my office, if you like."

"Thanks."

Kate sat in Mrs. Lang's swivel chair. She dialed the number and waited.

"Hello?"

"Oh. Hi, Mom."

"Kate, how are you? Is everything okay?"

"It's fine."

"So, what have you been up to?"

"Alison's taking care of some baby birds she found after the storm. She and her dad are working on the boat a lot. It's almost finished. Mrs. Lang has a couple of new jobs. Is Dad there?"

"No. He's gone over to the Fitzgeralds'. Should I have him call you? Kate, is this something I can help you with?"

Kate had really wanted to talk to her father, but she was anxious to have answers now. She explained to her mother about the painting.

"Okay," said her mother, "let's think this through. You say there are papers stored at the Art Association."

"Yes."

"And they're in a mess but the director of the Art Association won't be able to sort them out for a while."

"Yes."

"And you're looking for a bill of sale or some record that the painting was legitimately sold to Martin whatever-his-name-was."

"Quinlan. But, Mom, there might not be one."

"Let's not assume that right now. The main thing is, somebody has to go through those papers carefully."

"Uh-huh."

"Someone who would do a thorough job."

"Uh-huh."

"Why not you?"

Kate was taken by surprise. "Mom, Mrs. Perry isn't going to let me look through those things."

"Have you asked her?"

"No, but—"

"What's the worst thing she could say? No, right? And then you'd be no worse off than you are now. And she might say yes."

"Mom, I—"

"Let's role-play this thing. I spoke to Mrs. Perry a couple of times when I signed you up for the class. I'll be her."

"Mom, this isn't—"

"Come on, just try it. She's sitting in her office and you come in."

Feeling silly, Kate started, mumbling the words. "Mrs. Perry, I know you won't like this idea, but I'd like to see—"

"Can you start on a more positive note, Kate? For instance, is there anything about your request that benefits Mrs. Perry?"

Kate thought for a minute. "Well, she wants to find out about the painting, too."

"Right. Start with that."

"Mrs. Perry, I know you'd like— Mrs. Perry, we need to clear up the mystery about this painting. I know you're too busy to sort papers right now, so I would like to take on the job."

"Good, Kate." Kate's mother resumed her Mrs. Perry voice. "I'm sorry, but we don't allow children access to these materials."

"I know you're worried that I'd lose or damage things, but I'd be very careful not to."

"I'm sure you would, but it's my responsibility to keep these things safe."

"Mrs. Perry, I know these papers are important, so I'd take special care."

"Kate," said her mother, momentarily herself again, "is there anything else you can do besides reassuring Mrs. Perry that you'd be careful?"

"Um. What if . . . what if I had a grownup with me? Miss Franklin or Darlene?"

"That's an idea. Who are they?"

"The secretary and the girl who answers the phone."

The Mrs. Perry voice came back. "Miss Franklin and Darlene have work to do. I can't spare them to supervise you."

Kate suddenly had the best idea yet. "How about Laura?"

"Laura?"

"Laura Everett, my art teacher. I'll see her on Tuesday."

"Kate, that's a terrific idea, if she'd do it. Mrs. Perry knows her."

"And I could say that, since Laura studied art, we could straighten out the papers as we go, and that would help her. Mrs. Perry, I mean."

"Excellent point. Remember that one."

"Mom, if Martin Quinlan stole the painting, is it still mine?"

Kate heard her mother take a deep breath.

"I'm afraid not, Kate. If it was the artist's property at the time of her death, it would belong to whoever she willed it to. Did she have any children?"

"No, she didn't."

"When did she die?"

"In 1961."

"The estate would probably have been settled years ago. She might have had distant relatives, or she might have left her work to some institution."

"Like the Art Association?"

"Maybe. Should I have Dad call you when he gets back?"

"Yes. And, Mom, thanks for the help."

"I was happy to do it, Kate. Let us know how things work out."

Kate's father called about an hour later. "The main thing to keep in mind," he told her, "is that the burden of proof is on the Art Association if they want to claim that the painting was stolen. Even if no bill of sale is found, that could simply mean it was lost or never made out."

"But why did Mrs. Perry talk to their lawyer?"

"Probably to see what their situation was, how strong a claim they could make. I don't see that they've got much of a case."

"Couldn't they prove that Martin Quinlan didn't have the money to buy the painting?"

"I don't see that they could. If he did odd jobs, he was likely paid in cash. He might well have kept more of it in his house than anybody knew. Kate, for your own peace of mind, I hope you find some record of the sale, but don't worry if nothing turns up."

"Okay, Dad. You sound a lot better."

"I feel a lot better, too. I've cut way back on the pain medication, and I'm starting to feel like a real person again."

"That's great, Dad."

Later that afternoon, Kate decided to call Churchill Avery. Despite what she'd said to Mrs. Perry, she had begun to worry about doing the job right. After two rings, his energetic voice came on the line.

"Hello."

"Mr. Avery? This is Kate Harris. You gave me some advice about—"

"Kate! What a delightful surprise. How is the cleaning going?"

"Fine. I'm almost done."

"You are a prodigy. I must say, I thought you'd find the prospect too daunting."

"I'm calling to ask if you would please look at the painting and tell me if I did it right."

"Have you been wringing out the cotton the way I showed you?"

"Yes."

"No mopping?"

"No mopping."

"Have you had any cracking or peeling?"

"No."

"In that case, I'll bet you're doing just fine. Of course, I'd love to see the painting. I have to confess, a little bird at the Historical Society told me that what you've got may be a Whitney. Who would have guessed it? Or did you already know?"

"Mrs. Perry said it might be." Kate found she still didn't want to mention about discovering the signature, even though Mr. Avery would soon see it. "I can bring it over anytime."

"No, no," he said. "Let's not cart this thing around unnecessarily. I'll come to your place. If that's convenient, of course."

"Just a minute. I'll ask."

Mrs. Lang was in the living room reading the paper. "Sure," she said when she heard Kate's request. "Any time tomorrow is good."

They settled on the following morning at eleven.

Sunday began with a heavy rain. Mr. Lang left to work on the boat right after breakfast. Kate went back to the painting. She wanted it to look as good as possible before Mr. Avery saw it. By the time he arrived, she had removed all but a few inches of the black border. She could hear him at the front door, greeting Alison's mother. Kate waited nervously. Then she realized that Mr. Avery had stopped to watch Alison feed the birds.

"I started feeding them solid food on Friday," she said. "It's really Cat Chow, but you can use it for birds."

"They are demanding, aren't they?" he said. "Can they fly?"

"Not yet," said Alison. "But yesterday I saw them hanging on to the sides of the box and fluttering their wings."

"The back porch is this way," said Mrs. Lang. They walked into the living room, setting the birds into a round of frantic peeping.

"Aquariums! I've thought of setting one up, but I'm afraid of winding up with a lot of dead fish. Are they very difficult?"

"I could show you how," said Alison. She pointed out the various species of fish and plants she'd introduced. The tour seemed to take forever.

"I'm still not finished adding all the fish I want," she said.

"I see, a work in progress. In fact, an aquarium is like a work of art, isn't it?" he said. "Only you're working with living material. They're fascinating."

"Thanks. I'd better get back to the gang."

After that, Alison's mother and Mr. Avery came directly to the back porch.

"Kate, how nice to see you again." His pants were wet from the knees down.

"Thanks for coming in the rain."

"Not at all. I love the rain, and a good thing, too, considering how much of it we get here."

Mr. Avery leaned over the table. "Ah, you've uncovered the signature, so it's definite. My, this is a beautiful thing. Look at that handling of the paint, especially in the clouds and on the cape. On a first glance, I'd say you've done an excellent job with the cleaning, but let me have another look."

Kate hardly breathed while Mr. Avery pulled out a pocket magnifying glass and a penlight and examined the entire surface. He turned the painting over and examined the back. Then he turned to the front again, moistened a cotton ball, squeezed it out, and rubbed a circle near the center of the canvas. He checked the cotton, then tested several more places.

"I do see a little area here and another one here," he said, outlining the places with a fingertip, "that could use a tad more attention. But this is a first-rate job. My congratulations."

"Thanks." Kate felt herself go limp with relief.

Mrs. Lang brought out a tray of tea and cookies. Alison followed, and the four of them sat on the porch and talked. Kate thought about the day she'd begun the cleaning. It had rained on that day, too. Was it possible that was only two weeks ago?

"What are you going to do with the painting?" asked Mr. Avery, reaching for a cookie.

Kate had been thinking about that question ever since Alison had brought it up at lunch on Thursday.

"I don't know."

"Would you consider selling it?" said Mr. Avery.

"No," Kate said.

"Well, you certainly didn't have to think twice about that," he said with a smile.

Kate was slightly embarrassed. She must have sounded emphatic, but the one thing she didn't want to do was give up the painting. She felt a special attachment to it, and not only because of the hours she'd put into cleaning it.

"Mr. Avery," Kate said, "I want to ask you something."

He looked at her expectantly. "Is this to do with the question of the painting's ownership?"

"Yes." Kate described Mrs. Bennett's visit and the phone conversation Kate had had with her father afterward.

"I'm with your father," he said. "I doubt they'd have a case. But I can see that you're concerned about this. It would be nice to put an end to the speculation once and for all."

Kate guessed that Mrs. Perry knew Mr. Avery very well, and Kate was the outsider, but she felt she could trust him. "My mom had an idea about that," she said. She explained briefly what her mother had suggested.

"Capital idea," Mr. Avery said. "Your mother sounds like a sharp lady. In fact, why don't we call Laura right now?" He turned to Alison's mother. "May I impose on your hospitality and invite her over?"

"I'd love to meet her. There's a phone next to the fridge, and the book is on the counter."

"Back in a sec," he said.

Kate figured that Laura would probably be out.

"Let's see . . . Everett . . . Everett. Here it is . . . Laura? Churchill Avery. I'm calling from the Langs'. You know, where— That's right. Kate has done a wonderful job on this painting, which just happens to be a Maude Whitney . . . Yes, I knew you'd be thrilled. Care for a look? Mrs. Lang would love you to come . . . The corner of Winthrop and Thorn. Orchid house with flower boxes. See you."

Minutes later, Kate saw Laura, raincoat billowing, pedaling a bike down Winthrop Street. She was about to continue on to the front door when Mr. Avery jumped up and called to her through an open porch window.

"Laura! We're here."

She swerved around to the back door, dismounted, and leaned the bike against the steps. Alison opened the door. Laura seemed completely out of breath.

"Mom, this is Laura Everett."

The women shook hands.

"I'm dripping water all over the place," said Laura, slipping out of her raincoat sleeves.

"Don't worry about it," said Alison's mother. She took the raincoat and hung it on a peg. "Can I offer you a cup of tea?"

"Thanks." Laura pulled a tissue out of her pocket and blotted her hair. Then she spotted the painting. "What a find."

Kate showed her and Mr. Avery the copy of the 1913 newspaper article she had found.

"And to think," he said, "that this might have been thrown out with the trash if Kate hadn't gotten it and made the effort to clean it."

"And that," said Laura, "would have been a tragedy. Kate, you got this at the auction, didn't you?"

Kate told the story of how she had recklessly bid on it, sure that she was in no danger of succeeding. With the cleaned painting sitting a few feet away, the whole thing seemed quite funny. Her audience clearly thought so.

Mr. Avery gave Laura a brief summary of the situation. "And Kate would like to approach Mrs. Perry with this idea, if you'll agree to work with her."

"Agree to? I'd beg to if necessary. Seeing Maude Whitney's papers would be a privilege." She looked at Kate. "When do you want to make the pitch?"

"Um. I figured I wouldn't see you until Tuesday, so I was thinking Tuesday after class."

"Why not tomorrow?"

"Tomorrow? Don't I need to make an appointment?"

"That would be a good idea," said Laura. "Mrs. Perry's always there to open the door at nine-thirty."

"Don't worry, Kate," said Mr. Avery. "Laura and I will back you up."

"We sure will," said Laura. "We'll hound her relentlessly. Actually, Mrs. Perry's a very fair-minded person. She just comes off a little forbidding."

"Exactly," said Mr. Avery. "She isn't against you, Kate. She simply has the best interests of the Art Association in mind at all times. Which is appropriate, in her position."

That was probably true, as far as Kate could see, but it wasn't going to make dealing with her any easier.

The Perfect Opportunity

THE NEXT MORNING, Kate had barely finished her toast and jam when Alison handed her the telephone.

"Wait. I want to think about this for a minute."

"What's to think about? Call. Here's the number." Alison held out a scrap of paper.

Darlene answered. Kate stumbled out a request to talk to Mrs. Perry for a few minutes.

"She's got time this morning at eleven-thirty," said Darlene.

Alison, standing next to Kate, nodded emphatically.

"I'll be there," said Kate. She hung up.

"I'll come with you," said Alison.

When Kate hesitated, Alison said, "If you don't want me there, it's fine."

"No, you should come." Suddenly, Alison's being there seemed like a good idea. Kate wasn't sure why.

They got to the Art Association exactly on time. Darlene was sitting at her desk in the outer office. The streak in her hair had undergone a change over the weekend from blue to violet.

"Mrs. Perry's on the phone," she said. "Why don't you sit on the bench over there? She'll be with you in a minute."

The minute turned into three, then five, then seven minutes. Kate tried to take her mind off her nervousness by reading a brochure on the history of the association.

Meanwhile, Alison had been looking at Darlene. "How do you do it?" she said at last. "The color, I mean."

"Isn't it great? Fruit drink powder, that's the best."

Alison asked a number of questions about the exact method. Kate had no interest in turning any part of her hair a candy-box color, but listening to the conversation passed the time.

Finally Kate heard the phone being replaced in its cradle.

Darlene leaned toward the open door to the inner office. "Mrs. Perry, your eleven-thirty is here."

"My eleven-thirty?" Mrs. Perry came to the doorway and glanced around the outer office. She smiled briefly at Kate when she saw her. "Oh, hello. Darlene, didn't you say the person was here?"

"People." Darlene nodded toward Kate and Alison.

Mrs. Perry looked confused, but she quickly recovered her professional demeanor. "I'm sorry, did we have an appointment?"

"I called about an hour ago," Kate said.

"Oh. And this is in regard to . . ."

"The painting I'm cleaning. The one you saw last week."

"The painting. Yes. Why don't you come into my office?"

"This is Alison Lang," said Kate. "Can she come, too?"

"Of course."

Mrs. Perry's office was small and densely packed with file cabinets, books, plants, and a number of small sculptures and paintings. "Please sit down."

Alison slid back into one of the chairs and looked around. "Who are they?" She pointed to a photo of a young woman holding a baby.

"That's my daughter Jennifer and my granddaughter Danielle."

"Your daughter doesn't look like you," said Alison in her usual blunt manner, "but the baby does."

Somewhat to Kate's surprise, Mrs. Perry smiled and nodded. "You know, that's true. My daughter is the image of her father, but Danielle looks exactly like me at that age."

Kate was grateful for the entry Alison had provided to the conversation. She sat forward in her chair.

"Mrs. Perry, I found the signature. You were right about the artist."

"The signature—well, that does clinch the identification. Is that what you came to tell me?"

"Not exactly." Kate paused. "On Saturday, someone named Mrs. Bennett came over. She's a second cousin of Martin Quinlan. She said that some people think that her cousin stole the painting. Do you think he did?"

"Well, I—I have to confess," said Mrs. Perry, looking flustered, "I've been a bit remiss. I should have told you this earlier. I did find a catalog from a show that was held here in 1961. A painting described in that catalog is almost certainly the one you have."

"*Red Sky at Morning.*"

"Yes, how did you know?"

"I found an article at the library." Kate handed the photocopy to Mrs. Perry. She skimmed it.

"Yes, this has to be the same one."

"Mrs. Bennett was really upset," said Kate. "She grew up with Mr. Quinlan, and she says he was a very honest person."

"Martin was very dependable—and likable. I hired him for small jobs myself on a number of occasions. However, he wasn't capable of exercising mature judgment, you have to keep that in mind."

"That doesn't mean he stole things."

"No." Mrs. Perry sighed. "It's just that this painting is so out of step with the other paintings in the house, and according to what I've heard, I don't see that Martin could have afforded it. And then when I saw his signature on the receipts as the person who delivered the art to the artists after the 1961 show, well, it gave him the perfect opportunity."

"If Martin did steal the painting, it belongs to the Art Association, doesn't it?"

"Yes, it does, but I certainly wouldn't claim something I didn't think belonged here."

"I guess you think it does belong here."

"I understand that you bought it in good faith, and you've put great effort into restoring it, but I do feel its true home is the association. However—and I'm not sure why I'm telling you this—you needn't worry that I'm going to try to get the painting. I've spoken to our attorney."

"Arthur Burke?"

"My," said Mrs. Perry, "word certainly does get around quickly. Yes, I spoke to Mr. Burke. He has informed me that our case is very weak without clear evidence of theft."

Kate saw an opening.

"If there were a receipt or a bill of sale that proved Mr. Quinlan bought the painting, that would be good, wouldn't it? I mean, everybody would feel better, wouldn't they? And the rumors would stop."

"Yes, that would settle the matter. And I fully intend to organize the Whitney papers as soon as time permits."

"Mrs. Lang said that wouldn't be until after September."

"That's correct."

"And other things might happen to keep you busy."

"It's possible. I can't guarantee I'd get to the job right then."

Kate took a breath. "Mrs. Perry, I'd like to do it. You probably think I'm too young, but I'd be very careful not to lose a single scrap of paper, and I wouldn't ask to do it alone. Laura Everett said she'd work with me the whole time. She's especially interested in this artist. The job would get done, and you wouldn't have to spend any time on it yourself."

Mrs. Perry seemed at a loss for words. Several seconds went by before her professional manner got the upper hand over her surprise.

"I'm afraid that wouldn't be possible. As you said yourself, you are very young. No, I can't allow it."

"But Laura would be there every minute."

"No, it's quite out of the question."

"Mrs. Perry, Mrs. Bennett isn't the only person who's upset about the rumors. If I don't find something that proves Mr. Quinlan owned the painting, people are going to say I took something that didn't belong to me."

Kate saw that she had made an impression. Mrs. Perry fiddled nervously with her bracelet. "Of course, there would be no basis for anyone saying that."

"But people would say so anyway."

"Kate, when school starts in the fall, you'll be far away from those people. You'll forget about them."

"What if Kate comes again next summer?" said Alison.

Alison was probably saying that to help, but Kate was surprised to hear the remark.

"Good point," said a voice from the outer office. Mr. Avery leaned in the doorway. "Phyllis, you are looking at a golden opportunity. You saw the work Kate did on the painting. Where are you going to find such conscientious help—for free?"

"Churchill, you have to understand that I—"

"Plus someone with training in art history? Can you afford to turn down a deal like that?"

"Well, I—" Mrs. Perry turned to Kate. "You have to realize that there're boxes and boxes of material, and organization was not Ms. Whitney's strong suit."

"That's okay," said Kate. "Now that the painting is clean, I'll have a lot of time to work on something else."

Mrs. Perry drummed her fingers on the desk for a minute. "I hope I don't live to regret this, but have Laura get in touch with me and we'll work out the details."

"Thank you, Mrs. Perry," said Kate. "You won't regret it."

Mrs. Perry managed a smile, then she turned to Mr. Avery. "Churchill, did you want to see me for some reason?"

"Oh, I just dropped by to return that book on Japanese art you lent me."

"There was no rush on that, Churchill."

"That's all right. Now it's off my mind. Well, I've got to be going."

From where she sat, Kate could see Mr. Avery pass Darlene at her desk.

"That was lucky," said Alison on the way down the steps of the Art Association a few minutes later, "Mr. Avery stopping by when he did."

"I don't think it was luck," said Kate.

"Why not?"

"I saw him give Darlene the victory sign." Kate held up her index and third fingers to make a V.

"Oh."

They took a detour to the beach to hunt for shells. Interesting fragments were all they found, but Kate was too happy with the results of the meeting with Mrs. Perry to feel discouraged. They sat on a boulder and watched the waves for a while.

"Alison, thanks for coming along. And thanks for saying what you did." They sat in silence for a minute.

"So, are you?" said Alison at last.

"Am I what?"

"Coming next summer?"

"I don't know. But I'd like to come again." The words came out of a reflex to be polite, but as Kate heard herself say them, she realized they were true.

"Do you mean it? You were so quiet last week, I thought you weren't having a good time here, or maybe you were angry about something."

Kate didn't know how to explain what was wrong. She hardly understood it herself. "No, I'm not angry about anything."

They watched a seagull circle overhead.

"Alison, do you ever think about people dying? I mean people in your family?"

"Sometimes. Then I just figure, it won't happen. My parents aren't even forty years old yet. I know that sometimes young people die, but not usually. Is that what you were worried about?"

"I think about it sometimes."

"But your dad's okay now. And your mother isn't sick or anything."

"It isn't only people dying. It's other things, too."

"Are you afraid there's going to be another storm?"

"No, I didn't think about that. Do you think there will be?"

"No, not this year at least. But if we keep living here, we'll probably have another one sometime."

"Isn't that kind of scary?"

Alison shrugged. "We'll just have to fix everything again."

As they walked in the Langs' back door a little while later, they almost crashed into Mrs. Lang.

"Close the door, Alison!"

Kate ducked as a dark form swooped over her head, careened past the open door, and shot back toward the living room. A second bird was doing figure eights around the kitchen, while two others circled the dining room.

"They're flying!" said Alison. "We have to get the windows covered before they clobber themselves trying to fly through the glass."

They ran around pulling down shades and closing shutters. Corralling the birds on the front porch took a while longer.

"What do we do now, Dr. Dolittle?" said Mrs. Lang.

"The books said to allow the birds to fly outside when they're ready but leave a way for them to get back in. We can leave one window and screen open a couple of inches."

"What about bugs?"

"We'll have to keep the door to the porch closed. It'll only be for a few days."

Just before lunch, Kate phoned Laura to tell her the news.

"Kate, you've made my summer! I'll call Mrs. Perry right now. I work in the afternoons giving tours of historic houses, but I'm free every morning—except Tuesday, of course."

Minutes later, Laura phoned back. The sorting would begin at nine-thirty Wednesday morning.

Kate made one more call. She hoped they were home. This was not a message she wanted to leave on the answering machine.

"Hello?"

"Mom, you were right . . ."

A Privileged View

WHEN KATE AND ALISON arrived at the Art Association the next morning for the fifth lesson, the lobby had been transformed. Instead of being a dark and confining space, it was flooded with light. Wood panels that had made up the back wall had been removed. Glass-paned double doors stood in their place, framing a view of the courtyard beyond. Next to the doors stood an easel holding a hand-lettered sign, "Drawing Class" with an arrow pointing to the courtyard, where Laura was setting up more easels.

"Come in, come in," she said, waving them on enthusiastically.

As they descended the three stone steps to the courtyard level, Kate felt as if they had leaned against a secret revolving panel to find themselves in an enchanted garden. Surrounded by ivy-covered brick walls was a space carpeted with lush grass and crisscrossed by winding flagstone walkways, the perfect setting for the sculptures in bronze and marble that filled the courtyard. In the enclosed space, the light had a particular radiance.

"Isn't this just heaven?" said Laura. "I was afraid they wouldn't get the renovations done before the summer was over. Of course, the official opening isn't until Thursday evening, but Mrs. Perry said we could sketch out here today."

A succession of "ohs" and "ahs" came from the direction of the steps as the rest of the class filed in.

"Well," said Miss Longwood, "I certainly feel that my donation has been put to good use. There were times when I wasn't sure."

"We haven't any chairs," said Laura, "just a few benches, so I'll make this quick. Today I want you to think about light and shadow on the basic forms. I've made up a series of drawings to show you the effect of a single light source, like the sun, on a cube, a cone, a cylinder, a sphere, and an egg—which might be considered as a variation on a sphere but is useful in drawing portraits." She set out a succession of drawings clipped to poster board.

"There are two kinds of shadows. Cast shadows and form shadows. Everybody is familiar with cast shadows. They are caused by an object blocking the light to another object or surface. Form shadows are a little trickier. On rounded forms, which include everything but the cube, they begin gradually as the object's surface curves away from the light.

"But consider this sphere I've drawn. Think of it as an apple on a table. The darkest part of the form shadow on the apple is about three-quarters of the way back from the light source, not exactly opposite the light. That's because, even in the shadows, light is bouncing off the table onto the apple. You'll find objects look more three-dimensional if you show this reflected light in your shadows."

Everyone crowded around the easels for a look. After a few minutes, people began going off to find something to

draw. Near the back wall, Kate noticed a marble portrait, *Head of a Woman*. She had always thought of marble as a cold material, fit only for use in cemeteries. At that moment, she saw that marble wasn't opaque and cold at all. It was translucent and alive, like skin.

The model for the portrait had been young, with large sensitive features. Her serene expression had an undercurrent of sadness. But perhaps that was only a chance effect of the light and would pass.

Kate read the information card. The sculptor was a local artist, now dead, whose work was in the collections of some famous museums.

She sat on a nearby bench and blocked in the first faint lines, concentrating on the form of the head as an egg. As she worked, Kate found herself wondering who the woman was. A friend? A sister? Someone the artist was in love with? Or just a model whose face he liked? From the date on the card, she'd be old now, if she was still alive.

Had she ever come to the sculpture court to see her portrait? Did she stop someone and say, *This is me. This is me when I was young and beautiful.*

Kate had sketched in the eyes and the mouth, with an indication of where the shadows were, and had started on the nose when she noticed a slight shift in the light. She'd have to work faster. The second lesson came back to her—how she'd had to capture the moment. This time, the model was holding perfectly still. It was the light that was moving.

She hurried on to the hair, a mass of swirls, translating it onto the paper as a few sweeping lines.

Then she hesitated, unsure of what to do next. She had more time before the shadows changed completely, but not enough to finish the whole drawing to her satisfaction. Kate signaled to Laura and explained the problem to her.

"You could try working up only the eyes and defining the mouth a little more. Then leave it. Remember, an unfinished drawing—"

"Gives the viewer something to fill in."

"Right."

For the next five minutes, Kate focused intensely on the shadows that gave the eyes their arresting expression.

Passing clouds blocked the sun for a few minutes, erasing the shadows that Kate needed to see. When the sunlight returned, she saw that the moment had passed. The marble had lost some of its translucence, and the expression, while still beautiful, didn't seem as riveting as before. Maybe she was simply tired from the concentration.

She thought of taking a break and finding something else to draw, but Alison probably needed to eat. As Kate looked around for her, she came up the walkway.

"I'm going to start drawing a sandwich if I don't get one soon," Alison said.

Laura was standing nearby. "That's a perfectly good subject for a still life. It doesn't always have to be grapes and apples." She turned to Kate. "See you tomorrow morning. Mrs. Perry said we could have the library until noon every day."

On their way downtown, waiting for a pedestrian light, Alison showed Kate her drawing of a bronze lion. Its anatomy looked more like a dog's or maybe a sheep's, but the mane, a wild mass of smudges, was wonderful.

"My people aren't so good, but I do okay with animals. I wish I could draw better. For a couple of minutes, the sunshine made the mane look like flames."

The traffic light changed.

"Alison," Kate said as they crossed the street, "do you ever see something that you've seen lots of times before and all of a sudden it looks completely different? The shape isn't different or anything like that. It's the same but—"

"But what?"

"It's perfect."

At first, Alison didn't reply. Kate was afraid the idea sounded too strange. They stopped to look in a store window.

"Once in a while," Alison said at last, "like the day I found the birds. I guess they were sort of funny-looking to everybody else, since their feathers weren't grown in. When I picked each one up, I could feel it breathing, and I thought, How could it be alive, it's so small. But it wanted to live, I knew it." She shrugged. "I don't know. Maybe that's not the same thing."

"I think it is."

"Do you think," said Alison, "that that's when you see what things really are, when they're perfect? Or is it like a dream, and when you wake up you realize it wasn't true?"

They walked another half block.

"I think that's the way things really are," said Kate. "We just don't see it most of the time."

That evening, Kate wrote her fifth letter home:

Tuesday, August 2

Dear Mom & Dad,

You already know my news, so this is going to be a short letter.

This morning we had our art lesson in a really wonderful place—the sculpture court at the Art Association. It was closed for repairs, but now it's open again. I'd like to spend the rest of the summer there. The drawing I did today was the best one so far.

We picked up the photos of the painting after class this morning. They came out okay. At least you can get an idea of what it looks like.

Love,

Kate

P.S. Thanks again for the advice, Mom, about talking to Mrs. Perry.

On Wednesday morning, Kate and Alison had just finished breakfast when they heard a knock on the back door.

Mrs. Lang answered it. From the voice, Kate guessed that the visitor was a boy about six or seven years old.

"Is this the place where the person lives who knows about taking care of animals?"

"That's me." Alison went to the door.

"My older sister found a baby rabbit in our yard. It won't eat. It's really little."

"What are you trying to feed it?"

"Clover."

"No, it needs formula."

"Could you come over? We're afraid it's going to die."

"Mom, can I?"

"You're the Dolans' boy, aren't you?" said Mrs. Lang.

"Uh-huh. I'm Brian. My sister's Rosemary. We live in the blue house over there."

"Sure, you can go, Alison."

Alison grabbed a paper bag from under the sink and went to the front porch. From the clatter, Kate could tell that she was throwing together the paraphernalia from the birds' first days in the house.

"The birds don't need all of this stuff anymore," Alison said. "Mom, have we got any rags?"

For the next five minutes, Alison and her mother looked like players in a scavenger hunt, as Alison remembered things that might be useful. She paused at the door. "Kate, I'll see you when you get back. If I'm not here, I'm across the street. Bye!"

"I wonder how the Dolans heard about Alison," said Mrs. Lang, closing the door. "Come to think of it, I did mention the birds to Mr. Menahan, the pharmacist. Well, I guess it's going to be a quiet morning around here. Oh, I should stop at the post office. I'll walk with you, Kate."

Kate said goodbye to Mrs. Lang at the steps of the Art Association. She walked into the library to find Mrs. Perry shoving cartons together on the floor. Kate counted seven.

"Good morning, Kate. I hope you're ready to work. As you see, there's quite a lot of material."

Kate smiled and nodded.

"Hi!" Laura brushed by Kate carrying another carton.

"You know," said Mrs. Perry, dusting off her hands, "it's a great privilege to see someone's private papers."

"Mrs. Perry, I'd never tell anybody anything I shouldn't about what we find," Kate said.

"I know you wouldn't, Kate. If I didn't feel that, I wouldn't have agreed to your seeing them." Mrs. Perry looked at her watch. "I've got a meeting now, so I'll leave you to it." She walked out briskly, closing the door behind her.

"I didn't know there'd be so much stuff," said Kate in a low voice.

"Neither did I," said Laura. "Nothing's labeled, so we might as well start anywhere."

They hoisted a carton onto the table and opened the flaps. Laura scooped out a wad of material. Kate saw an address book, ticket stubs, envelopes, newspaper clippings, and a spiral-bound notebook. A handwritten list fell onto the table. *Birthday card to Aunt Amy, Call Barbara re: lunch, Pick up jacket at dry cleaners, Stamps at P.O.*

Laura looked up. "This is kind of a presumptuous thing to be doing, isn't it?"

Kate nodded. She felt as if they had burgled someone's home and were pawing over the stolen goods.

"Well," said Laura, "if we don't do it, somebody else will." Hesitantly, she picked up the notebook labeled "Aug. 1936" and flipped through it.

"Should we try to organize things according to date?" said Kate.

"We might not find dates on a lot of things," said Laura. "We could put them into piles by what they are, like catalogs in one pile and newspaper clippings in another."

"That's good."

For the next few minutes, the only sound was the shuffling of paper.

Kate flipped open a small sketchbook. The first page was covered with geometric designs in pencil. She put the sketchbook flat on the table so they could both see it.

"I hope there are more of these someplace," said Laura. Then she pulled out a typed list of names and addresses. "This looks like a mailing list," she said. "Hey, my great-aunt Miriam is on this list."

Kate found the catalog from an art show. They started to read Maude Whitney's entry.

"Wait a minute," said Laura. "We're like the guy who puts newspapers on the floor so he can paint the walls and winds up reading the papers instead of painting." She handed the catalog back to Kate. "We've got to lay down a strict rule—only enough reading to identify the item."

After that, the table filled up quickly with tax records, shopping lists, catalogs from art supply houses, appointment books, calendars, medical records, journals, and canceled checks. Bills of sale turned up, too, but not the one they were looking for.

"I'm going to find a bag or something for the receipts," Laura said, after a handful of them slid onto the floor.

She returned with a pack of folded stationery boxes. "Darlene saved the day. We can use these."

As Laura put the receipts into their own box, she said, "I should double-check these just in case we've already hit pay dirt." She sat down and paged through the sheets. "What's this?"

Kate waited. Their privileged glimpse into Maude Whitney's life might be over if something had turned up.

Laura shook her head. "False alarm. This is just a receipt for some oil paints. My eye caught the word red."

They opened a second carton. At the top was a snapshot labeled "Summer 1938—Islesboro" on the back.

"Islesboro is off the coast of Maine," said Laura.

The photo showed people in a yard bordered by long-needle pines.

Laura pointed to a woman with short hair wearing a plain blouse and slacks. "I think that's Maude Whitney."

Kate had been picturing a tall woman with striking features. Judging by the height of the people standing next to her, Maude Whitney wasn't tall. The color of her hair was difficult to judge in the black-and-white photo, but it seemed neither dark nor blond. Her features, shadowed by the sun, appeared unexceptional.

Bundles of letters, minus their envelopes, filled most of the box.

"I wonder why she didn't save the envelopes," said Kate.

"Maybe just to keep the paper to a minimum. There certainly are a lot of letters."

They were down to the last few items in the second carton when Laura looked at her watch.

"Ten minutes to noon. I've got to hit the road."

Mrs. Perry walked in. "Put all the unsealed cartons in my office. There should be room on the floor next to the file cabinet. The ones that are sealed can stay here."

As Kate went down the Art Association steps a few minutes later, she noticed that the sky was as crystal blue as she'd ever seen it here. And the temperature was perfect. She decided to stop at Perry Street beach before heading back to the Langs'.

As she watched the breakers roll in, Kate realized that this was the first time since her arrival she'd been to the beach, or just about anyplace else, alone. Back home, she'd been used to spending whole days by herself, her parents nearby but their attention elsewhere. She missed the opportunities to let her mind roam without the need to keep part of herself available to other people, like having to stay dressed in case somebody rang the doorbell.

Now, her thoughts floated free. For the first time since her father's surgery, she was sure he would be all right.

She spent a few minutes looking for shells, then started back, veering left, toward Winthrop. At Shore Road, she stopped. Feeling like she was playing hooky, she turned right and walked downtown.

Plywood still covered the Purple Cow. Here and there, dried seaweed rippled in the wind like prairie grass. Kate looked in a few store windows and browsed the aisles at the reopened variety store. On the way out, she noticed the time. Twelve forty-five. She began to walk faster.

The fledglings were flying in and out of the open window on the front porch as Kate came up to the house. Soon, they'd be ready to live on their own.

As she went around to the back door, she heard Alison's voice from the kitchen. "That's great, Mrs. Edgar. I'll ask my dad to stop by for it on the way home from the job he's doing today. He always phones in at lunchtime if he's not here. Thanks. Bye."

She turned to Kate. "Oh, there you are. I thought you'd be back earlier."

"Was that Mrs. Edgar from the library?"

"Uh-huh. She's giving me the cage they used for the baby raccoons they raised. Well, lending it to me anyway, for the Dolans' rabbit."

"Were you able to feed it?"

"Yup. After the birds, it was easy. I showed Brian and Rosemary how to do it, but they asked me to come again this afternoon to make sure everything's okay. I want to bring the cage with me. Mrs. Edgar's leaving it on her front porch. How'd you make out?"

"Well, there's more to sort than I thought, but we're doing okay."

"Want to come with me to the Dolans' this afternoon? The rabbit's really cute."

"Sure."

Mr. Lang came home with the cage a little after three that afternoon. Kate and Alison carried it the half block to the Dolans'.

When Kate was introduced to Rosemary, she realized she had seen her a few times.

In a cardboard box lined with an old flannel shirt, the rabbit was huddled in one corner. It seemed impossibly fragile.

"Have you fed it?" said Alison.

"I tried," said Rosemary, "but I'm afraid I'm not doing it right. Maybe you could show me again. The formula's right here."

Alison scooped up the rabbit and slipped it into Rosemary's hand. Then she gave her an eyedropper full of formula.

"You're doing fine," said Alison. She helped steady the dropper. The rabbit licked furiously at it. Suddenly it didn't seem fragile at all. "See?"

Kate pulled her sketchbook out of her pocket. "Is it okay with you if I draw while you're doing that?"

"Uh, sure," said Rosemary.

With the rabbit tucked in Rosemary's hand, the form of its body was almost impossible to see, so Kate concentrated on the head and the front paws, the way the rabbit grasped

Rosemary's fingers while it gulped formula from the dropper.

While Rosemary finished the feeding, Alison prepared the cage, adding a soft towel next to a plastic bottle filled with water. "Careful with the water," she said, tightening the bottle cap. "Warm, not hot." As soon as Rosemary released the rabbit into the cage, it wiggled into a fold of material.

As Kate and Alison were leaving, Rosemary called after them, "You're coming tomorrow, right, Alison?"

"Sure am."

✿ Photographs

ON THURSDAY MORNING, Kate walked into the Art Association library to find Laura studying a large book.

"Mrs. Perry found this. It was published by the Art Association in 1978 for the one hundredth anniversary of Maude's birth. Look! Color reproductions of some of her paintings."

Kate was fascinated to see the portraits of fishermen and dockworkers, their dark-eyed children and careworn wives, their humbly furnished cottages.

The residences of the wealthy were here, too, with their grand entranceways and dark interiors pierced by gleaming highlights of silver and crystal.

In art books, Kate had seen portraits of the accomplished women who presided over these homes—corseted figures of triumph launching themselves into richly furnished rooms as if they were figureheads on the prows of ships.

But Maude Whitney didn't paint them that way. She showed them in private moments—bathing, reading letters, daydreaming, recovering from illness, playing with pet dogs—their faces expressing doubt, wonder, loneliness, feelings, Kate guessed, that they never spoke about at their glittering dinner parties.

"Fortunately, the reproductions look high quality," said Laura, "because we're not likely to see many of the originals."

"Because people have them in their living rooms?"

"Right. Of course, if this period of art has a revival at some point, a lot of these may come on the market." Laura closed the book. "Okay. Back to the salt mines."

They sorted three cartons by noon.

After Laura left, Kate stayed on for another look at the color reproductions. When she finally checked the clock, it was twelve-fifty. She packed up quickly. By running every other block, she managed to be just on time for lunch.

"The rabbit's even fluffier today," Alison said. "You should've seen it."

At lunch, Alison suggested that she and Kate go downtown.

"At least we could see which places are open."

Kate hesitated. "Well, I took a quick look on the way home yesterday, just on Main. A lot of places are still boarded up."

"Oh."

"So what's on the docket for this afternoon?" asked Mrs. Lang, passing around the bread.

"Well, I'm not finished cleaning the frame on the painting," Kate began.

The phone rang. Alison picked up the call in the kitchen.

"Hi, Dad. Uh-huh . . . Okay. Kate's working here, but you can count me in." She came to the doorway. "Dad could use help sanding the boat. He's picking me up in half an hour."

Kate thought of saying she'd come along, but she felt that the door had been quietly shut in her face.

Friday morning, Kate walked into the Art Association library to find Laura unloading another carton. "It's the mother lode of the photos," she said, pulling out handfuls of envelopes. One envelope contained two professional photographs in folders. The first showed a group of about twenty young women in formal gowns with gloves above the elbow. A caption was written on the folder in gold ink: "First ball of the debutante season, 1896—Maude, middle row, second from left."

A number of the girls were beautiful, a few, remarkably so. Maude wasn't. Even the bloom of youth, which gave her face an appealing softness, couldn't disguise her plainness.

The second photograph showed Maude by herself in a white lace blouse and dark skirt. Her right hand had been posed on the back of a chair in an attempt at graceful ease.

In the left, she was holding a spray of roses as if it were a wet umbrella.

The other envelopes contained snapshots, many of them labeled on the backs: "Elizabeth and Bert, summer cottage, 1949," "Paul at Colby's Ice Cream Parlor, Age 6, 1927."

The most fascinating of all were the ones taken during Maude Whitney's years of study abroad. After Laura left to get more boxes at Kennon's Office Supply, Kate spread out the contents of all the envelopes marked "France."

Here was the shy girl from the stiff studio portrait transformed into an energetic young woman with a sketchbook under her arm on the steps of the Louvre, the ruffled blouse replaced by a crisp tailored shirt. Here she was at an outdoor café, at Notre-Dame Cathedral, at Monet's studio in Giverny.

Kate turned to the envelopes marked "Italy." Here was Maude Whitney "With Rebecca on the Spanish Steps in Rome." Here they were "Tossing Coins into the Trevi Fountain" with its rampaging winged horses. Kate knew from a travelogue she'd seen that that was supposed to ensure a return someday.

Here were Maude and Rebecca "At the Colosseum" with a young man identified as Vittorio. Kate double-checked the "Italy" envelopes. All empty, except one. She shook it. A small portrait photo of Rebecca fell out.

Kate studied the photo, and all the others in that set. Then she scooped them up and slipped them back into their envelopes just as Laura came in, carrying two shopping bags.

"Find anything interesting?"

Before Kate could answer, Mrs. Perry leaned in the doorway and asked them to bring all the boxes and cartons to her office.

"Tomorrow afternoon's the annual tea for our donors. We're intending to use the sculpture court, but we'll need the library in case of rain. Just leave me an aisle to my desk."

"Can it be noon already?" said Laura. "That trip took longer than I figured it would."

Ten minutes later, she and Kate stood on the front steps.

"See you on Monday," said Laura, waving as she headed east on Magnolia Street.

"See you."

Kate went west. Then, instead of turning north at Winthrop, she turned south to the beach.

The ocean reflected the leaden sky. Kate's mind went back to the photos she and Laura had discovered that morning—most of the people smiling at the camera must be gone now, the birthday parties and holiday dinners and backyard picnics only a thin film of chemicals on stiff paper.

Who were Elizabeth and Bert? Beloved friends? Or only casual acquaintances? Who was Paul? When he was grown up, did he remember that ice cream cone, how he'd been made to stand for the photo while ice cream dripped over his fingers and onto the hot sidewalk? Maude Whitney was at the junction of all those lives. Without her, the aunts and uncles and cousins and friends lost their places in the scheme of things and joined the army of nameless people in other people's family albums.

How long would the photos and sketchbooks last? What about the paintings? Even Mr. Avery had said *Red Sky at Morning* might be on a garbage heap now if Kate hadn't rescued it. A message in a bottle probably had a better chance of surviving.

Alison wasn't at home when Kate got back. Mrs. Lang said she'd been asked to help out with another animal—a stray kitten this time—by a girl who lived across town. Her parents were friends of the Dolans.

"I don't know why this town bothers to have a newspaper," said Mrs. Lang. "The grapevine is so much faster."

When Mr. Lang got home just before one o'clock, Kate explained to him about the kitten.

"Looks like Alison's expanding her practice," he said.

Alison pounded up the back steps thirty minutes later. They had started lunch without her.

"Sorry I'm late," she said, slipping into her chair. "The kitten didn't want to eat at first. But she's okay now."

"Alison," said her father, "you've heard of the latest technological marvel, the telephone? Call if you're going to be late."

"Okay, Dad. I didn't think anybody would miss me."

Kate was almost sure that Alison shot her a glance as she said that.

That afternoon, Kate decided she'd been neglecting the garden. Alison said that the water in one of the aquariums looked a little cloudy. Somehow, their separate jobs took until dinnertime to finish.

On Saturday morning, Kate slept later than usual. By the time she got downstairs, Mrs. Lang was wiping crumbs off the table.

"Alison's gone over to the Dolans'. They called this morning and asked if she could come now instead of this afternoon. I think she's going to see the kitten after that. Want some breakfast?"

"I can get it. Where do the kitten people live?"

"Their name is Beck. On Elliot near Simmons. I think it's a green house with yellow trim."

Kate took a bowlful of oatmeal. She ate quickly, forgoing her usual toast and jam, but when she got to the Dolans', nobody was home.

She could have tried finding the right house on Elliot, but Kate didn't want to go without an exact address. Alison would cheerfully have knocked on the doors of complete strangers and asked where the family with the stray kitten was, but Kate had never been able to approach people that way.

She went back to the Langs'.

"Alison wasn't at the Dolans'?" Mrs. Lang called from her office.

"No."

Kate retrieved the mail from the front porch, pulled out her letter from home, and brought the rest to Mrs. Lang.

"Should I see if the Becks are listed in the phone book?" Mrs. Lang said.

"That's okay. I have some things to do here."

"You're sure?"

"Yes. Thanks."

Kate took the letter to the back porch.

Thurs., Aug. 4

Dear Kate,

We were quite bowled over by your drawing from the sculpture court. The original will be framed as soon as it makes its appearance on our doorstep.

Congratulations on completing the cleaning of the painting. I always knew you had determination. If the photos are any guide at all, this is a wonderful piece.

And congratulations on your success in gaining access to the Whitney papers. As I have said, the proof you are looking for probably doesn't exist, but I know you want to do this search very much.

I now walk without the cane most of the time, except when I want to feel like Sherlock Holmes. I believe the well-to-do men of his day carried beautifully carved canes at all times, presumably for slaying dragons should the need have arisen.

Love,
Dad

Kate was still on the back porch working a crossword from her puzzle book when Alison walked in.

"Oh, hi," she said. "Didn't my mom tell you where the Becks live?"

"I overslept," Kate said. She went back to her puzzle, stumped on a six-letter word for "curtains, to Mugsy" with "T - - - - D" filled in by crossing answers. She could hear Alison telling her mother about the baby rabbit and the kitten. Kate wondered if she'd have another chance to see them.

Lunch was hurried, since Mr. and Mrs. Lang had to shop for a mattress that afternoon.

"Alison, you and Kate are welcome to come with us, but it would be boring for you, I think."

"That's okay," said Alison. "Kate and I will stay here and play croquet."

"Kate," said Mrs. Lang, "is that okay with you?"

"Oh. Sure." Kate didn't particularly want to play. As she watched Alison's parents drive away, she thought of calling off the game. Instead, she wheeled the croquet cart out of the toolshed.

Every time Kate put a wicket in place, Alison moved it to a different spot. Just establishing the course took twenty minutes. Then Alison changed her mind three times on which color she was playing.

"Just pick one," Kate said irritably. "It'll be dark by the time we start if you keep messing around like this."

"I want my lucky color. I just can't remember which one it is."

They argued over the rules of the game. A bee flew past Alison's face as she took a stroke and the ball rolled under a bush. She insisted on taking the shot over. Kate wouldn't have asked for a concession like that. Then Kate took time to line up a stroke. Alison rolled her eyes and said that Kate treated even a game as if she were being graded on it.

By the time Kate finally won the match, she was too aggravated to enjoy it.

On Sunday Alison maintained a relentlessly nonchalant manner while Kate studiously ignored it, taking refuge first in her sketchbook and then in her crossword. Just before dinner, she figured out the six-letter answer she was looking for: "T-H-E-E-N-D."

When Alison turned down her father's suggestion of a game of dominoes, Kate saw him exchange a glance with Alison's mother. Then they both shrugged.

At breakfast on Monday, Alison announced that she was going to the Dolans' that morning.

"Why don't you go in the afternoon, when Kate can go with you?" said her mother.

"Brownie probably needs a feeding."

"Can't Rosemary do that?"

"I'm better at it."

Kate busied herself taking plates to the sink.

At the Art Association, Laura was setting out bundles of letters on the library table when Kate arrived. "I phoned Mrs. Perry on Saturday and asked if I could work on the papers on Sunday afternoon. She was nice enough to drive over and let me in. I went through all the bills of sale and the tax records. Nothing."

"Thanks for doing that."

Laura set one of the letter bundles on her side of the table and one in front of Kate. Neither of them said anything for a moment.

"Do you feel as weird as I do?" said Laura at last.

Kate nodded.

Laura sighed. "Keeping in mind that somebody will do this even if we don't . . ."

They sat down and read in silence. The letters in Kate's stack had dates from the 1950s and contained family news—the graduation of a friend's daughter, a cousin's premature baby, the death of an elderly great-uncle.

As she read, Kate began to recognize handwriting styles—Aunt Estelle's star-pupil penmanship, Barbara's bold script, Cousin Beth's backhand slant. Amy mixed printing and cursive letters, while Sofie decorated her capitals with great flourishes.

Kate got to the bottom of the bundle without finding any reference to painting. Laura, hardly looking up from the letter she was reading, passed over another bundle.

These were from the 1940s, full of the same kind of news as the others, but with more words and phrases that were foreign to Kate. Aunt Estelle complained about someone who was hogging their party line. Barbara told about losing some ration coupons for meat.

When Kate looked up after several minutes, Laura was pulling a notebook out of her bag.

"Find anything?"

"Not about the painting, no," said Laura. "But this is a really interesting letter. Listen: 'What you said about Jack's work is quite accurate, I think. He doesn't have much technical ability, but he does manage to go directly to the heart of the subject. I find his charcoal drawings in particular very moving.' This might be from another artist."

"Who?"

"It's signed Gerry." Laura drummed her fingers on the table. "Gerry, Gerry. Hey, there was a Geraldine Fitzsimmons who was working around the same time as Maude Whitney. I think she mainly sculpted." She set the letter to the side. "If you find any others that have anything to do with art, put them on top of this one."

Kate was hoping to find letters like the one Laura had. She came across one bundle all from the same person, Peg. Kate couldn't tell if she was an artist or not. Her letters were full of family news, mostly about her children, but she seemed to have a keen interest in art.

January 15, 1925

. . . We stopped by the gallery in Newport on our way home from the visit to Aunt Evelyn. Am I imagining this or is your latest work showing some influence of Cubism? I'm referring in particular to "Lighthouse, Rocky Point." Although I prefer the drama of pieces like "Approaching Storm," I'm sure these explorations feed the creative mind . . .

November 8, 1928

. . . I agree with you that German Expressionism has produced some powerful work. While I freely admit this, I find I do not like it at all . . .

Kate set the bundle in a separate stack.

Every now and again, she glanced up. Laura seemed to be going slower and slower. She had separated out more of the letters from "Gerry" and was reading them intently.

"This is like an art lecture," she said at last. "I'd love to see Maude's replies to these letters. Here." She pointed to a paragraph.

I am amazed at how much simpler my work is, at least on the surface, than it used to be. The more I learn, the more expression I am able to put into a single mark. Remember Mr. Henderson's class? Don't say the same thing three times when once will do. Now I appreciate what he meant.

Laura reached into the carton. "There have to be more like this."

There were. Maude Whitney—whom, Kate noticed, Laura was beginning to refer to by her first name—had kept up a correspondence with a number of artists. The ones she hardly knew were the easiest to identify, since they often signed their full names. Her close friends were likely to sign off with "Love, Nan" or "Best, Jim" or even "Yours, M."

Laura's special stack grew. Every few minutes, she would stop reading long enough to jot something in the notebook.

Then Kate found a letter from an art school friend thanking Maude—Kate found herself thinking of her the way Laura did—for coming to his opening.

. . . I think you are right. The portrait of the old woman in the shawl is better than the one of the newsboy. I cleaned up the second one when I should have left it alone. As you said, those first searching lines should be allowed to stand, involving the viewer in the process of drawing . . .

Kate showed the passage to Laura.

"I wish," Laura said, reaching for her pen, "we had ten cartons of letters."

Mrs. Perry opened the door and leaned in. "Laura, I thought I'd better point out that it's five after twelve. You don't want to be late to work."

"Oh, gosh. Thanks, Mrs. Perry." She sighed. "Duty calls."

Kate helped her get the boxes back to Mrs. Perry's office. She didn't make any side trips this time, just went straight back to the house. Maybe she should make a point of spending time with Alison. That might make things easier between them.

"It's just you and I for lunch today," said Mrs. Lang when Kate got to the house. "Alison phoned and said she's getting a bite downtown."

"By herself?"

"I think Rosemary Dolan is going with her. Alison said something about looking for a book on rabbits."

"Oh. That's good," Kate said quickly. "You were hoping Alison would make friends around here."

"Yes, I was."

Kate carried the lunch plates to the table.

"Kate," said Mrs. Lang, spooning egg salad onto the plates, "is something wrong between you and Alison? Things have seemed a little tense these last few days, in fact, ever since you started this project at the association."

"Well," Kate said, "we both have jobs now."

"Yes," said Mrs. Lang, "I think that's part of it."

As she settled down to getting the last traces of soot off

of the frame that afternoon, Kate thought about what Mrs. Lang had said. That was exactly when the trouble had started between her and Alison, when that first carton had been opened and Kate had entered a world where Alison couldn't follow.

The sorting had made a bigger claim on Kate's time and attention than she had thought it would. Maybe Alison's feelings were hurt.

Naturally, they weren't spending as much time together since they'd both gotten involved with other interests, but that was a good thing.

She wadded a bunch of damp cotton balls in her hand and rubbed them along the frame.

When Alison came home, they should have a talk. Kate checked the clock. Just after three. Alison and Rosemary had probably gone to the bookstore.

The good thing about this time to herself was that Kate was doing a really good job on the frame. But if they didn't get back soon, she might not have the chance to talk to Alison before dinner.

This was the kind of thing Alison didn't think about. She was careless in certain ways. Like not bothering to consider that it was nearly four and Kate might have been waiting for her.

When Alison walked in the door at four-twenty, they were too close to dinner for any private talks, even if Alison hadn't brought Rosemary with her. The two of them breezed by Kate and headed for the front of the house.

"Rosemary wants to see my fish."

Kate threw the cotton ball she'd been using into the bag. If Alison wanted to talk about anything, she'd have to make the first move.

✺ Lost and Found

AT THE BEGINNING of the next art class, Laura opened her bag and set out three pictures taped to heavy cardboard.

"We've talked about achieving a sense of three dimensions in your drawings through the use of technical perspective, but the principles of this method were not worked out until the early 1400s, mostly in Italy. For most of history, artists found other means of showing depth."

She held up a landscape. "Let's talk about the differences between the foreground and the background in this illustration."

"The mountains are blue," said Alison. "Mountains in the background are always blue."

"Yes. Do you know why that is?" said Laura.

"No."

"Water vapor and dust in the air diffuse the light, similar to the way the atmosphere of the earth makes the sky blue. It's not important to know that, of course. The thing you need to remember is that colors get cooler the farther away they are."

"The elk in the foreground," said Miss Dixon, "are in very sharp focus, and the ones in the background aren't."

"Right. Of course, once in a while, you'll come across a photo or a painting in which the foreground is in soft focus and the background is sharp, but usually it's the other way. What else can you say about the background?"

"Nothing's very dark or very light," said Mrs. Randall.

"Yes," said Laura. "Water vapor and dust soften the contrasts.

"There you have the three characteristics of subject matter as you move into the background—it loses warmth of color, sharpness of definition, and contrast.

"If you're doing a drawing in black and white, of course, you can't show the color shift. But you can still get a lot of mileage out of the techniques you have available.

"Chinese painting, for instance, is often done in blue-black ink. You see how this landscape is divided into three levels, almost like levels of a stage set—foreground, middle ground, and background. Each level is painted lighter than the one in front of it."

Laura passed around a tiny sketch of a country scene with windmills.

"Here's the same idea applied to a line drawing. Notice how much bolder the line is on the elements that are nearest the viewer, and how much more delicate it is on the background elements. I guess you could say that Rembrandt knew what he was doing.

"Keep in mind, your eye will tend to go to the area with the boldest lines and the hardest edges, that is, the most abrupt transitions between dark and light. Usually that's the area of greatest detail as well. That area could be small.

It could be away from the center of the picture. It will still attract your attention.

"Of course, it's equally important what you leave out. A naïve drawing—what's sometimes called primitive art or folk art—will try to show every last detail, foreground or background, with the same importance."

Kate immediately thought of the paintings she had seen at the auction—the painstaking leaf-by-leaf rendering, each leaf facing forward.

Laura began to stack the prints again. "For sketching today, we're going to the garden behind the Historical Society."

As the other students filed out, Kate went up to the table. "Laura, may I see the Rembrandt drawing again?"

"Sure. You can give it back to me later." She picked up her bag and followed the last person out the door.

Kate was in no hurry to leave. She studied the Rembrandt drawing, trying to memorize every mark. Like handwriting, each stroke looked as if it had been made quickly, but not a single one had been made carelessly. In quite a few places, a line had been reconsidered. Kate could see the first attempt, a kind of ghost next to the line that was wanted. Where had she seen something about "searching lines"? The phrase was in one of the letters to Maude Whitney, that was it—how those first marks involved the viewer in the process of drawing. It was true. Kate could follow the energetic movement of the pen as the artist rethought a line.

She glanced at the clock, grabbed the drawing, and hurried out the door.

When she got to the Historical Society Mrs. Travers was at the desk, once again reading a paperback.

"Another Inspector Trask?" said Kate.

"No," said Mrs. Travers. "You were absolutely right about the author keeping too much information from the reader. Very irritating." She escorted Kate to the back entrance, which led out to the garden.

Kate handed Laura the drawing and looked around for Alison.

She was sitting on a retaining wall, apparently sketching a hydrangea bush in front of her. She looked like she was frowning, but that might have been from the sun. Kate saw her scrub her eraser across the paper. Ordinarily, Alison hardly touched an eraser.

"Are you having trouble?" asked Kate, walking up to her. She started to slip off her backpack.

"We can't all be natural-born artists, you know."

Kate started to say something, then slung her backpack over her shoulder again and looked around the garden.

At the far end was a patch of tiger lilies. As Kate set up there, she imagined the dreary, exhausting days remaining in her visit if she and Alison weren't getting along. She missed their long walks and their conversations at the beach.

She turned to the lilies. Which of the approaches she'd learned was the best one here? Should she start with drawing the basic forms? If so, which one applied to a lily? Was each petal a separate form? Or should she do a gesture drawing showing how the flowers swayed in the breeze? Did perspective apply to things that weren't man-made?

Time was passing. Kate had resisted it up to now, but wasn't crating the thing to try? The cube and the sphere were no help, but a cylinder contained the blossom with little wasted space. A cone worked even better.

She decided on a composition with three lilies, remembering what Laura had said about flowers in a cluster looking like people at a parade, each one facing a different direction.

By the time Laura announced the official end of class, Kate had sketched in the main construction lines of the lilies. The blossoms looked sturdy rather than delicate, but Kate decided she liked that. This was a different way of thinking about a flower.

Quickly, she darkened a few of the lines on the petals in the foreground. Inevitably the pencil didn't exactly repeat the initial lines. Kate automatically reached for her eraser. Then she stopped.

The lilies seemed to be in motion.

She looked over to the retaining wall. From the expression on Alison's face, she had not had a good morning. Before Kate could see her drawing, she'd closed the pad.

On their trip to Kennon's Office Supply and back home they hardly talked. They were still blocks from the house when the sound of a power saw reached them. Kate turned to Alison.

Alison broke into a run. Kate kept walking. She got to

the Langs' intersection just as a massive limb from the maple hit the ground. Immediately, two men attacked it with saws, stripping it of its leafy branches. The limb, bristling with stumps, was heaved up onto the back of a flatbed truck. The branches were tossed into a chipper. A spray of wood bits blew out the nozzle.

Kate heard the back door slam, then, as she came up the steps, Alison's voice, shaking with anger.

"You did this on purpose when I was away so I couldn't stop you."

Mrs. Lang answered, sounding as if she might cry. "Alison, it wasn't like that at all. When Mr. Ryan looked at the maple this morning, he saw that the inside was rotted. It wouldn't have lasted much longer anyway."

"So? Why not let it live a few more years?"

"Because big branches could have started falling off at any time. He said someone could easily be killed. He said to take it down as soon as possible."

"He said. He said. He doesn't know everything."

"Alison, I'm as upset as you are about losing the maple. But this had to be done."

Alison thumped up the stairs to her room. Kate waited on the steps for a moment, then went in. Mrs. Lang turned around, a helpless expression on her face. "I can't make Alison understand. Can you talk to her?"

Kate climbed the stairs and knocked gently on Alison's door.

"It's Kate."

"If you need to get in, go ahead."

Kate pushed the door open. Alison was lying facedown on her bed.

"Alison, your mother didn't know about the tree having to be cut down until this morning. She wasn't keeping it a secret."

Alison's voice was muffled by the pillow. "I know."

"Are you coming down to lunch?"

Alison nodded. Kate quietly set her drawing pad in the closet and went downstairs.

Mr. Lang was out on a job site, so the table was set for three. The unnerving blare of power saws continued all during lunch, joined by the rasping sound of branches being fed into the chipper. Nobody ate much. As they were clearing the table, the doorbell rang. Alison's mother picked up her checkbook and a pen.

Kate ventured a glance toward the front door. The porch and the living room seemed unnaturally bright. Alison's mother thanked the man and handed over a check. Then she closed the door and looked around.

"I guess we'll get used to this. It is nice to have the light, of course."

"No, it isn't," said Alison. "This is ugly." She went back upstairs to her room.

Kate looked out from the front porch. All that remained of the maple was a ground-level stump and a scattering of sawdust.

———

A half hour later, Alison came downstairs again.

"I've got to check on Brownie and Tiger. Has anybody seen my sandals?"

"I haven't," said Mrs. Lang. "Is Kate going with you?"

Alison shrugged. "If she wants."

"Alison, that's unkind. What's going on?"

"Nothing. I just thought Kate might have something else to do."

Mrs. Lang turned to Kate. "Would you like to go?"

Alison might not want her company, but Kate wanted to see the animals.

"Yes, I'm going. Alison, your sandals are under the sofa."

Even though they walked in silence to the Dolans' and the Becks', Kate was glad that she'd decided to come along and that she'd remembered to bring her sketchbook. Brownie looked different already, the fur thick and glossy, the body filled out.

By contrast, Tiger seemed all motion with no fixed form. She stretched herself out like a piece of taffy, then tucked herself into a tiny ball. Alison was clearly surprised by the kitten's progress from the day before. On the way home, they broke their silence and talked about it.

"Babies don't change that fast, do they?" said Alison. "I mean human babies."

"I don't think so. That's probably because people can live much longer."

"You mean everything goes slower for people than for cats?"

"I think so."

"Why? Why should some things live longer than other things?"

"I don't know," said Kate.

Alison's father announced at dinner that night that he had lined up someone to help him get rid of the stump in the front yard.

"I want to see a new tree in that spot as soon as possible. I'm going to get some information at Anderson's Nursery about what to plant."

Alison made a face. "No matter what you get, it's going to be a baby tree. I'll practically be an old lady by the time it's grown."

"Better than a stump, though, right?"

Alison stabbed her fork into her green beans. "I guess."

After dinner, Kate wrote her sixth letter home:

Tuesday, August 9

Dear Mom & Dad,

Laura and I have sorted almost all of Maude Whitney's papers except for the letters she saved. We found a lot of those. Nothing has turned up so far, at least not a bill of sale or anything. But some of the letters are from other artists. They're really interesting, even if they aren't what we're looking for.

The maple tree in the front yard was cut down today. Everybody's upset about it, especially Alison. I can't think of anything to say to make her feel better because the yard does look pretty bad, and her room doesn't seem like a tree house anymore.

I don't think *Alison* would be interested in anything I have to say anyway. We haven't talked much this week. She's been taking care of two orphaned animals, a baby rabbit and a kitten, or helping with the boat, which is fine, except that she purposely makes plans to do things in the afternoons without including me. Meanwhile, she knows I'm busy every morning with this new job.

The drawing of the tiger lilies isn't finished because I had a hard time figuring out what to do first.

Laura is a good teacher. All the same, drawing was easier before. Now I'm thinking about a lot of things at the same time—basic forms, light and shadow, movement, perspective, foreground and background. When I look at my drawings, all I see is what I forgot to do.

I guess when you've taken lots of classes and you're very good, you can think about all these things at the same time, or maybe you don't have to think about them at all.

Sometimes, I'd like to draw the way I did before, but I can't forget what I've learned. I guess I wouldn't want to forget it now, anyway.

Love,

Kate

The next morning, Alison was already downstairs when Kate woke up. When she got to the table, Alison and her mother were paging through a catalog.

"We're picking out a tree," said Alison.

"How about some kind of fruit tree?" said her mother.

"I just want something that grows fast," said Alison.

224

When Kate got to the association library, Laura was already halfway through a new bundle of letters. She wondered if Laura still remembered the reason they'd started reading them.

"Aha!" Laura jotted in her notebook. "Just what I've tried to tell beginning painting students: 'If all of the colors are bright, there is no brightness.' "

Kate realized she must have looked puzzled.

"It's like putting a gemstone in a setting," said Laura. "If you don't do it properly, the gem won't sparkle. If you want to make a color vibrate, tone down what's around it. Of course, there's always an exception. The Impressionists could slam bright colors together and get the most amazing effects. But that's genius."

That reminded Kate of her painting, how the colors seemed to shift, but she didn't want to interrupt Laura's train of thought.

A bundle of letters was already set at Kate's place. Once again, they were all from Peg, but these were written at least twenty years earlier than the others, when Peg and Maude had both been at school, although not the same school. Peg referred to someplace called Briarwood and a starchy headmistress named Miss Tannenbaum, who once caught Peg and two friends sneaking off to an amusement park when they were supposed to be in class.

She bemoaned the obligatory afternoon teas with the faculty and related funny stories about her instruction in something called "deportment." Kate couldn't figure out exactly what kind of school this was. She passed one of the letters across the table.

"It sounds," said Laura, "like a finishing school, where young ladies from well-to-do families were sent to learn how to be proper society matrons. One of the advantages was that they stood a good chance of meeting suitable husbands through friendships they made there."

That seemed to have happened to Peg. After three years at Briarwood, playing practical jokes on staff and students alike and dodging the ever-vigilant Miss Tannenbaum, Peg wrote to Maude that she was engaged to be married. Her new status was the occasion for a round of parties and visits to family.

April 18, 1897

Aunt Evelyn put Michael through the wringer, but he survived the interrogation, I'm happy to report . . .

September 25, 1897

. . . Fall is definitely the time for a wedding, I don't care what they say about being a June bride. The day was crisp and beautiful, no beads of sweat running down anybody's face. Even Aunt Evelyn looked radiant—or was that my imagination? We actually got through the day without major mishap. The minister, who is getting on in years, did omit part of the ceremony, but that just made it mercifully shorter. At any rate, I trust I am legally married and that I can now, with confidence, add the "H" to the monogram on the guest towels . . .

Wonderful news about your taking first place in the student Life Drawing show. Not that I'm surprised, of course. I'm just glad the judges had the sense to recognize talent . . .

So H was the first letter of Peg's married name.

Kate gathered all the bundles from Peg H and set them in a long row according to dates. None were earlier than the ones from Briarwood. Kate guessed that the women had lived near each other until Peg was sent there and Maude began art school. After that, they wrote once or twice a month until the autumn of 1961.

Laura broke off from the letter she was reading and looked at the row of bundles.

"Some reason you're separating those from the rest?"

Kate was embarrassed. The only reason was that she'd become intrigued by the writer and wanted to know more of her story.

"Well, this sounds like a really close friend, maybe her best friend. Don't you think there might be a chance that something's in one of her letters?"

"Maybe." Laura went back to reading. A minute later, she was jotting furiously again.

Kate turned to the letters in the next bundle.

December 12, 1897

. . . the move to New York will have to be made despite the snow. Our town house awaits and will probably become the Kingdom of the Mice if we don't plant our flag soon . . .

December 10, 1899

. . . James Andrew made his appearance in the world Tuesday morning and has ascended to the throne already. All household activities are now directed toward His Highness' welfare and comfort . . .

October 4, 1901

. . . The house is under official quarantine for diphtheria. Jamie's fever hovers around 105. I try not to give in to tears, especially in front of Michael, who frets terribly over the slightest furrow in his beloved son's brow . . .

May 20, 1903

. . . The arrival of Rachel Catherine has sent Jamie into a tumult of emotions. For the past three and a half years, his rule has been undisputed . . .

August 11, 1912

. . . Jamie adores his new sister, Patricia Anne. Rachel is somewhat less enthusiastic . . .

February 12, 1917

. . . this European war is a terrible thing. A cousin of Michael's has just lost a son in the conflict. I am so thankful that James is too young for the draft. Large amounts of guilt accompany my gratitude. Other mothers are not so fortunate . . .

October 30, 1929

. . . My chief concern is for Michael's health. He feels a personal responsibility to the investors and is devastated by their losses. No amount of reassurance, pleading, or argument has penetrated his sorrow . . .

March 12, 1930

. . . Michael came home from the sanatorium last week. He is much improved, although still in delicate condition. I do all that I can to make sure the household runs smoothly . . .

. . . I wish that Michael had lived to see the war over and his grandson safely home from the Pacific . . .

Laura looked across the table. "You look a little spacey. Why don't you call it quits for now?"

Kate nodded. She said goodbye and left. Hardly thinking where she was going, she headed for Perry Street beach.

A strong wind was blowing off the water when Kate got there. The exact horizon was lost in dancing reflections from the hazy sun. Kate felt as if she'd just stepped off a roller coaster, staggering as she reentered the world of normal speed. In two hours, she'd raced through a half century of someone's life.

She turned to the tide line and automatically began searching for shells. The familiar sweeping glances helped steady her. A few yards away, a godwit scurried up and down in the surf, jabbing repeatedly into the wet sand.

Suddenly Kate stopped in midsweep. Her eye had caught a shape, no bigger than a plum. She raced to grab it before the next lap of surf sucked it back into the ocean. As she poured water and sand out of the shell, she turned it over and over. It was perfect. She slipped it into a pocket and started back to Shore Road.

Mrs. Lang was just hanging up the kitchen phone when Kate walked in the door. "Kate, I'm glad you're back. That was the dentist's office. I forgot I have an appointment. I'm going to be late if I don't leave now. Alison's at the Dolans'. Why don't you go over there for a while? Then you can come back together. Tom should be home in about a half hour."

"I have a couple of things to do, then I'll go," said Kate.

"Okay," said Mrs. Lang, "but don't stay here too long." She picked up her purse. "See you."

"See you." Kate closed the back door. A few minutes alone was ideal. She hadn't decided when to tell Alison about the shell. Going to the beach by herself was such a small matter. But Alison would be upset when she found out.

The shell book was with the field guides in the living room bookcase. Kate took it to the recliner, putting the shell on the lamp table next to her. She flipped through page after page of shells with the basic shape of the spiral. The job was going to be impossible.

Then, at the beginning of the book, she found maps of the coastal areas of the world, listing the shells that were common in each. Some of the prettiest were found on the beaches of Asia and Africa. Next to their intricate forms and patterns, Kate's shell was plain. But she liked the way the bands of reddish-brown encircled the off-white spiral, accenting its simple shape. After studying the drawings of the most common shells in the area, Kate guessed that hers might be a kind of whelk called a New England Neptune. She wondered how old it was. Years probably. A shell grew slowly, like the trunk of a tree. Instead of rings, ever-larger spirals recorded the passage of time.

Footsteps came up the front walk. That had to be the mail carrier. Alison usually came in the back door. But it was Alison.

"Oh, hi. I wasn't expecting you to be back from the association." She tossed a handful of envelopes onto the sofa. "It's mostly junk. Is that a complete shell?"

"I was trying to identify it."

"Where did you find it?"

"Perry Street beach."

"When were you there?"

"Just now," said Kate. "It's a New England Neptune, I think. What do you think?" She got out of the recliner and handed the shell to Alison.

"It could be. It's your first whole shell. Congratulations." She handed it back.

"How is the rabbit?"

"Good."

"Is it bigger?"

"Yeah."

Kate tried to think of a question that would demand more than a one-syllable answer. "How can I tell for sure what kind of shell this is?"

Alison shrugged. "Find somebody who knows more than I do."

Kate saw that Alison was about to go upstairs. "Alison, I wish I'd found it sometime when we were together."

"Yeah, well, you can go to the beach by yourself. There's no reason why not."

"And there must be times you want to go places without me."

"No."

Kate fumbled for a reply.

"You know," said Alison, "if you don't want me along with you, why don't you say so?"

"Because most of the time, I do want you along."

"But you don't want me to know about the other times."

"I figured you wouldn't like it. And I was right. You don't."

"I don't care one way or the other."

"That's not true."

"I thought you'd like having somebody show you around town. I guess I was wrong about that. Well, it won't happen again."

"I did like it. But now I don't need so much help. Going to the beach myself isn't something I planned. I just did it one day. You went downtown for lunch with Rosemary and didn't tell me about it."

"I knew you were going to be busy at the Art Association."

"Not in the afternoon."

"You'd be there all day if Laura didn't have a part-time job. What's so terrific about looking through a lot of old papers anyway?"

"You know I'm looking for something important."

"You don't really need to find a bill of sale. Mrs. Perry can't take the picture away from you. That's not why you're spending so much time there. Do you even notice what happens around here anymore?"

"Like what?"

"Like the birds aren't here anymore."

"They still come back to the porch. I've seen them."

"Not since Sunday."

Kate started to object, then stopped. She hadn't noticed the fledglings' departure.

"You think I'm spoiled because I'm an only child, don't you?"

Kate was caught off guard by the sudden shift. She hesitated before she spoke. "Sometimes."

"People who have brothers and sisters are always thinking that. They think that if you're the only one, everything's great and you always get your way."

"Alison, you get your way a lot."

"When did we ever do anything you didn't want to do?"

"That's not it exactly."

"So what is it exactly?"

Kate thought for a minute. "You usually know what you want to do. I have to figure it out. By the time I've done that, we're already going someplace. When I'm by myself, I just sort of wander around until I figure out what I want to do."

"How was I supposed to know that?"

"Well—you aren't. But that's how I feel anyway."

"So, what am I supposed to do? From now on, am I supposed to wait for you to say what you want? And how long do I wait? How do I know if you like my idea or if you're just going along with it? If you were me, what would you do?"

The questions were like an unexpected volley of tennis

balls. Kate didn't know which one to swing at first. She had never thought of the problem from that point of view.

"I don't know," she said at last.

"Well, neither do I," said Alison. She turned and started up the stairs. "My dad can help you identify that shell. He knows more about them than I do."

Kate heard the bedroom door shut. She sat back down in the recliner, surprised to find herself shaking. She almost never got into arguments. Anger buoyed her up at first, but that soon deflated, leaving her confused and empty.

✹ Puzzles

ON THURSDAY MORNING, only three bundles of letters from Peg H remained to be read. Kate had given up hope of finding evidence of the painting's history. But finishing the letters, which she would surely do today, would be like saying goodbye to a wonderful friend.

Letters in the first two batches announced the marriages of three grandchildren and the births of five great-grandchildren.

Kate pulled the string tie on the last batch. These were dated from 1955 to 1961. That was the year Maude Whitney had died. Reading through the letters, Kate found no mention of illness or frailty. In fact, both women seemed to have been in excellent health.

August 9, 1960

Dear Maude,

Alaska is magnificent. My only regret is that I didn't see it sooner. This morning, the more intrepid of us hiked to a plain where caribou are migrating by the thousands. I cannot describe the feeling this spectacle caused in me . . .

April 16, 1961

. . .When you are in Rome, throw a coin into the Trevi Fountain for me. It seems to have worked for you, although it took sixty years . . .

A few minutes later, Kate reached the bottom of the stack. She picked up the last letter, not wanting to read it.

October 8, 1961

Dear Maude,

I understand completely about the painting. Under the circumstances, it was the right thing to do. No need to apologize. I never regarded it as mine anyway. *A work of art doesn't really belong to anyone, does it?*

Yes, it would be lovely to have a copy, but we both know our remaining time is too valuable to spend any of it repeating what was already done. Besides, you know better than anyone that the inspiration isn't there a second time. I'll always treasure the memory of having posed for it.

See you at Thanksgiving. The burgundy guest room is yours again if you want it. I've banished Cousin Sofie to Outer Mongolia

235

in the blue room at the end of the hall so our talking won't disturb her beauty sleep.

Love,

Peg

Without a word, Kate passed the letter across the table. Laura read it quickly, then they both rushed out the door, almost crashing into Mrs. Perry, who was coming in from the sculpture court.

"Sorry," said Laura. "Look what Kate found."

Mrs. Perry put on her glasses and took the page. "Who is Peg?"

"We don't know yet," said Laura, "but she was a close friend of Maude's."

"If Maude Whitney saved Peg's letters," said Kate, "Peg might have saved Maude Whitney's letters. Maybe we could find them."

"It's a long shot," said Mrs. Perry, "but I'll do what I can. And you two should start making inquiries."

That meant placing phone calls and ringing doorbells. Kate saw the opportunity she was looking for.

"Mrs. Perry," said Kate, "I'd like to call Alison and tell her about this letter, if that's okay with you."

Mrs. Perry handed the letter back to Laura.

"I don't see any problem with that. You can use my office phone."

The impulse, which had seemed right a moment before, began to seem like a bad idea when Kate actually picked up the phone. Alison wouldn't want to help. She resented the whole project.

She probably wouldn't be home anyway. This was exactly the time she'd be at the Dolans' or maybe the Becks'. If everybody was out, leaving a message was pointless, since Alison wouldn't check the answering machine.

If Kate talked to her at all, she could wait until dinner. She put down the phone. In her mind, she heard Alison's voice. *Call.* Kate picked up the phone again. She waited through five rings, then started to hang up.

"Hello?" Alison sounded out of breath.

"Alison, I didn't think you'd be home."

"I was coming up the back steps when I heard the phone."

Kate couldn't make out anything from the tone of Alison's voice. "We found something. Not a bill of sale. A letter."

"Uh-huh."

Kate forced herself to continue in the face of Alison's lack of interest. "We need to find out who wrote it."

"Why are you calling me?"

"Because you're good at talking to people you don't know."

"Oh. Well, after you do it a couple of times, you'll see it isn't that hard. Besides, Laura can do it."

"I know. But I want you to come with me."

"I thought you said I was always running everything. Or something like that."

"Well, you do, sort of. But I shouldn't have expected you to read my mind." Kate paused. "Alison, I wasn't spending all that time at the Art Association to get away from you."

"So what was it?"

Kate struggled to find a comparison. "It was like working a jigsaw puzzle, only you don't know what the picture is supposed to look like."

"That's fun?"

"Not at first. But when you get a few pieces together, you figure you'll get a few more, and then you start to see something. You can't quit until it's finished."

"I guess it isn't finished."

"Not yet. That's why I'm calling you." A silence followed. "Alison?"

"I'm here. I was just thinking about it."

"What's to think about?"

"That's my line." A longer silence followed. "So what's in this letter?"

Kate read the first paragraph aloud.

"Alison, why don't you meet me downtown at the Purple Cow? It's supposed to be open again."

"Just so you know, this doesn't mean I'll ring any doorbells for you."

"That's fine. When can you leave?"

"Now."

"I'll probably get there first. I'll grab our table if it's free."

Packing up took longer than Kate had calculated. When she got to the intersection of Magnolia and South Main, she looked up the block and saw Alison at the entrance to the Purple Cow, anxiously scanning the street.

"Alison!" Kate broke into a run. "Sorry I'm late. I thought for sure I'd get here first."

Alison turned around. Relief washed over her face before her usual offhand manner took over. "I've never heard you yell before. I wasn't sure you could do it."

Kate pushed open the door of the Purple Cow. A riot of color greeted them. The cool, shimmering black-and-white planet had turned tropical. A constant stream of excuse me's and sorrys came from customers trying to maneuver towering sundaes and double-scoop cones safely through the crowd and out the door.

"Is this the end of the take-out line?" asked Alison. They were barely past the entrance. The woman in front of her nodded.

As they shuffled forward, Kate saw that a counter had replaced the marble-top tables. From "44 Fabulous Flavors," the ice cream selection had been trimmed to twenty-five.

"We're sure to finish all the flavors now," said Alison. "Hey, is that a real parrot?"

Kate looked in the direction Alison was pointing.

"It's fake," said the woman in front of them. "I was assured of that when I phoned the health department yesterday. I had no intention of risking feathers in my vanilla frappe."

Kate and Alison looked at each other, then looked away as they suppressed giggles.

As soon as they'd gotten their cones, they headed for the beach. A light mist was falling.

"I guess this is lunch," said Alison. "We can get something else later."

Kate described the rest of the letter she had found.

"Why don't we ask Mrs. Travers at the Historical Society for help?"

"That's a good idea."

"You're sure none of those letters had Peg's last name?" said Alison.

"I'm sure."

"There's a Peg in my class at Parker. It's short for Margaret."

"It is? How can that be?"

"I don't know. It just is."

"I wonder if Mrs. Perry knows that."

Margaret H. The expanded name somehow gave a different impression of the person. It also jogged a memory, but Kate couldn't pin it down.

"I miss the old Purple Cow," said Kate as they walked back to Shore Road.

"Me, too. But I really miss the Wheelhouse."

At the Historical Society, a woman who introduced herself as Mrs. Lacey was filling in for Mrs. Travers, who was on vacation. She suggested that Kate and Alison come back the next day, when the librarian of the society would be there.

The light mist had turned into a steady rain by the time they left. They alternated running and walking on the way home, getting thoroughly soaked anyway.

After they changed clothes, Kate sat down with the crossword from that day's paper. The weather forecast on the same page called for clearing skies overnight. Moonrise would be at 10:29 p.m., with Jupiter visible in the southeastern sky before dawn.

At dinner, Kate and Alison took turns describing the new decorating scheme at the Purple Cow. Suddenly, the whole experience, including the fake parrot and the woman who'd called the health department, seemed riotously funny.

"Glad to see that the white flag has been raised," said Alison's father. "I was about to buy a flak jacket."

Kate saw Mrs. Lang give him a glance and shake her head, then turn to Alison. "So, what flavors are gone?"

A discussion ensued that turned into a memory game with the wager of a single-scoop cone. Alison predicted she'd win handily.

"My memory's better than anybody's if it's about food," she said.

That night, while Alison was in the bathroom washing up, Kate was suddenly overtaken by sleepiness. She stretched out on the sofa bed. In a minute, she'd get up and change into her sleeping shirt. In a minute.

She awoke in confusion. The promised clearing had taken place. Stars were visible, and Jupiter shone in the southeastern sky, below the crescent moon. Alison's head was halfway under the covers. The digital clock read 4:48.

Kate turned over and stared at the ceiling. Margaret H.

Why did that name seem familiar? She slid out of bed and tiptoed across the room to the desk. In the faint light, she wrote the name in longhand across an index card and studied it.

She set the card on the desk to look at in daylight. Then she picked it up again. In neat letters, she printed the name.

Didn't the Historical Society have cards like that? "Donated by _____," "Estate of _____." Was one of the women a Margaret?

But even if one of them was, how could anybody tell for sure if that Margaret and Peg were the same person? Margaret was a common name.

Kate lifted the painting off its hook and brought it to her bed. At first, the woman's silhouette appeared almost featureless, but as the sky outside brightened, details emerged. Every bit of the work had been so carefully done. Even the brooch that secured the cape was painted as skillfully as if it were the only subject of the painting.

Kate sat up. Wasn't the brooch itself sitting on a glass shelf? So many exquisite objects were displayed, she couldn't remember.

Kate was so excited, she felt like waking Alison up to tell her. She felt like waking everybody up. But that would have to wait. She sat on the edge of her bed watching first light extinguish the stars until even Jupiter was lost in the glow.

✹ Coming About

"DO YOU WANT ANY JAM?" Alison held out the jar. "Kate?"

"Uh, no."

"By the way, it's thirty seconds later than the last time you looked at the clock."

Kate turned around. "Sorry. Are you sure the Historical Society opens at nine-thirty and not nine o'clock?"

"I've got a brochure somewhere," said Alison's mother. "Should I look for it?"

"Thanks. No, that's okay."

When they arrived at the Historical Society at nine-twenty, Mrs. Lacey was unlocking the door.

"Miss Peters won't be here for another half hour, but you're welcome to come and sit in the reception area."

"Actually, Mrs. Lacey, we'd like to look at the glass cases on the second floor," said Kate.

"Well . . . I suppose that would be okay. Let me get some lights on."

Mrs. Lacey disappeared into the coatroom. Kate could hear switches being snapped. Lights flickered in the dark hallway and the stairwell.

"Thanks," said Kate. She and Alison sprinted up the spiral staircase.

"You start from the right and I'll start from the left,"

said Kate. For the next few minutes, the only sound was Alison's quiet singing.

I come from Alabama with my banjo on my knee, I'm bound for Lou'siana my Susanna—

"Find it?"

"No. Sorry. Thought I had it for a second."

—for to see. It rained all day the night I left, the weather it was dry, the sun so hot, I—

"Alison, I found it."

The brooch lay on a low shelf with several others. Kate stooped to read the tiny print at the bottom of the display card, *Estate of Margaret Hathaway.*

As they came downstairs, Kate heard Mrs. Lacey talking to someone, a young woman, from the sound of the voice.

"Oh, Kate, I was just explaining to Miss Peters about the person you're trying to identify."

"We know who it is now, Mrs. Lacey. Margaret Hathaway."

Kate explained about the letters from Peg H and the brooch.

"I'd say that clinches it," said Miss Peters. "I'll see what we have on the Hathaway family."

Miss Peters disappeared into the maze of bookshelves. She returned with a thin manila folder.

"I'm afraid this is all we have."

Then Kate remembered. "Hathaway was her married name. I don't know what her name was before that."

Miss Peters shuffled through the contents of the envelope. "Here's a wedding announcement. Fairchild. She was born Margaret Fairchild." She disappeared into the maze again, emerging with a flat box. It turned out to contain a family tree of the Fairchilds, beginning in 1789, an engraved portrait of Margaret's grandfather, captain of a clipper ship, and memorabilia from his voyages, including maps and a pocket watch.

All very interesting, but none of it helped locate any descendants of Margaret Hathaway. Kate remembered from the letters she'd had three children, a boy and two girls. James would have been a Hathaway forever, but Rachel and Patricia would have acquired new names as married women.

"Here's one more thing," said Miss Peters, "an inventory of the pieces willed to the Historical Society by Margaret." The inventory noted the date of receipt, July 18, 1962, and the date of Margaret's death, February 22, 1962. She had not outlived her friend Maude by many months.

"I have an idea," said Miss Peters. "I've only been librarian here for six years. You should talk to Marion Haywood. She had this position for decades."

A phone call confirmed that Mrs. Haywood would be happy to talk to Kate and Alison. Her home was a short walk from the society.

The woman who was pulling weeds in her front yard as Kate and Alison came up the sidewalk was not even as tall as Kate, wiry and tan. She smiled broadly, pulled off her gardening gloves, and shook hands.

"I've been searching my memory since Miss Peters called. Come." She led them up the steps to the open front porch. "Please sit down." She pulled off her straw hat. "A number of years ago, the society had two visitors from New York City, a woman who was probably in her middle thirties and her daughter, who looked about eleven or twelve. The woman was Margaret Hathaway's granddaughter. She wanted to show her daughter the jewelry and other items that Margaret Hathaway had left to the society. As I recall, they were also interested in any information we had on the Fairchilds. That turned out not to be much, but we had a lovely talk about her family."

"Do you remember the woman's name?" said Kate.

"Unfortunately, I don't. I might recognize it, but I can't bring it to mind."

"Wouldn't her last name have been Hathaway?" said Alison.

"No. This woman was the daughter of Margaret Hathaway's younger daughter, so the last name was changed when each of them married." Mrs. Haywood shook her head. "If I could remember the approximate date of the visit, we'd have a way to get the name."

"How could we do that?" said Kate.

"From the guest book. The society keeps every one of them, back to 1881, when it was founded. Some people just sign their names, but other people enter comments." Mrs. Haywood rocked back and forth in her chair. "Let's see . . . we talked about her great-great-grandfather, who was a sea captain, and about the wonderful things he'd brought back. A number of them are in our exhibit, of course.

"Oh, I recall something. She said that, at the reading of

the will, she had been upset that so many pieces were going to the society, in particular, a pair of opal earrings she had wanted to wear at her sweet-sixteen party that spring."

"Her grandmother died in February of 1962," said Kate. "We just read it."

"If the woman I spoke to was sixteen in the spring of 1962, that means she was born in . . ."

"1946," said Alison.

Kate was surprised that Alison could do arithmetic in her head so fast.

"Right," said Mrs. Haywood. "And if she was in her middle thirties, the visit was . . ."

"Around 1981," said Alison.

"That's right." Mrs. Haywood seemed as surprised as Kate.

Miss Peters looked up when Kate rushed into the library short of breath, Alison a few steps behind.

"I thought you two were going to Mrs. Haywood's."

"Been there and back," Alison said.

In between breaths, Kate described the conversation.

"I'll be right back." Miss Peters made another foray into the bookshelves.

"Alison, did I thank Mrs. Haywood?"

"Only about six times."

Miss Peters reappeared with an armload of albums. She set the 1980 book open on the library table. Together they scrutinized the columns for "Home/Business Address" and

"Purpose of Visit." A few New York addresses turned up, but the purposes of the visits were not recorded.

A search of the 1981 book was equally inconclusive.

They were up to June 1982 when Kate spotted the entry: "To see the Margaret Hathaway bequest." The address was given simply as "Riverside Drive, New York City." The visitors were "Margaret Rutledge Foster & Daughter Tricia."

"Eureka!" said Miss Peters.

"I'll bet," said Alison, "there are about ten thousand Fosters in the New York phone book."

"But how many live on Riverside Drive?" asked Miss Peters.

"Unless they moved. Don't you think they would have moved by now?" said Alison.

"Possibly," said Miss Peters, "but the bigger problem is that phone numbers are still often listed only in the husband's name, and we don't know that. But you might find more information on the Internet. We're not online here, but the public library is." She wrote "Margaret Rutledge Foster, Tricia Foster, National Phone Book, Internet" on a slip of paper and handed it to Kate.

Kate had hardly followed the conversation. She felt slightly dazed. On the way to the public library, she had only a vague idea of what they were supposed to ask for.

"Alison, did I remember to thank Miss Peters?"

"About eight times."

When Kate handed the slip of paper to her a few minutes later, Mrs. Edgar smiled. "I don't need to see the phone book. I know exactly where you can find these people. On Chandler Street. Margaret and her daughter applied for library cards when they moved to town a couple of years ago. They take out books every few weeks. Margaret likes mysteries."

"More tea?" Mrs. Foster held up the teapot, hidden under a quilted hood that she referred to as a "cozy."

"No, thank you, Mrs. Foster," said Kate. She already felt shaky.

"I'll have another cup," said Alison.

Kate wondered what Alison's tea tasted like. When Mrs. Foster had said, "One lump or two?" Alison had said, "Four, please."

Mrs. Foster poured tea for herself and Alison, then sat back on the sofa.

"I can't tell you how thrilled I was to hear you had located my grandmother's letters. I've been almost certain all along that the Art Association had them somewhere. Unfortunately, I got little help from the former director. He told me that a search had failed to locate the Whitney papers, but he'd contact me if they turned up. Naturally, I never heard from him."

"I think that Mrs. Perry is trying to straighten out a lot of things," said Kate.

The back door opened.

"We're in here," called Mrs. Foster.

A woman who looked about the same age as Kate's mother walked into the room.

"Trish, these are the young ladies who phoned, Kate and Alison. This is my daughter, Tricia."

"Excuse the work clothes," said Tricia. "Finding Great-Grandma's letter box is going to require some rooting around in the attic."

"Cup of tea, Trish?"

"Maybe later, Mom. I'll shove a few boxes around first." She waved to Kate and Alison. "With any luck at all, you'll see me in a few minutes."

"Well," said Mrs. Foster, "where did I leave off the story?"

"Your grandmother had just gotten married," said Alison.

"Oh, yes. Her husband was starting a career in investments, so they moved to New York. That's where they raised their three children, and that's where I was born and raised. But I was always drawn to the idea of living by the sea. Oh, I know that New York is on the water, but one doesn't feel the ocean's presence the way one does here.

"I'm sure my fascination with the seacoast came from listening to my grandmother's stories, especially the ones about her grandfather."

"The one who was captain of a clipper ship?" said Kate.

"That's right. My grandmother and I were particularly close. As you see, I was named after her. Her stories made the town where she had been raised sound so romantic. I have to say, 'romantic' is not an adjective I'd apply to every place around here. 'Down at heel' would be a generous description of a few areas. But the magic isn't entirely gone, is it? I mean, how could it be, with the ocean a stone's throw away?

"I prevailed upon my husband to move here after he retired. The next thing I knew, he had unretired himself and taken up photography." That explained the framed photos of the seashore that filled almost all the available space on the walls.

"Mrs. Foster," said Kate, "is the house your grandmother grew up in still standing?"

"More's the pity, no. It was torn down in 1935. By then, it had been inherited by my grandmother's only sibling, a younger brother. Her father, you see, assumed that the brother would marry and need a house for his family. Well, he never married and never had children. The house itself became too much for him to maintain, and the property was more valuable cut up and sold in pieces."

"Where was it?" said Alison.

"On Kirk near Perry. The land is very high there, and the house had three stories. The view from the widow's walk must have been spectacular."

"We're pretty sure that's where your grandmother posed for the painting," said Kate.

"Yes, the painting you described to me is almost certainly a portrait of my grandmother, although from the title, I'd guess it was intended to represent all women who had sons and fathers and brothers at sea.

"You know, Grandma mentioned having posed for a

painting. Of course, I have photos of my grandmother, even one of her in her wedding dress, but I'd love to see the painting. Would that be possible?"

"Sure," said Kate. She didn't see what else she could say, although she suddenly wondered if tracking down Margaret Foster would simply add a new claimant to the painting.

Kate heard footsteps coming down the attic stairs. Tricia appeared carrying a large wooden box. "Is this it, Mom?"

"Indeed it is. Isn't it beautifully made? Rosewood, I'm almost sure. And the carving and joinery look Japanese to me."

Just then, Kate was too eager to get at the contents of the box to spend time remarking on the craftsmanship. Tricia set it on the coffee table.

"I think the lid's stuck, Mom."

"Oh, dear, no. It's locked. I have a key somewhere . . ."

Alison came over. To Kate's surprise, she turned the box upside down. "Here it is. It was taped to the bottom."

"Of course, now I remember, I put it there myself. Thank you, Alison."

Tricia scraped the dried tape off the key, then inserted it into the lock and turned it with a satisfying click. When Mrs. Foster raised the lid, Kate saw bundles of letters, much like the ones at the Art Association, but tied with blue satin ribbon, not string.

Mrs. Foster began setting them out on the table. "These are from Maude Whitney. And these."

"Thank goodness," said Tricia, fingering her way

through a bundle. "From the postal marks, they seem to go by dates."

"These are from 1961." Kate handed her the packet.

Tricia opened the envelope on top and skimmed the two pages inside. "Listen to this—

September 25, 1961

Dear Peg,

I might as well get this over with up front. I gave away "Red Sky at Morning." I am keenly aware that I always said it would go to you someday. Let me explain the circumstances and try to bail myself out.

Last Thursday evening, we had a storm. Torrential rain and winds that made the house feel like the deck of a ship under full sail.

I heard a crash out back about ten that night. When I played a flashlight around the yard, I saw that a section of shingles had been ripped off the studio roof by the wind and more were about to go.

It's a miracle I wasn't blown to Rocky Point getting from the house to the studio. When I got in, rainwater was puddling on the floor under the unprotected roof planks. More worrisome was that a line of minor (at that point) leaks was opening up right across the ceiling. I rolled a number of drawings into a throw rug and stowed them in the house. Then I came back for more. I took the drawings first, thinking they'd fare the worst if the roof took off for parts unknown. I'd made about three or four trips when I saw headlights in the driveway. It was Martin Quinlan's truck. He'd come out because he was worried about me, alone out here in the boondocks.

I was never so glad to see anyone in my life. He had a tarp in the truck. Between the two of us, but, in fact, mostly thanks to Martin, we got every last drawing and painting into the house.

How do you thank someone for saving so much of one's lifework? I told Martin to take any piece he wanted. At first, he kept saying that I didn't owe him anything, but then I told him that I'd feel terrible if he didn't take something. That won the day. He went into the front room and brought back "Red Sky." He knew exactly where he'd put it. He said he'd always liked that one best of all my paintings because the woman in it reminded him of his mother. Remember Eleanor Quinlan? You do resemble her, especially in profile.

I was about to tell him that I'd already promised it to someone, but seeing the expression on his face when he looked at the painting, I simply couldn't.

I'll paint you another from my sketches and thumbnail roughs. It won't be exactly the same, but it might be interesting to see how the experiences of the intervening years have affected my approach to the subject.

The roof is in the process of being repaired. I have in front of me the prospect of transferring all the pieces back to the studio. Fortunately, I won't be working against time. This is undoubtedly an opportunity to update the inventory file, which I am perpetually behind on.

Confession is said to be good for the soul, so I anticipate feeling better any day now.

Wonderful news about your latest great-grandchild.

Love,
Maude

Kate hung up the phone and checked off the last name on her list. She had read her photocopy of the letter to her parents, Churchill Avery, Mrs. Perry, and Mrs. Bennett. Laura was at work, but Kate read it into her answering machine. By then, she could recite whole sections of it from memory.

"Done?" asked Alison, dropping into a chair.

"Done." Kate sat back on the porch sofa.

Alison's father came in the back door.

"Did somebody leave the phone off the hook, or was that your mother's chatty cousin Sheila?"

"I'm sorry," said Kate. "It was me."

"Show my dad the letter."

Kate handed it to him.

"Well," he said after he'd read it, "I'm flat-out amazed. Let me get this load of lumber into the workshop, then you can tell me how you did it. I might just have a little announcement of my own, but I'll save it for dinnertime."

"It's about the boat, right, Dad?"

"What boat?" He raised his eyebrows in mock innocence.

"Did you get the certification?"

"The who?"

"Did you, Dad?"

Alison followed her father out to the workshop. Kate stayed where she was. The excitement of the morning was ebbing, replaced by a pleasant exhaustion.

At dinner, Mr. Lang's announcement was more of a formality. Alison's mother clearly knew about the certification already, and Alison was so happy, Kate knew that the news could be only one thing. Nonetheless, making the event official was the occasion for applause and cheering.

"She's in the water, right, Dad?"

"As we speak."

"When do we sail?"

"Is tomorrow soon enough?"

"As long as it's early tomorrow."

When Kate came downstairs the next morning, Alison was sitting across from her father, who was on the phone.

"Dad's listening to the marine forecast," Alison whispered.

Kate got a bowl and silverware for herself and joined them at the table.

"Okay," said Mr. Lang, hanging up the phone, "we set sail at eight-thirty. That will take us out on the morning tide."

The bedroom door opened. Mrs. Lang shuffled out in a robe and slippers. "So what's the order of the day?"

"We sail at eight-thirty, Mom."

"So why are we up at the crack of dawn?"

"I couldn't sleep," said Alison, "and Dad was up even before me."

Mrs. Lang yawned. "Well, this will give us plenty of time to get our gear together."

"I got mine together," said Alison. "Last night."

Kate hadn't seen the boat since the afternoon she and Alison had walked to the shop. Now, with the wood sanded smooth as glass and the brass fittings gleaming in the sun, the boat was even more beautiful than before.

By eight-thirty, everybody was covered with suntan lotion and outfitted with life jackets, visors, and sunglasses. Mr. Lang hopped into the boat first and assisted the rest of them onto the deck.

"Quick review of the rules," he said. "What's number one?"

"Duck when you say 'coming about,' " said Mrs. Lang. She turned to Kate. "Ask me how I know that."

"Well," said Mr. Lang, "you were a quick learner. We only ditched once." He pointed to the arm that held the bottom edge of the mainsail. "Kate, this is the boom. It swings from one side to the other when we change direction. Don't get clobbered. Now, what's rule number two?"

"Do everything the captain tells you," said Kate.

"Good. And rule number three?"

"When in doubt," said Alison, "refer to rule number two."

"Now, here's another piece of vital information." With a flourish, he pulled a piece of paper out of his shirt pocket and appeared to be reading it. " 'Port is left. Starboard is right.' "

"Very funny, Dad."

Then Alison's father put the paper back in his pocket. Kate could tell from his manner that the joking was over.

"Kate, when you need something to hold on to, use the gunnel here," he said, gripping the edge of the boat. "Alison, you go forward. Release the bow."

She unfastened a rope, and the bow started to drift away from the dock.

Her father released the stern.

Using the two ropes that controlled the small sail, Alison pulled it to catch a breeze that filled the sail. At the same time, her father unfastened the rope on the mainsail, holding on to it as he pulled on the tiller.

With both sails turned now to catch the wind, the boat began to move forward.

Slowly, they maneuvered past a small navy of sailboats, motorboats, rowboats, and dinghies, all bobbing at anchor.

When they passed the jetty, nothing was before them but ocean. Kate pulled down her visor to secure it as the boat began to skim through the water.

A minute later, Mr. Lang called, "Ready about!"

Alison undid a rope from its cleat and held it. Her father unfastened the mainsail. Alison let out her rope.

"Coming about!" Kate ducked. As the boom passed directly overhead, the canvas snapped for a second or two before the sail caught the wind again and continued its arc to the opposite side of the boat.

"We're tacking," Alison called over her shoulder to Kate.

Nothing disturbed the gentle undulations of blue-green water except the wake that the boat stirred up. The sails rippled each time they came about. Otherwise, the only sounds Kate was aware of were the bow cutting through the water and the wind in her ears.

On the horizon, waves shattered the reflected sun into a blinding shower of sparks. Despite the visor and the sunglasses, Kate squinted.

The wind picked up. The boat seemed to be flying, barely touching the water. Kate held tight to the gunnel, but even as she did, the boat seemed to fall away, and she was the one who was flying.

In the days that followed, Kate was happy and relieved. At least that was what she told anybody who congratulated her on finding the letter. That seemed simpler than saying she felt as if she had awakened to find herself suddenly at her train stop and now was standing, shaky and disoriented, on an empty platform with hastily grabbed suitcases.

While her attention had been dominated by the painting, everything else had been pushed aside, but when she thought about the situation, what was different now?

The one solid thing she could point to was that her father had gotten safely through his surgery and the weeks of recovery.

On Monday morning, the weekly letter from home arrived. Kate sat down in the bamboo chair on the front porch to read it.

Fri., *Aug. 12*

Dear Kate,

I was sorry to hear about the maple. It was a bad day around here when we had to have the crab apple tree removed. I don't think you remember it. It was in between the river birch and the magnolia. It had been raining dead branches for months, but we hated to see it go.

Here's some good news. I'm back to driving. I feel like a teenager with his first license, although I must be driving like a senior citizen. At any rate, I get more impatient honks from the cars behind me than I used to. It's wonderful how major surgery changes your priorities. Having to wait through a red light doesn't seem like an undue burden anymore, certainly not worth risking a collision to avoid.

On the other hand, I've pulled out the draft of the novel I started three—or was it four?—years ago, the one about growing up in a mining town. I don't want an almost-finished manuscript sitting in my file cabinet.

Your drawing of the lilies is quite interesting, perhaps the most interesting that you have done this summer. Your flowers have dimension and structure.

Regarding your problems with Alison—you may feel that she is more responsible for them than you. But who started it, etc. is unimportant. Somebody has to make the first move to work things out. Don't be too proud to do it.

We are counting the days until we see you again.

Love,

Dad

The remark about the almost-finished manuscript caught Kate's attention.

She took the letter upstairs, put it in the pouch of her flight bag, and took out the photocopy of Maude's last letter to Peg. She skimmed nearly to the end before she found the sentence. *I won't be working against time.* But she had been. She had died only a month later. The inventory never got done. And the Thanksgiving visit, with its long talks and laughter late into the night, never happened. The holiday must have been a sad one for Maude's friend.

Kate folded up the letter and slid it into the pouch.

✿ What the Eye Sees

ON TUESDAY MORNING, Laura caught up to Kate and Alison as they reached the steps of the Art Association. Besides her usual canvas bag, she was carrying a stack of books.

"Can we take some of those?" said Kate.

"That's okay. I'd better not let go. Guess what. Mrs. Perry wants me to stay on and do a complete cross-indexing of all Maude Whitney's papers, including the letters that Margaret Hathaway's granddaughter has."

"Is Mrs. Foster going to give them to the Art Association?" asked Kate, as they all started up the steps.

"Well, that hasn't been decided yet, but I've talked to her, and she said that she'd definitely give us photocopies."

"So you'll be working on the letters every morning," said Kate.

"And afternoon. That's the best part. Mrs. Perry is hiring me to do the work full-time as soon as my tour guide job is over at the end of the summer."

"What about the job you were applying for at the bank?" said Alison.

"Well, I'm rethinking that."

When they got to the library, the rest of the class was already there. Laura leaned over the table and let the books she was carrying spill onto it. "Why don't all of you gather around the table to see these?" she said.

Laura picked out several books and opened them at the paper markers.

"As I mentioned last week, the principles of technical perspective were worked out in Italy in the early 1400s. While it's not perfect, in terms of creating the illusion of three dimensions, this method worked better than any other had before. It became the norm in European art."

The open books showed a tiled floor, a domed ceiling, the interior of a cathedral, and a spiral staircase.

"As you see, artists have often worked with subject matter that pushed the method to its limits." Laura opened another book.

"Then, about a century and a half ago, Japanese prints like this one began to be exported to Europe. They became quite the rage."

The print showed a woman in a kimono sitting next to a tea table. Kate had seen Japanese prints before. She had found them intriguing but strange.

"Does anybody want to guess where the vanishing points for the table would be?" said Laura.

"There wouldn't be any," said Mr. Banfield after a minute. "The lines that indicate the front and back edges of the tabletop are parallel to each other. They'd never converge."

"Right. Remember last week when I referred to other systems for creating the illusion of depth? This picture uses one called 'oblique projection.' You'll see it in Asian art.

I won't go into the specifics of it, except to say that it doesn't use vanishing points."

Laura pulled a piece of paper out of her sketch pad. "I made a drawing by tracing the table in the Japanese print. Then I drew the table in two-point perspective."

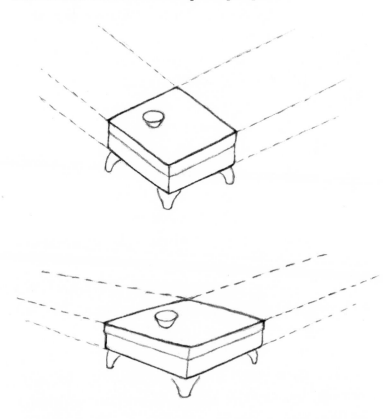

The first table seemed to be tilted, as if someone were starting to topple it over toward the viewer. The second table appeared to be resting comfortably on the ground.

"As you may notice," said Laura, "oblique projection

doesn't give as great a feeling of real space as technical perspective.

"The two systems differ in one other important way. In the class on two-point perspective, we talked about how that system puts the viewer in a particular place, looking in a particular direction. In that sense, the viewer becomes part of the picture. Asian art deliberately avoids that."

Laura opened several more books at the bookmarks.

"A number of the Impressionists began to incorporate elements of Asian art into their work.

"Here's a painting of farm fields by van Gogh. Do you see depth here—or something more like a mosaic of colored tiles fitted together? Believe me, van Gogh was highly skilled at creating depth, as we can see from earlier paintings. He flattened this scene because he wanted to.

"Artists like Matisse took this idea even further. To a great extent, this flattening of the picture space is the story of modern painting."

Kate found it difficult to believe that anyone would prefer flatness over depth. She had always been attracted to paintings that made her feel as if she could step through the frame into another world as boundless as the one she inhabited. All other paintings seemed inferior, produced by artists who lacked the skill or the energy to create a believable world.

Laura opened another book. A table was featured, this one covered with fruit, pottery jars, stemmed glasses, and a wine bottle. Again, the table seemed to be tilted toward the viewer.

"This is a print done in France in 1926," said Laura. "As some of you may know, it's an example of Cubism."

"I've always wondered how anybody could like that kind of painting," said Miss Dixon.

Miss Farley nodded. "Me, too."

"Can you pin down what it is that you don't like?" said Laura.

"We seem to be in two places at once," said Mrs. Dixon. "Or maybe three. We're looking down into the glasses and jars but seeing them from the side at the same time."

"Now some people would say that is truer to the way we actually see things," said Laura. "Remember, you take in a scene by shifting your eyes."

"Isn't the perspective method better?" asked Mrs. Shelley. "I feel as if all these glasses and jars are about to come crashing down from the tabletop."

Kate was glad she wasn't the only one to dislike the odd, dizzying world of Cubism.

"Well," said Miss Longwood after a minute, "I don't know about anybody else, but I find the shapes of the objects quite . . . interesting. The whole picture reminds me of a quilt."

"Or a jigsaw puzzle," said Mr. Banfield.

"Yes," said Laura, "this is a pleasing arrangement of interlocking shapes, but I think that the artist had a deeper purpose in working this way."

She reached into her bag, pulled out a butter carton, and held it up. "From where you're standing, each one of you sees only certain faces of this box. But you know there are other faces that you can't see." She unfolded the box, tore off some of the flaps, and arranged the pieces of cardboard on the table in a design. "By making these hidden faces part of the composition, Cubist art shows what the mind knows, not what the eye sees."

Kate had never thought of that before. She studied Laura's reconfigured box.

Laura stacked the books to the side of the table and pulled a sketchbook and pencil out of her bag.

"For drawing today, I thought we might try a method I haven't talked about yet, contour drawing. It's excellent training in hand-eye coordination. Mrs. Randall, may I ask you to be the model? Just sit down in one of the chairs in the front row. Thanks."

Laura opened the sketchbook. Keeping her eyes steadily on Mrs. Randall, she moved her pencil around the paper. Kate saw that she was drawing an outline of the seated woman, the chair legs, and the handbag on the floor.

"Don't look down," said Laura, "and don't lift your pencil off the paper until you're finished, except to put in what are called negative spaces. For instance, if the model is standing with her hands on her hips, the area between her arm and her torso is a negative space."

Kate found the drawing odd but appealing.

"I've been looking for a good opportunity to introduce

contour drawing, and now that we're talking about flattening the picture space, this seemed the ideal time. As you see, the figure looks like a cardboard cutout."

One by one, the people in the class stood or sat in front of the group for five-minute poses.

As she worked on the first pose, contour drawing seemed like an interesting novelty to Kate, like trying to write backward, but as she continued to draw, she felt she was entering that place where her pencil point and her eyes seemed to be moving as one.

"I got some weird drawings out of that," said Alison on the way to Kennon's. "How about you?"

"Very weird. But I like them."

"Me, too."

"We're home," said Alison, as they walked in the back door a few minutes later.

"Kate!" Mrs. Lang's voice came from her office. "Pick up the kitchen phone!"

As she put the receiver to her ear, Kate could hear her mother's voice and the sounds of a hospital.

". . . and they wheeled her straight from the car into the delivery room. The baby was born eighteen minutes later."

"Mom?"

"Kate? I was just telling Diane the good news. You're an aunt as of nine forty-seven this morning. Steven Harris Delassandro decided to make a surprise appearance nine days early. He was eight pounds, nine ounces."

"Is that big for a baby?"

"Plenty big. And, Kate, he's got the Harris cleft chin, plain as day. Anne thinks he looks like you. She's sleeping just now or I'd put her on."

Her mother and Anne were being nice as usual, telling Kate there was a resemblance. How could anybody see a resemblance in a face that was hardly formed?

"That's great news, Mom."

"Kate, I'll be staying with Anne and David for a few days to help out. I'll be in touch later in the week."

At lunch, Kate was the object of good-natured teasing from Alison and her father, who agreed that they should call her Auntie Kate from then on.

"So," said Alison, "do you feel like an aunt?"

Kate thought she should say something appropriate, but she didn't know what that was.

Mrs. Lang came to her rescue. "I think it won't sink in until you meet him."

Kate wasn't at all sure that seeing her nephew in person would make a difference.

She wrote her seventh letter home that evening.

Tuesday, August 16

Dear Mom & Dad,

 I like the name Steven. What color eyes does he have? And what color hair?

268

The class this week was on modern art and how artists since the Impressionists have flattened out their subjects on purpose. I don't know if I'll ever like this kind of painting very much, but after Laura explained a few things, I think I get the point of what the artists were doing.

We did contour drawings today. That means drawing the outline of the subject without looking down at the paper. You should try it just for fun.

Love,

Kate

In the following days, Alison got a crash course in sailing. Every day her conversation featured new terms: "reefing," "points of sail," "in irons," "halyards," "winches," and "turnbuckles." Books on sailing piled up on the nightstand and Alison's desk.

Kate came along in the mornings, but she asked to be dropped off at the marina by noon. She explained that she needed to finish a special drawing project, leaving the impression that the drawings were for her family. That was partly true. Some of them were.

After lunch each day, while Mrs. Lang was occupied in her office, Kate walked around the yard sketching the house and the workshop from various angles.

The weekend—two perfect August days—was spent, much like the first weekend of Kate's visit, playing sports. Kate tried Rollerblading again. Alison won the second Harris-Lang croquet tournament.

On Monday morning, Kate hesitated before opening the letter from home, knowing it was the last one she would receive on this visit. She slit one side of the envelope and pulled out a stack of photos. The one on top showed Anne cradling the baby. It was clearly taken right after the birth. Anne's face was flushed and shiny. She was gazing at the baby as if no one else existed.

The next two photos had been taken in the hospital nursery. Steven was identified by an arrow inked in the margin. Without that, Kate would have found the tiny face indistinguishable from the others. No wonder babies were sometimes given to the wrong families.

The remaining photos detailed the homecoming. Zee was still away at the riding school, but both sets of grandparents were in attendance. Every possible grouping of people seemed to have been recorded. The only consistent element was the baby, presented as if he were a wondrous creature, never seen before.

At the bottom of the stack was a photo of Steven by himself, lying on a blanket, facing the camera. The upper lip had a downward-pointing peak in the middle. Kate recognized that peak. Zee had one just like it. The nose was a button, the least distinctive feature. But, plain as day, as her mother had said, was the Harris cleft chin. This was not an interchangeable unit in the human race. This was Steven, the new baby of the family. Suddenly Kate realized, that wasn't her anymore.

She unfolded the letter.

Dear Kate,

Here are the vital statistics on your nephew. He has gained three ounces this week, so he's now tipping the scale at eight pounds, twelve ounces. He was twenty inches long at birth, although I'm not sure how they can tell that—as far as I can see, babies don't uncurl for weeks.

His eyes are brown. His hair, what there is of it, is dark brown, almost black, so you see that he takes after his father as far as coloring is concerned, but the Harrises are well represented in his features. I predict that the button nose will evolve into the noble arch Grandma bequeathed to the family.

Although his vocabulary is limited, I'm virtually certain that I heard him say he can hardly wait to meet you.

I have to warn you, your normally rational, sedate parents are making complete fools of themselves over their grandson. We'll try not to let the cooing get totally out of hand.

We're now counting the hours until your return.

Love,
Dad

Once again, a note from Kate's mother was included.

Dear Kate,

I asked your father to let me give you the news. The clan—including the three of us, plus Zee, Anne, David, and our amazing grandson, Steven—is gathering for an eight-day visit to the farm, starting the day after you get home. I know this isn't the trip you had hoped for, but I think we're going to have a ball.

My folks sound a bit edgy over the idea of our descent en masse, but they're so delighted with the prospect of seeing their great-grandson that I believe they've already put the extra leaf in the dining room table.

Love,

Mom

Kate would have to get a new drawing pad and a small sketchbook to bring with her to the farm. Suddenly she had lots of ideas for things to draw.

✿ Passing It On

AT THE BEGINNING of Tuesday's art class, Laura stood in front of the table instead of going to the blackboard.

"We're going to do something a little different today, since it's the last class. First, I want to tell all of you how much I've enjoyed teaching it. I hope we can continue next summer. I've spoken to Mrs. Perry, and I believe there's a good possibility of that."

Everyone applauded.

Laura smiled. "Let's get on to today's class. Remember what I said in the first class—in order to express what you see in your imagination, you need tools in your kit. You've been introduced to some of those tools this summer. But the reverse is also true. In order to make good use of tools, you need imagination, moments of special clarity, when you see into the heart of things. We all have these moments. Most of us can't express them to others.

"If you've ever experienced one, you know that it's brief. After it's over, all you're doing is gathering information about your subject, its shape, its texture, and so forth, and even that's chancy. The model will move, the light will change. Meanwhile, you must try to hold on to your first vision.

"Now, I want you to go wherever you want and draw whatever you want. Come back here in an hour. We'll look at all the drawings and talk about them."

The room was quiet for several minutes. One by one, chairs were vacated as people thought of destinations.

"I'm going to draw our sailboat," said Alison at last. "It probably won't come out, but I'm going to try it anyway. Do you want to come along?"

"Thanks, but I've thought of a place."

"Bet I know where."

They walked to the corner of Magnolia and Preston. Alison turned toward the marina. "See you in an hour," she said.

Kate turned the other way, up the hill.

A five-minute walk took her to the Quinlan house. Once again, Kate sat down on the stone wall across the street, but now she understood how to alter the perspective.

She opened her pad to a fresh page and drew a horizon line, then considered the roof lines. She sketched them in three times, each time at greater angles from the horizon. Each time, the sense of drama increased.

As she extended the roof lines down to the horizon to

locate the vanishing points, she realized that the points were off the paper. Laura had said that could happen.

From the estimated left and right vanishing points, Kate sketched in the top and bottom lines of all the window openings. The sides were straight verticals. So were the lines indicating the corners of the house. Then, by accident, Kate discovered that tilting all the verticals slightly made the house look taller. The main structure was established.

The house still didn't seem solid. Shadows would fix that. She drew the shadows cast by the window ledges as dark slashes on the front wall, which seemed to rise like a sheer cliff out of the chaotic garden, dominating it. But that was an illusion. Without the power of growth and change, the house could do nothing as mosses and vines and ivy worked their way along its clapboard siding, ruining the wood they clung to.

Somebody would probably buy it soon. They'd yank out the vines and ivy, wash away the moss, paint the clapboards, and plant grass in the yard. Her drawing would be the only record of the house at this moment.

Didn't the lions, peering out from their private jungle, express the essence of the place as she had seen it that morning—what Laura would call her vision of it? If she'd thought of that sooner, Kate could have altered the perspective to make the lions more central in the frame. But now she knew another technique that might be useful. She began to work up first one lion and then the other in terms of the basic forms. That told her how to shape the form shadows and where to put the shadows cast by the manes, the muzzles, and the bared teeth. The lions became the area of greatest contrast and sharpest detail.

Then she turned to the tangle of plants in the yard, rendering a few foreground clusters with precision, suggesting the rest with scribbles.

She checked her watch. Eleven-twenty. Kate gathered up her things and walked quickly down the hill.

That evening, Kate wrote her last letter home.

Tuesday, August 23

Dear Mom & Dad,

Today was the last art class. We all went out and drew for an hour, then had a really interesting discussion when everybody got back. Alison drew the boat her father built. The drawing is the best thing she's done the whole summer. She said that after sanding every square inch of it with five grades of sandpaper, she could draw it in her sleep.

I'm not sending a copy of my drawing this time. I want you to see the original. It won't be much longer now.

I'm sorry the lessons are over.

Love,
Kate

"I don't see a single flavor that we haven't had," said Alison as they stood in front of the Purple Cow's ice cream list on Wednesday afternoon. "Let's get two different flavors and mix them together."

"Okay."

They got their orders and took the two counter seats facing the front window. Alison spooned up some of Kate's ice cream and mixed it into hers. "Hmm," she said, licking the spoon, "I guess Pistachio Raspberry isn't going to be the new flavor of the week. Are you going to show your sketchbook to Laura?"

"Laura's seen all my classwork."

"No, I mean the little sketchbook. The one you don't think I notice you drawing in," Alison said with a mischievous smile.

Kate was embarrassed. "Sorry."

"It's okay. Laura said to practice. I'm just too lazy to do it. Can I see it, too?"

"Sure."

"What about Laura?"

"I'll have to think about it."

"What's to—"

"I know, I know," said Kate.

On Thursday morning, after Alison and her father left for the marina, Kate dialed Laura's number.

"Kate! I was about to call you. I just remembered that you'll be leaving soon."

"Sunday. Before I go, I have some sketches I'd like to show you. If you have time."

"I'm waiting for a package to arrive, so I can't leave the house, but you're welcome to come here. I'm only a few blocks up the hill from you. Kane Street and Winthrop. It's the white house on the corner. Number sixty-five. Go in the side gate."

Kate told Alison's mother where she was going and grabbed her sketchbook.

Kate had never seen an artist's studio before, not in person.

At Number 65, a flagstone walkway led to a separate entrance, where Laura was standing in the open doorway.

"Isn't this a glorious day? I can hardly wait for the deliveryman to get here so I can go out and paint."

Laura's apartment was four simply furnished rooms. The studio occupied what would otherwise have been the bedroom. A drafting table dominated the space. Floor-to-ceiling shelves were crammed with bottles, jars, tubes, brushes, and books. Pencils stuck out of coffee cans. An easel was fitted into the space, along with a rack for storing paintings.

Now that Kate was about to show her sketches, she had a last-minute rush of doubt. They weren't good enough.

Laura paged slowly through the book. Kate had forgotten how many drawings she had done—shells, shoes, figurines on a shelf, the milk pitcher, a wicker basket, the kitchen, the pantry, Alison's room, her father in the workshop, drinking a cup of coffee, watching a ball game, her mother on the phone, cooking, reading a book, the three of them playing cards, Alison asleep, feeding the fledglings, talking on the phone, holding the baby rabbit and the kitten.

"You've made a lot of progress this summer. Your drawing has really improved. I'm sure you see it."

Kate nodded.

Laura flipped back through the book until she got to the one of the Langs watching a baseball game on TV. "You've told me more about these people in this one drawing than you could have said in a paragraph."

Laura handed back the sketchbook. "Will you be taking art classes in school next term?"

"Yes, but they aren't like the ones you taught."

Laura pulled a well-thumbed volume off the shelf. "This is a terrific book on perspective. It's got examples of how to violate the rules to achieve an effect without the viewer being aware of what you're doing."

The book looked interesting, and Kate could have stayed all day, but Laura probably had things to do, and Kate needed to work on her drawings. She described them to Laura.

"I've thought about doing them for a long time, but I sort of put off starting them until last week."

Laura rolled her eyes. "Tell me about it. Starting can be murder. All the good things you've ever done seem like flukes."

Kate was surprised. Laura had always seemed the picture of confidence.

They walked to the gate. "Wait a minute." Laura ran back into the house and came out with the book on perspective. "Take this with you."

"Oh, thank you. When I get through with it, I'll send it right back."

"No, keep it. I've got it memorized." Laura opened the

gate. Kate started to thank her again, but Laura put up her hand. "Someday you'll pass it on to somebody else."

Kate was almost half a block away when she heard Laura's voice. "Thanks for showing me your sketchbook!"

At breakfast on Friday, Mrs. Lang suggested that Kate start thinking of what she wanted to pack in her carry-on and what she wanted mailed back.

"I'll see if I have any boxes to hold the painting," said Mr. Lang.

"They'll let Kate carry it with her on the plane, won't they?" said Alison.

"We still need to pack it well. Would a flat box be good? Kate?"

"Oh, sorry, I was just thinking about it. Yes, a flat box."

Kate noticed Alison's mother looking at her intently for a moment.

Alison decided to go downtown with her father to look at some books on navigation. Kate said she had things to do at home.

"Don't eat before we get back," said Alison. "Today is probably our last chance to get lunch at the Purple Cow. Tomorrow's the waterfront festival, and the place'll be jammed with tourists."

After they left, Kate went upstairs, sat down on Alison's bed, and studied the painting for a long time. Then she got up, tore out the last three clean sheets from the back of her drawing pad, and stacked them on the sofa bed. She set the painting facedown on the paper, folded the sheets carefully around the frame, and tied up the package with a piece of string.

She found Alison's mother in her office. "May I borrow a shopping bag?"

"Sure. There's one on the hook in the pantry."

Just then the phone rang. Mrs. Lang picked it up.

"Oh, hello, Edith. I've got those figures for you."

Kate knew that this would be a long phone call. She scribbled her destination on a note and put it on the desk in front of Mrs. Lang. Without interrupting her conversation, Mrs. Lang nodded. Kate took the shopping bag upstairs and slipped the neatly tied parcel into it.

Then she walked to the Art Association.

Darlene, her forelock a deep magenta, looked up when Kate came in. "Hi. Did you find more papers to sort?"

"No. I came to see Mrs. Perry. If she has time."

"I'll ask," said Darlene. She slipped into the office and reappeared a moment later.

"Go on in."

Mrs. Perry was partially hidden by the stacks of paper on her desk.

"Please sit down, Kate. I'm still trying to get our files into some semblance of order." Kate noticed that her gaze rested briefly on the shopping bag.

"Thanks. Mrs. Perry, I've been thinking about what to do with the painting, and I've made up my mind. I'm going to loan it to the Art Association if you'll put it on display. It would still be mine, but this way, a lot of people can see it, not just me and my family and friends."

"Kate," said Mrs. Perry, sitting back in her chair, "I hardly know what to say. This can't have been an easy decision for you. Are you sure?"

"I'm sure."

"Of course we'll put it in a place of honor. Naturally, your loan will be acknowledged on the information card."

"That's okay. I only want to know that it's going to be seen."

"I had in mind—just daydreaming, mind you—that space to the right of the entrance to the sculpture court."

Kate turned around. "That's a good place."

"Now—if you're really sure—I'll have Arthur Burke draw up a letter of agreement right away and have copies sent to your parents. They'd have to sign for you. In the meantime, shall we see what the painting looks like in this setting?"

They cut the string and pulled away the white paper.

"Darlene," said Mrs. Perry as they passed her desk, "would you hold this up against the wall here?"

They studied the effect.

"I think it looks perfect," said Mrs. Perry.

"So do I," said Kate.

When Kate got home, Mrs. Lang was in the backyard, clipping an azalea bush.

"I can't believe how much this thing has grown this

summer." She glanced at the empty shopping bag. "Did you drop something off at the Art Association?"

"Yes. The painting. I'm leaving it there. It's still mine, but I want people to see it, and this way they will. It will be in the lobby from now on."

Kate waited for Mrs. Lang to raise some objection to the plan, but she only nodded, then clipped another branch. "I thought you might do something like that."

"I got the idea from one of the letters Margaret Hathaway wrote. She said that a work of art doesn't really belong to anybody."

"That's an interesting way to look at it. I think I agree."

"Mrs. Lang, may I use the phone? I'd like to call a few people and let them know where the painting is going to be."

"Of course."

"Well," said Mrs. Foster, when Kate gave her the news, "that makes up my mind. I'm definitely going to give my grandmother's letters to the association."

"Oh, thank you so much for letting me know," said Mrs. Bennett. "I'll call my niece. She works for the newspaper."

"That's splendid," said Mr. Avery. "I hope that means you'll be coming back to us very soon."

Kate started to call Laura, then decided that she wanted her to be surprised.

Alison and her father were home by noon.

"Wow," said Alison when Kate announced the news,

"Mrs. Perry must have flipped. I want to hear all about it. You can tell me on the way downtown."

Kate and Alison split the house special sandwich as they sat at the Purple Cow's front counter and watched people go by on South Main.

"There are a lot of tourists in town," said Kate.

"Wait till the cold weather starts. The place'll be dead. A lot of stores and restaurants close after November."

They ordered ice cream cones and went to Perry Street beach.

"Maybe they'll have some new flavors by next summer," said Kate as they walked along the shore.

"A lot of things will be different by then. We'll have a new tree in the front yard. I'll be a junior skipper. The Wheelhouse might be back in business."

"Really?"

"My mom heard something about it."

"Where it was before?"

"I think so. It won't be like it was, though. Everything will be new."

"I suppose," said Kate, "that the Quinlan house will be sold."

"Probably. My dad says it needs a lot of repairs. I think they ought to tear it down and put a new house there, but some people love the historic stuff." Alison picked up a scallop shell, looked it over, and slipped it into her pocket. "Do you think you're going to miss the painting? You could still take it back."

"No, I'm not going to do that. Besides, people at the Art Association know about taking care of paintings."

"I'll bet your folks are going to be pretty amazed to see your drawings. Nobody else in your family draws or paints, do they?"

"No. Only me."

"You're lucky."

Kate looked at Alison.

Lucky? Alone with her toys in a houseful of adults, watching and listening, struggling to understand—that wasn't lucky.

Or was it? On the day Maude Whitney stood in the middle row, second from left, knowing that she'd never join the ranks of poised and beautiful young women—did she feel lucky then?

But she was—because of the very differentness she would have changed at that moment. She was a watcher, too, Kate was sure, off in a corner with her sketch pad.

"I guess so," said Kate. "I guess I'm really lucky."

✺ Flying Home

ON SATURDAY MORNING, Kate came downstairs to find Alison on the back porch, reading a sailing manual. She looked up from the page. "You're sure you want to stay here this morning? It's going to be a scorcher. You'll be a lot cooler on the water."

"I'm sure. I've got a few more sketches to do before we go to the festival."

"Mom? What about you?"

"I've got a telephone meeting with a client this morning."

After Alison and her father left and Mrs. Lang went to her office, Kate got her drawing pad and went outside, filling page after page with sketches of the yard until the pad was almost used up.

Just before noon, she went upstairs, tore most of the sketches out of the pad, and stacked them. Across a clean sheet, she scrawled in big letters "Thanks for a Wonderful Summer! Love, Kate." Then she tore that sheet out and put it on top of the stack. A shelf for blankets in the back of Alison's closet made a good hiding place.

Kate came downstairs and slipped into the recliner with a crossword puzzle just as Mrs. Lang came out of her office and Alison and her father came in the back door.

"Kate and I will get something to eat at the waterfront," said Alison when she saw her mother setting out plates for lunch. She started up the stairs, then thumped back down. "Kate, is that okay with you?"

"Sure."

On the way down Winthrop, Alison described the morning's lesson, turning the boat around to retrieve an object or passenger fallen overboard. "Jibbing" was the new word for the day.

At the waterfront, lines of white canvas tents housed the booths selling a variety of crafts. Despite the heat and the blazing sun, Alison was inexhaustible, looking at everything, chatting with the people tending the booths.

They bought fried clams, lemonade, and strawberry ices as they moved slowly up the waterfront, while fishing boats and sailboats gathered in the inner harbor. Up front, black letters identified the harbormaster's boat. When Kate and Alison got to the fisherman statue, they stopped. Kate had always meant to study the plaques. She began reading the names. They were listed by year, starting in the 1600s. Alison had been right. Almost every year, people were lost.

After a few minutes, Alison said, "It's almost five. There's always a parade to the memorial. If you want to see the start of it, we should go up to the Legion Hall."

They turned away from the waterfront and walked half a dozen blocks up Elliot Street.

About a hundred people were there, some of them dressed up, some of them in shorts and T-shirts. One man was wearing a clerical collar. A number of people, men and women and children, carried bouquets of flowers. The mood seemed quite festive for a memorial service. Kate was surprised to hear joking and laughter, along with occasional static from a walkie-talkie. A boy about eleven was trying to play tag with his older sister while their mother was pinning the girl's hair into a French twist.

At five o'clock, four men carrying drums gathered behind a police car parked in the middle of Elliot Street, facing the harbor below. The man with the walkie-talkie held up his hand. Conversation and laughter died away. The four drummers stood with sticks poised. The man gave a nod, and the police car rolled forward. The drummers took up a beat. Kate looked over her shoulder as she and Alison started down the sidewalk. Behind them, the formless crowd was assembling itself into a procession.

At Shore Road, the procession turned right. Ahead of them, at the memorial, a small crowd of people waited. When the procession arrived, the drums fell silent. Alison took Kate's hand and slipped into a place in front of a makeshift wooden podium. A man climbed the steps of the podium and tapped the microphone. As a cold breeze began blowing off the water behind him, he introduced himself as Jack Stacy, chairman of the memorial committee. Kate kept glancing around at the other onlookers, wondering which ones had friends and family members listed on the plaques. She caught only bits of his speech. *This beleaguered industry . . . the soul of the town . . . the heroic men and women who . . .*

A student who had won an essay-writing contest sponsored by the memorial committee—concerned that the younger people of the town were losing touch with its traditions—read her essay. Again, only a few phrases penetrated Kate's consciousness. *The courage of these brave . . . never to return . . . lest we forget the sacrifice . . .*

The mayor spoke. *No members of his family were fishermen. Nonetheless, he felt a deep connection to . . . as a boy, he had dreamed about . . . that gave the town its character . . .*

In between speeches, a choir sang hymns about peril on the sea and travelers looking for safe harbor.

Then a white-haired man was introduced, the retired captain of a fishing boat. He told how, many years before, a snowstorm had delayed his arrival in town. The *Johnny D* had left port without him. Ten days later, the boat was lost with all hands. Kate began to pay attention.

A woman about the same age as Kate's mother talked about the father she had never known, gone missing in a storm when she was less than a year old. No trace of the boat or its crew was ever found.

Mr. Stacy announced that more names, not originally known when the plaques were put up, would be added soon. From the hoarseness that came into his voice, Kate thought that the deaths would be recent ones, some of the men perhaps known to him. The first name was from 1838, then two from 1934.

With the sun low in the western sky, Father Philip Pacheco of Mary, Star of the Sea parish said a prayer for the families who had suffered losses and for the safe return of all sailors.

Then he and the mayor lifted a wreath off its stand and handed it to the family Kate had noticed at the Legion Hall.

"That's the Materas," Alison whispered. "Rafael Matera was one of the men who was lost last spring."

Mr. Stacy repeated the information, an unmistakable catch in his voice. Kate was sure he knew the Materas.

She looked closely at each member of the family. How could there not be some distinguishing mark, like a scar from an operation, to tell even a stranger that something terrible had happened to them, that one day they had received the worst news they could get? A half hour ago at the Legion Hall, the Materas could have been any family. Kate had always pictured grief as a locked cell, but maybe it wasn't. Maybe it was a private room one sometimes left, then came back to, in time to be visited less and less often.

As the choir began singing "Amazing Grace," the Materas lifted the wreath over the guardrail and tossed it onto the water. Then other people stepped forward, throwing bouquets and single flowers.

Alison took Kate's arm and steered her to the rail. When they looked down, the wreath was already lost in a raft of flowers bobbing gently on the outgoing tide. More flowers kept cascading in, a waterfall of red and yellow and white.

A heap of flowers had been put out near the rail for people to throw. Alison took a red one for herself and handed a white one to Kate. At first, Kate felt awkward. She hadn't lost anyone at sea.

But eventually, everybody lost something or somebody, or maybe missed something they'd never had. She tossed in her flower. It floated by itself at first, then caught onto a cluster of flowers. That cluster joined another and another.

As the carpet of blossoms moved away from the seawall, Kate lost sight of her flower. She imagined it crossing the inner harbor, floating past the breakwater, past Rocky Point lighthouse, past the last bell buoy, out to open water.

The next morning, Kate was awake before anybody else. She took the stack of drawings out of the closet and tiptoed downstairs. Using the step stool, she put them on top of the refrigerator. Nobody would think to look there. When she got home, she'd tell the Langs about the present.

Then she went upstairs, slipped back into bed, and waited for sunrise.

The airport terminal was full of people in various stages of sunburn, carrying tennis rackets and wearing golf caps.

"One more weekend and the summer's over," said Mrs. Lang. "Hard to believe."

"We're a century early," said Alison. "They haven't even posted a gate yet."

Mrs. Lang talked about the excellent possibility of Alison's visiting the Harrises during the semester break. "It'll be here before you know it."

Alison sighed. "That's months away."

Mr. Lang pointed to a monitor. "Gate 17. They just posted it."

"Ticketed passengers only," said an attendant as they approached the X-ray conveyor belt.

Mrs. Lang hugged Kate tightly. "I feel like I've had two daughters this summer."

"In fact," said Alison's father, "we're thinking of trading Alison in. She already knows all my jokes."

Alison punched his arm. "Very funny. I'm going to shop for a new dad who's got jokes I haven't heard a million times."

"Kate," said Alison's father, putting an arm around her shoulder, "joking aside, we're going to miss you terribly."

Kate stood uncertainly for a moment, as people maneuvered suitcases around them. Then she stepped forward and hugged Alison. "This was the best summer ever."

"Really?" said Alison. "You're not just saying that?"

"I mean it."

Mr. Lang lifted her bag onto the conveyor belt. Kate walked through the metal detector, picked up her bag, and hoisted it onto her shoulder.

"I left a present for all of you," she said, stepping away from the luggage chute. "Look in the kitchen when you get back." She started down the concourse. Then she turned around.

"Thanks for everything!" she called. The Langs were still waving as she turned toward her gate. She didn't look back again.

Having to present her ticket and identification, as well as answer questions and keep track of her boarding pass, prevented Kate from focusing on her own thoughts until she strapped herself into her seat. With a series of slams, the overhead compartments were shut. As they began to taxi the pilot said something about perfect flying weather and an on-time arrival.

The plane pivoted at the end of a runway, then paused. Kate felt vibrations as they began to roll down the pavement, faster and faster. The ground fell away. Water appeared under them. They swung up and around in a great spiral. Below them, sailboats, lobster boats, ferries, and tugs navigated the harbor. Then they flew into a cloud and the harbor disappeared. The sunlight diffused into a haze, white and silver, as they circled, higher and higher.